Paweł Huelle, born in 1957, is a novelist, playwright and newspaper columnist who has lived most of his life in Gdańsk, which is often the setting for his work. He worked as a press officer for the Solidarity trade union, as a university lecturer in philosophy, and later headed up Gdańsk's local television centre before becoming a full-time writer. His novels *Mercedes-Benz* and *Castorp* have also been published by Serpent's Tail. Both novels were shortlisted for the *Independent* Foreign Fiction Prize.

Praise for *Mercedes-Benz*

"Wonderfully droll, offbeat, both touching and farcical"
Independent

"An exhilarating, liberating, brief and delightful novel with a story at every turning… Antonia Lloyd-Jones's translation sustains the mischief and verve of the original… Huelle's wit and his subtle gift for measuring absurdity stand comparison with Hrabal or any of the other great central European ironists" *New Statesman*

"Quirky, thoughtful and often poetic, it opens a subjective and fascinating window on to the recent past" *The Times*

"Huelle writes in such an engaging, chatty style that you hardly notice the fraught circumstances underlying every tale"
Guardian

"A little gem of a book... the prose glides along, buoyed up by a faintly ironic tone which is both refreshing and endearing, *Mercedes-Benz* has an understated intelligence and dignity"
OXview

"Huelle has a light touch, weaving his stories about French and German cars in pre-war Poland with adventures in post-Soviet traffic so artfully that you do not see where he is taking you until it's too late to turn back"
Books of the Year 2005, *Independent on Sunday*

Praise for *Castorp*

"A writer whose work is full of depth and allusion... pulses with irony that Mann would have been proud of... wonderfully absurd humour" *Independent on Sunday*

"An intelligent, intriguing and atmospheric novel worthy of its inspiration. It is admirably served by Antonia Lloyd-Jones' nuanced and readable translation" *Independent*

"A delightful period piece... His style is charmingly effective, the book written with an understated wit very much of the era in which it is set, and gently, deceptively provocative" *Observer*

"Engaging... Huelle is a skilful ironist who displays great subtlety of touch as he embraces the absurd" *Financial Times*

"A breezy and ingenious comic prequel to *The Magic Mountain*" *TLS Books of the Year*

"Book lovers queue here" *Scotland on Sunday*

Paweł Huelle

The Last Supper

Translated by Antonia Lloyd-Jones

A complete catalogue record for this book can
be obtained from the British Library on request

The right of Paweł Huelle to be identified as the author
of this work has been asserted by him in accordance with
the Copyright, Designs and Patents Act 1988

Published by Wydawnictwo Znak in 2007
in Krakow, Poland

First published in this English translation in 2008
by Serpent's Tail, an imprint of Profile Books Ltd
3A Exmouth House
Pine Street
Exmouth Market
London EC1R 0JH
www.serpentstail.com

Designed and typeset by Sue Lamble
Printed in Italy by L.E.G.O. S.p.A., Lavis, (TN)

1 2 3 4 5 6 7 8 9 10

for Jerzy Keiling

The author who wrote this history was so eager for the names within it to be concealed that he chose not to identify the country where it took place, for reason of the great monstrosity that occurred there, and his preference not to shame the country, families and relatives apparently still living; he adds, however, that wherever it may have occurred, suffice to say – in his words – it is true

Michał Jurkowski, *New and Unusual Histories*, circa 1714

For them I was life, but for me they were death
Mani Psalms, CCXLVI

CHAPTER I

The strange consequences of a strange awakening

THE NEWS THAT YUSSUF BROUGHT from the other side of the river was alarming. Government men were combing the lower town and not a single corner could give refuge. The shiny black motorbikes that looked a bit too heavy to jump across the narrow stream in the valley or to chase a rebel down some back-street steps were actually as nimble as dragonflies. Any poor wretch who was counting on them being cumbersome and took it easy on his legs, or else ran out of puff, paid with his life. The killing was nothing like an execution. Once the insurgent was within small-arms range, he fell from a shot that sounded like a crisp thwack. Sometimes, when the rider was feeling bored with his monotonous job and decided to have some fun, the passers-by were given a free street theatre performance. On these occasions the motorcyclists liked best of all to use bare wire made of thin steel. It strangled a man faster than a Spanish garrotte. The time by the Fountain of Liberty when one of the motorcyclists threw a noose around the neck of an escaping rebel and then dragged his corpse around the square, the members of the public sitting at the tables outside the Café El Rashid stood up and gave the display an ovation.

"It's true," said Yussuf, poking in his gums with a toothpick as usual, "everyone hates them. I do too. They're dogs that need to be taught a lesson. But why do it in broad daylight? In front of the journalists? And the citizens? They could round them all up at night when the city is asleep, take them to the port, put them on board one of the old Panama-registered ships that have been rusting by the wharves for years and simply drown them five miles out to sea. Just as Mao Tse Tung did with all the whores in China. Don't you think?"

Yussuf liked giving vent to such issues. He always turned out to have read this and that, or at least knew something from one of his teachers.

"As far as I remember the film," I said, summoning the waiter, "those five or ten thousand prostitutes were drowned in a river. You understand, Yussuf? In a river, not in the sea."

He was served a coffee and a glass of cold water.

"It's all shit," he said slowly, drawling every word. "This is, and that is. Infidel shit too," he added, so there could be no doubt what he thought of it all. "What's the difference?"

"The difference is that those women's bodies were carried along by the current for hundreds of miles. But in the sea?"

"Sharks," he sniggered, "a great big feeding ground for the

sharks. Though the insurgents are carrion – they stink while they're still alive. I don't feel sorry for a single one of them. You get it? Not one. If I'm hacked off," he said, pointing at the sun's orb, "it's because on this sort of occasion, in broad daylight, they always do a few peaceful people in. But the journalists are no worse dogs than them. Just like the government people." He handed me a letter from Ariston and asked: "You said something about a film? Do you remember the title?"

I didn't. Ariston, who never used a telephone, fax or computer, had written to tell me that our lesson would not take place today or over the next few days, and not just because of the situation. "I am leaving for the village of Oasin on a matter of great urgency" – that was the entire explanation, after which he had noted down a dozen new sentences for me to translate. "Better sit at home with a dictionary and not get mixed up in anything – I'll be in touch when I get back," the letter ended in English again.

Without getting an answer about the film, Yussuf pointed a finger at the ancient script; in Ariston's handwriting the paragraph had something truly majestic about it.

"Did you come here to study? And what does that old man know? It's none of my concern. I'm just the messenger. But do you know what they say? He isn't called Ariston at all. And he isn't a Greek. You people from Europe always let yourselves get taken in."

I paid for the letter. I said there would be no answer. As he mounted his scooter he replied: "Even so I'm not going back down the hill. I'm not a fool!"

I remembered that in my flat above the café the air conditioning had broken. I put off the homework for Ariston and went outside with my camera again. The line running to the other side of the river, as far as the old Admiralty building, was out of service. The stop where a few days earlier a bus full of passengers had blown up was still one great big hole, ringed with police tape, perhaps purely for the sake of form. I went down the near deserted, sun-scorched street and reached the Hill of Prophets. At the huge binoculars where there were always a lot of tourists hanging about, there was no one. But, amazingly, the cog-wheel railway built here in the British era was running as it did every day. I noticed this immediately, seeing the two blue cars slowly passing each other mid-route, at exactly the point where the Coptic monastery appeared among the olive groves, surrounded by a palisade of cypress trees. Below, beyond the small bed of a dried-up stream lay the old city, girded by stone walls, with minarets and the towers of Christian shrines shooting into the sky behind them.

As the railway car from Queen Victoria's day crawled up the hill, I thought about Ariston, who arranged to meet each of his pupils separately, in various parts of the city, as if studying Greek required a deep conspiracy. This absurd eccentricity of his could be explained in many ways, but right now, as I waited for the blue railway car, that had gone past the Coptic monastery now and was climbing laboriously along the wall of the Jewish cemetery, I had a minor revelation: Ariston always tried to make sure the text he prepared was more or less indirectly connected with the place where he gave the lesson. But why had he taken me to this very hill one time, which seemed to have nothing to do with Aristides' *Apology*? And how did it go at the time?

> *And then Aristides of Athens addressed the Emperor Hadrian with these words: They represent Dionysos as a god and the teacher of drunkenness, who seduced the wives of his neighbours until he went mad, and was at last put to death by the Titans. So if Dionysos could not come to his own aid when they killed him, and in addition proved a madman, a vagrant and a drunkard, how could he be a god? And how can he help others, who could not bring aid to himself? Quite another is Jesus, noble Emperor...*

"However it might sound," I had said at the time, as I struggled to translate the final sentence in particular, "however it might sound, Aristides' argument makes no sense. How can one defend Christianity like that? Jesus' enemies used almost exactly the same arguments. To them he was none other than a vagrant, a madman, a drunkard and a lecher. They too said he did not help himself, so how was he to help others? What Aristides says about Dionysos is what Jesus' enemies say about him. Is this symmetry of arguments common in such cases?"

Ariston had not responded to my doubts. As the railway car full of tourists moved downhill, he had stood up from the bench, where we had already spent a good hour, and pointed out the Coptic monastery.

"Do you know that's the oldest church in this city? Maybe the oldest surviving Christian church in the world?"

Now, as I travelled down in the empty car, it occurred to me that his choice on that occasion was no accident either. The text he was tormenting me with at the time – or rather its hardest extract – came from the first *Apology* in history. Whether it was Hermias, or Theophilus of Antioch, whether Apollinaris of Hierapolis, Militiades, Tatian the Assyrian, Justin the Martyr, or even my teacher's namesake, Ariston of Pella, they all wrote their defences of the Christians after that famous, great and excellent speech by Aristides of Athens. Perhaps that is why the oldest *Apology* had to be deciphered in a spot overlooking the oldest church? What did I know about the Copts anyway? Just once, as a tourist, I had heard their singing at the Church of the Holy Sepulchre. It was powerful, archaic and so beautiful that I have never heard anything like it, not even in a Russian Orthodox church.

From the stop at the bottom of the hill I headed for the old city on foot. Outwardly, nothing seemed to be happening in the narrow alleyways. But the closed shop shutters, empty café terraces and low number of tourists creeping stealthily back to their hotels – all this made a rather gloomy impression. Only on the edge of the Armenian district did I catch sight of some boys kicking a ball in the street. They were happy, because there were no cars to get in their way.

The taxi I finally managed to catch drove slowly, as if on its way to a funeral. On a bridge, at a military checkpoint they wanted to turn us back, but though crumpled and expired, the press pass I found by some miracle in my jacket pocket cleared the way for us.

"It's all the fault of the Americans," said the driver, taking a close look at me in the mirror. "First they pay the rebels, then they order them to be killed, and finally they film it all. America is pure evil. If it weren't for America, this country would be happy. Like Lebanon used to be."

I nodded as I paid him for the ride outside the Admiralty building. The enormous square with the Fountain of Liberty in the middle, by which two dozing armoured cars were discreetly biding their time, was buzzing with life as normal. Only the skilled observer might have noticed fewer rickshaws and taxis than usual, all spinning in the great whirlpool of the roundabout, occasionally breaking free of it like insects leaving a swarm to land at one of two ranks – either at the Hotel Continental, where the striped awnings of the Café El Rashid recalled the days of Prince Albert, or outside the Admiralty building, where I had just alighted. The policemen I glimpsed out of the corner of my eye checking the ID of a passer-by as I slowly made my way towards the terrace of the Café El Rashid were a normal sight in this city on an ordinary day, so I became all the more determined to dispense with Yussuf's services for the future. There were several courier firms I could call in the city, so why should I have to listen to his fantastic ravings? The boy must have been to one of those suspicious dives in the suburbs the day before, where to the noisy beat of the horribly strident local version of techno, they sat under liberation movement posters, smoking dope imported from Afghanistan.

"He must have had some good stuff," I thought, as I

approached the terrace of the Café El Rashid, "if he was still having such weird visions on his way to me in the upper town." Nevertheless, recognising a couple of Russian tourists sitting at the next table, I asked in their language: "Have you seen any motorbikes here?"

"The Harley riders had a world rally in Rijeka," said the girl, addressing the man. "We were there last year," she went on, looking at me and smiling. "But here?"

"It's quiet here," said her companion. "The riots have been going on since morning, but in the port area. The army has the waterfront district so tightly surrounded a mouse couldn't slip through. See what I mean?"

As he spoke, he and everyone else stared up at the sky. Above the square, from somewhere between the tower of Ali's Mosque and the spire of the church of the Assumption of the Blessed Virgin Mary, three army helicopters had emerged. Flying very low, they were making a dreadful noise. At the height of the Admiralty building they abruptly changed course and flew straight over the port district. Soon after we heard the dull rumble of several explosions coming from the direction of the sea.

"Till evening," said the Russian, "then it'll all be over."

"Are you from the Baltic?" the girl asked me. "You've got such a hard accent."

I nodded as I leaned over the Café El Rashid's ice cream and dessert menu, which I already knew. My Russian neighbours were absorbed in each other again; young and sympathetic, they looked like a honeymoon couple.

Ariston lived in the port district – I had only been to his place once with a letter of recommendation from Professor Hannover; he had received me in a long, narrow hallway, read the letter and said almost in a whisper: "Never come here again – please remember that." Then, after a short pause, speaking louder he had added: "Once you have found somewhere to live, please send me your address. I'll let you know when the time comes. Please don't imagine you're my only pupil."

Later on, once we had met many times in various parts of the city, his dry manner did not bother me at all. He knew all the ancient languages, and this fact alone commanded the greatest respect. I never dared to inquire why he had not once asked about my dissertation, nor did I ever try to investigate why he used that bizarre system of his, informing me of each successive meeting in a short letter brought by a courier. Didn't he trust the post? The suspicion that he had a share in the city's courier firms seemed downright insulting. Perhaps it was Ariston's way of keeping his pupils isolated, so they'd never know anything about each other?

Instead of easing up a bit as the afternoon advanced, the heat was getting stronger. In the shade of the palm trees that ran around the Admiralty building colonnade sat a legless beggar. The only reason he had not been moved on from there today must have been the riots: the police, army and city guard had something else to do. I threw a silver coin into his bowl. The expression in his film-coated eyes was dreadful, because it wasn't really an expression, but the declaration of a void. I felt a shudder, as if it were a warning clearly aimed at me: don't go any further. But I walked on, quite at random, down a path in the botanical garden, which ran for several hectares behind the Admiralty building right down to Diocletian's Avenue, where it was fenced off by a wall with no way through to the other side of town. At this moment I couldn't help thinking of Madame Sorge: she was the only one of my teacher's pupils I had met, though of course it happened by accident. Ariston had told me to meet him in a part of the garden where terebinth trees and sycamore figs formed a circle. In the middle stood a stone bench with the carved face of a lion, and that was where I caught sight of them, poring over a book. She was reading something slowly, and he was listening, correcting a word from time to time or adding a comment in French. When he saw me I could no longer withdraw, so I glanced at my watch to emphasise that I'd come at the appointed time; Ariston beckoned me over, and then introduced us to each other in a dry, business-like way. Before we had sat down to our lesson, as I watched the bright splash of Madame Sorge's hat disappearing in the shade of the terebinths, I asked what language the book they were working from was in.

"It's an epic poem by Ferdowsi," he replied. "Have you heard of him?"

As I had not, he merely added: "It is in Old Persian." And in his usual way, he immediately asked me a question: "You see the path Madame Sorge has taken? It is stony, isn't it? So remind me, please, what would be the word for 'stony'? What did you say? *'Trachys'*? Good, but please correct your accent –

Greek is not French…"

It was the only joke I ever heard Ariston make, as at once we moved on to the proper name of the Trachonitis region, which Luke the Evangelist mentions as a land of pagans.

Now the bench under the terebinths was empty, and the foggy memory of Madame Sorge began to dissolve in the scorching afternoon air like the phantom of the strange city in the form of the Greek word *trachys*. From far beyond the stone wall, built from the remains of Diocletian's baths, came the sound of short bursts of gunfire, ambulance sirens and the rumble of heavier missiles. Founded in the last century by a philanthropist called Hersch, the garden took these noises calmly, as if the plants growing here belonged to an order in which politics and war had nothing to say. And yet it was an illusion. As I was crossing a Chinese bridge over a pond, watching the huge turtles among the water lily pads, a nearby explosion preceded by a piercing whistle shook the earth, the wooden footbridge, the air and the plants.

Only some fifteen seconds later, as I got up from the water once the last scraps of stone, wood, steel, earth and leaves had stopped falling with a splash onto the surface of the pond, did I realise what had happened: a shell had hit the garden wall. Chunks of rock, or the blast of the explosion, or probably both, had blown away the bridge. Not much of the Chinese-style structure was left. Somewhere at the bottom of the pond lay my camera. Beside me drifted two dead turtles. With some effort, I emerged from the waterside ooze. My muddy sandals felt as if each one weighed more than a kilo. Nor did I have my watch; the strap must have broken in the water. I wanted to light a cigarette, but there was nothing in my jacket pocket but a soggy wad of tobacco. My head was aching. I lay down on the lawn on my back and gazed up at the pure, bright sky, across which not even the smallest cloud was floating. I couldn't have cared less if a garden curator found me there, a policeman, a soldier or a rebel; now, at dusk, in the night or at dawn, tomorrow, the day after or in a week from now. I was hearing words I had learned with Ariston: *anagaion, philos, plous, iatros, estin, angelos, hora, peristera*. I could see the river mouth where my father and I used to fish together. We were sailing in a boat; around us lush meadows stretched along the riverbanks, then some sandy dunes were blinding us with their brilliant whiteness. A salty wind was murmuring, the pine trees smelled of resin, and we were happy.

When I opened my eyes, dusk had fallen. Then I saw the hole in the botanical garden wall. It was wide, shaped like a big letter "U". On the other side, an armoured car was slowly driving down Diocletian's Avenue. The beam of a searchlight flashed across the lawn; I heard some shouts, the car stopped, and there were two soldiers standing over me. I couldn't speak. Although they were pointing their guns at me, I slowly reached a hand into my inside jacket pocket, where my old press pass ought to be. The first one kicked me in the side. The other one kept screaming something, but I couldn't understand a word. Finally I managed to extract a sodden cardboard rectangle. It was the train ticket for my journey from the Hill of Prophets down to the old city. With my hands folded on the back of my neck they stood me against the wall while they conferred with their patrol commander. Only then did I say in English: "Do you want to shoot me? I was here by accident when the shell struck. I live above the Café Hillel in the upper town."

They were furious. But the commander made a call to summon a police car, in which I was briefly interrogated. Then they made another call to ask the owner of the house if he could confirm the identity of his lodger, which he did. We drove through the labyrinth of streets in the port area, through smashed-up barricades, and past burning cars, tyres, dustbins and warehouses.

"So what do you imagine?" asked the sergeant. "Think we're going to take you home? Or to the Hotel Ritz, perhaps?"

The policemen's laughter didn't last long. Out of a side street a motorcyclist emerged; instead of a helmet he was wearing a balaclava, and over his shoulder hung a Kalashnikov. Before the driver had time to perform any sort of manoeuvre, the motorcyclist had hurled a Molotov cocktail at the bonnet. He rode off like a daredevil, on one wheel, and as we leaped out of the car, now hidden behind a recess, he opened fire on us. I lay in the roadway until the firing stopped. Then I slowly walked the length of a building. None of the policemen got up from the ground to come after me. Although I had been in this district several times, I had completely lost my bearings. A familiar corner, where I thought I recognised a tobacco shop or a grocery turned out to be merely similar to the one I remembered. I wandered around like that for I don't know how long, returning a couple of times to places I had already been in fifteen minutes earlier. Finally, anguished to the utmost degree, I sat down on the pavement and leaned back against an empty container. A motorbike or an armoured car speeding down the street could no longer make any impression on me. I wanted to just stay like that until dawn, then head for the lower town – somehow get out of this labyrinth in the light of day.

Sleep did not overtake me, probably thanks to the fact that after a while I recognised a house on the other side of the street. I had only been in it once – when with a letter of recommendation and a trembling heart I had gone to see Ariston on the first floor. As my left foot had swollen up, it took me a long time to hobble the last dozen metres. The entryphone had been ripped out, the front door was not locked, and the stairs inside were not lit. I knocked at his door. He didn't answer, so I pressed the door handle. In the long hallway where he had once received me there was no furniture at all. The bedroom, and the study too, presented almost as pitiful a sight. An old bed, a small cupboard for books and a work table – that was all, not counting the clothing cast here and there on chairs and stools. In the kitchen there was an old sideboard, like the ones manufactured in our country in the early 1960s. Only when I put on the light did I notice the open pantry door. And there was Ariston, hanging from a clothes-line attached to the roof beam. I went back into the kitchen and opened the first drawer I came to in the sideboard to find a knife. Then the phone rang. I spent a long time looking for it, until finally I found it in the bedroom, hidden under the bed. I lifted the receiver and heard your voice.

It was more or less like this: I managed to get up, and with the receiver in my hand I wandered around the kitchen, making myself some coffee. As your sentences reached me from afar, I gazed out the window, watching a couple of cats steal by, one behind the other, in the deep snow, one ginger and one black, but in fact neither of the two realities – neither the one outside the window nor the one formed by your words – was getting through to me, as if I were still immersed in the world of my absurd dream. How could I answer your question about Mateusz's painting at a moment like that? About the academics, the critics, or the avant-gardists? What did I care about Monsignore just then, or what the Archbishop's assistant thought? The screams, denunciations, squabbles and scandals? I couldn't gather my thoughts, as if an invisible thread were still tying me to everything I had experienced over there, on the other side of consciousness. Why was there someone like Yussuf? How had Ariston made his way into my dream? Where was the city I had been wandering around? No dream had ever put me in such a state of confusion, though to be honest it was more than that – the feeling that in any place and at any time you can cross a boundary, on the other side of which the contours of things, matters and people form a different pattern. I didn't feel like talking, and you took that for peevishness. Today, as I write this chronicle, things are different, though, as the playwright Mrożek put it, I couldn't see what I wanted to, just what I was bound to.

CHAPTER II

or how I first came to talk to Mateusz about the Eucharist, in highly unsuitable, not to say morally and acoustically scandalous circumstances

OF COURSE I HAD BEEN TO Jerusalem, and that may well be why certain details of the dream I described to you in the previous chapter featured so clearly. The view from the Mount of Olives onto the dried-up bed of the brook of Cedron, with the walls and gates of the old city rising beyond, was an exact – so to speak – memory of the one I had admired as I leaned against a low rock wall at the observation point. I had taken a photograph of some boys playing football in the Armenian district. I had been to the Church of the Holy Sepulchre, and I had indeed heard a Coptic mass. A few days before I arrived the Palestinians had blown up two buses full of passengers. On Hillel Street, at a café of the same name, I had ordered a glass of chilled white wine.

I found it quite easy to trace the origin of some other

details of the dream to other cities. The railway I had taken down the hill came from Budapest: known as the *sikló*, it runs steeply uphill from Clark Square to the Royal Palace on Castle Hill, from where there is a fabulous view of the Danube, Pest, the Parliament building and the oldest bridge in the city, the Széchenyi Chain Bridge. The botanical garden was deceptively similar to the one in Zagreb, though there aren't any near-eastern terebinths growing there. However, beyond that I started having problems: the square, the Admiralty, the river and the port were all hard to locate and had no real prototypes, at least not in my experience. A photo album of Alexandria that I looked through specially for this purpose did not bring any solutions, nor did several albums of the excellent drawings by the nineteenth-century artist David Roberts.

You will say there's nothing odd about it, because dreams have their own inscrutable logic, and you're right – for instance, in this story (though I don't know if that's the right word for it), the Gethsemane church at the foot of the Mount of Olives had turned into the Coptic monastery, which is situated, at least in Jerusalem, in a completely different place. Then again you may ask, what has that got to do with it? I merely wish to show you how much effort and research I have put into explaining to myself something that probably doesn't need explaining.

So let's move on from these places. What I find far more astonishing about this sort of dream is the pre-set memory. What I mean is that if you encounter someone for the first time ever – in a dream, of course – you seem to have some knowledge of them, as if you have already met them lots of times before, even though you have never had anything to do with that person, whether awake or asleep. And so I could write about Yussuf that he "liked giving vent to such issues" because I knew it perfectly clearly, though in actual fact, how on earth did I know that, if it was the first time such a person had ever entered my dream – or my consciousness?

Ariston caused me even greater trouble. The fact that he had once received me at his flat and had given me lots of lessons, like the one I remembered, at the top of the hill, was not the actual subject of the dream, its plot – to put it crudely – obvious plan or moving image; on the contrary, all these bits of information came from somewhere in my memory, though perhaps not the kind we conjure up when we're having a conversation about a third person whom we have known since childhood.

Here I will take a short cut: Ariston came to me from a book I read a long time ago, which must have left a much deeper impression in my mind that I had suspected while reading it: do you remember the character Balthazar in Durrell's novel? He was old, eccentric and rather batty, with a circle of admirers to whom he lectured on the most obscure mysteries of cabbalistic doctrine. Transformed into Ariston, in the totally different time and space of my dream, he taught me Greek, which, as you well know, I have never adequately mastered. This discovery, if I can put it like that, gave me a sense of liberation, as well as an explanation of the trickiest element in the dream. If I were to go and see a psychoanalyst, he would immediately make Ariston into a father, whose death – no doubt necessary for the development of the patient's personality – had occurred prematurely, before he had passed on life's most essential experiences and mysteries.

When I met Mateusz, I had not yet read Durrell, and in those days I could never have even dreamed of travelling abroad, and yet my first visit to his studio, which I shall now attempt to describe to you, had a certain element which all these years later appeared in that dream in a slightly altered form.

The noise of the electric train came rattling through the open windows of the old German villa. Mateusz was standing in the kitchen alcove trying to find a corkscrew, while the Engineer stared about him with a look on his face implying that all the oils, sketches, drawings, water colours and gouaches filled him with total disgust. He went up to the easel, then the wall, almost pressing his nose against the canvas as if he were very short-sighted, then turned towards us wearing a grimace and lisped: "Dweadful, tewible, howendous!"

"What's your point?" asked Mateusz, as the cork finally popped from the bottle of Bulgarian wine and he poured it into some thick, tea-stained glasses. "Maybe you could paint it better yourself?"

The Engineer made a face that implied extreme irritation with a dash of contempt.

"The point is not whether something is well or badly

painted," he drawled. "The point is whether it's painted at all. Fucking hell, can't you understand that?"

"To be honest, no, I can't really," I said, looking the Engineer straight in the eye. "This man, nailed to the earth's sphere," I went on, pointing at the canvas, "is screaming so loud he can be heard in every galaxy. But God is not there."

"Fucking hell," said the Engineer, clutching his head and looking at our host, "who've you got here? A virgin incowupt?"

"This is his," said Mateusz, holding up a copy of my first book, which admittedly was at that point just a typescript in cardboard covers, "but you wouldn't understand it anyway."

"What an arsehole," snarled the Engineer. "Anything litewawy in art is a piece of shit."

Mateusz nodded indulgently, implying that he'd heard it all a hundred times before and did not necessarily agree with the Engineer, who had now gone entirely on the offensive; hopping about like a boxer, he was running up to each canvas and board in turn shouting: "And what the fuck is this? Fucking litewature! Paint is just dwied-up blood! It's ancient dwied-up sperm! Painting is kaput! It's over. Can't you see that?"

Suddenly he took a cut-throat razor out of his pocket, which, as I can see now, hadn't got there by accident, went up to the painting I'd just mentioned, "Ecce Homo", and, without a word, with long, slow strokes of the blade, ripped it into narrow strips. Mateusz was astonished, maybe even mesmerised at the sight of this destruction: the point being that it was planned, deliberately performed before his eyes, so patently and brazenly that it took your breath away.

"This is diwect action," said the Engineer, stepping back with a satisfied air from the canvas, which now resembled wallpaper, or a honeycomb – "new age art, and you can give that," he said, ripping off a strip of canvas and tossing it on the paint-spattered floorboards, "to the whores at the Beehive for sanitawy towels!" And he burst into nervous laughter, so loud that for a moment it drowned out the clatter of the trains.

Mateusz didn't move an inch. But as soon as the Engineer went up to the next canvas he blocked his path, and for a while they grappled in total silence. This was the first debate on the subject of modern art I ever took part in. In those days the Engineer, of whom you're going to hear a lot more, was assistant to Professor Śledź at the Academy, and the story of his final exam had passed into school legend – twenty-five canvases painted red and slashed with a razor, given top marks by the committee. So there I stood next to them, and to tell the truth I was horrified. Mateusz finally seized the razor from the Engineer's hand, put the blade to his neck and hissed: "You can cut off your own dick for all I care, but keep your hands off my stuff!"

Only then did the real fight begin. It would be too long and tedious to describe – I'll just tell you they gave each other a real beating, hitting hard and falling to the floor a few times. Luckily the razor fell on the ground too, and I got the chance to pick it up and hide it in my pocket. The two adversaries knocked over just about everything in the room: the easel, chairs, bedside table, lamp, cabinet and stool. The end was equally impressive. Mateusz picked up the Engineer like a heavy beam of wood and hurled him at the Venetian window. Can you imagine the racket? It wasn't just the advocate of revolution that went sailing onto the lawn from the first floor, but the window frame and a thousand slivers of glass went flying down too.

A draught came gusting through the studio, and dozens of sheets of paper were caught up by the wind, whirling between the walls and ceiling before finally coming to land on the floor like a flock of gulls.

"Should someone who calls themselves an engineer be preaching on the subject of art?" Mateusz was standing at the basin, washing the blood from his face. "I know it's a sign of the times: the city, the machine, the proletariat, but does it have to go that far?"

I was listening to him and not listening all at once. I was holding a sheet of paper on which a system of circles and parallel lines formed something shaped like a Christmas tree.

"Oh, that's the Kabbalah!" said Mateusz, distinctly cheering up. "At the top you've got the Crown, and right at the bottom the Kingdom!"

He opened another bottle of wine and, as if nothing had happened, gave me an introduction to this arcane knowledge.

"The Pillar of Balance is the most important one," he said, "but even more curious is the fact that before He made the world God must have had to shrink Himself for there to be enough room. You see? For there to be enough room! But why did you tell the Engineer God isn't there? Don't you believe in Him? Maybe you're an atheist?"

The conversation would probably have proved extremely interesting, if it weren't for the fact that just then three policemen entered the studio. Who called them? Mr and Mrs Zielenko, of course. They lived underneath the studio, and their crude, secretive nature was utterly offended by having to live next door to artists. Resettled here straight from the countryside, they only had one hobby: more or less once a week, whenever they heard anything louder than the patter of mice or saw something that surpassed their imagination, they called the police.

"Citizen," began the sergeant, "what's going on in here? Making noise again?"

As quietly as could be, Mateusz handed them his identity card, then lit his pipe and sat in an armchair, as if Mr and Mrs Zielenko and their entire backstage crew, including the Civic Militia, the Volunteer Reserve, the district Party committee, the allotment owners' club, the village homeowners' circle, the residential committee, the house committee, the Front for National Unity and the parish committee were of no concern to him at all.

"Bit of a tussle, was there?" said the sergeant, holding the identity card in two fingers and waving it above the defendant's head. "Should we withhold this document and summons you?"

Mateusz did not even deign to make eye contact with the

policeman.

"Windows flying out, are they?"

"Citizen Sergeant," said one of the constables, who while examining the paintings leaning against the wall had come across a picture of a woman's head with a woolly forest of spirally intertwining penises growing out of it, "perverts like this should be sent straight to the camps. Why the bloody hell were they closed down?"

"Shut your gob, Rydomski!" said the sergeant, rashly revealing the flatfoot's name to us. "You'd best keep your nose out of politics because you're a bit short on brains. And as for you, gentlemen," he turned to us, "we've had complaints about you singing songs!"

"We were singing the *Internationale*, as usual," I said without hesitating, "and please make a note of it in your report."

"Quite so," said Mateusz, breaking his silence from behind clouds of pipe smoke. "The *Internationale*, in the report, without question!"

Just then we heard the mighty thud of the Engineer's footsteps on the stairs. In his own way he proved a genius: to fall onto the lawn and then get up as if nothing had happened, brush down his clothes and make his way to the nearest bar, quickly down a couple of vodkas there and return in even better condition than before to the site of his missionary activities he must have had an undeniably potent categorical imperative driving him.

"Fucking hell, man," he said, throwing himself into the

sergeant's arms and covering him in soggy kisses. "The avant garde and the police, that's the best coalition!" As if he had a talent for that sort of clowning and some well practised tricks, quick as a flash the same bear hug was performed – actually without any protest – on the other two policemen. Then the Engineer stood in the middle of the studio, spread his arms as if about to fly and declared: "It was me, fuck it, thwough that window! The one and only me! That's what you call an expewiment! Hey, arseholes, don't you get it? Don't like that sort of art, do you? But it's the future! Not that." He nodded towards the partly painted canvases leaning against the wall. "Not that." And he blew his nose in their direction, which was clearly a hit with the policemen.

Once the sergeant had repeated a few official formulae and they had finally gone, Mateusz declared: "Engineer, get out of here. And never come back. Do you hear me? Never!"

He wasn't even offended. He poured himself a full glass of wine, drank it in one go, giggled and cooed as he was leaving: "Wilt thou be gone? It is not yet near day!"

Over the fretsaw and hardboard we returned to our interrupted conversation. Mateusz measured the window area with a piece of string, and as he positioned a stool to lean on, said: "The main thing was the flow of light! A spark that came floating down. At least that's how the authors of the Kabbalah express it."

"The Big Bang," I said, laboriously sawing at the hardboard as Mateusz held it up, "is even less imaginable than what you said just now."

"Exactly," he said, taking his turn at the fretsaw, "the density of matter before the explosion."

"One point six times ten to the power of minus twenty-seven," I recited, "according to Planck. A dot smaller than a pinhead. And all this came out of it. Even this wretched board, us, the grass, the clouds, the sun, the galaxies, everything. Can it be possible? They tell us to believe it. And you'd think it's just the Bible-bashers, but no, it's the scientists too."

"A gweat big fucker of a bang!" said Mateusz, parodying the Engineer, "a cosmic ejaculation!"

And once we had finally nailed the hardboard over the broken windowpane, in a few strokes he sketched the Pillar of Balance on it, with the other two pillars, of Mercy and Severity next to it.

"This diagram," he explained, "has been bothering me for ages now, though I have no doubt it was only created by a play of the imagination. Human curiosity, nothing more or less."

Then we left the studio. Do you remember the footbridge over the stream? Where the street with the old villas and mansions ends, there's a deep rift through the middle of town all the way to the sea, a gorge several metres deep with a small brook running down it. Right on that bridge Mateusz, who was leading the way, suddenly stopped, turned around, pointed a finger at me and asked in a loud voice, almost shouting: "And which scene in the Bible do you consider the most powerful, apart from the beginning, of course? Because in your book you make allusions, but you refuse to say anything clearly!"

It was funny, and try to imagine that situation simply, realistically, without any of the symbolism we're inclined to add years later: those two guys standing facing each other on the narrow bridge, while the one asking the question leans against the railing like a ticket inspector, barring the way for the one who has to give an answer – as I've said, it's about the Bible; below them there's a babbling brook whose postglacial age can be set at some ten thousand years, they're talking about a book that is not more than three thousand years old, the city surrounding them is not more than a hundred, and if you add up both their ages at the time, the speakers are less than seventy-five. You will ask why I'm so obsessed with numbers, so I'll say how could I not be, since – in that time long past – we had only just stopped talking about the Kabbalah, and now, as I give you an account of that afternoon, I'll move on to what happened next: so, without stopping to think for long, there on the bridge I started humming a line from vespers that I must have dredged up somehow from childhood memory: "You are a high priest for ever!"

At which Mateusz, who had turned around by now and was walking down the bridge, joined in, loudly singing the next line with me: "According to the order of Melchisedech!"

An old lady who came walking towards us from the Sierakowski mansion gave us an extremely worried look, then stopped on the bridge, turned around twice to look our way, and made the sign of the cross over the general area just in case, because – and you have to make allowance for the fact that we were already a bit tipsy – on the other side of the brook we repeated our tuneful chorus at the tops of our voices, then roared with laughter as we set off briskly round the gentle curve of the little street that ran downhill to the Golden Beehive. Naturally, I had to explain at once: why, wherefore and whence Melchisedech, when there are only two verses about him, while the rest of the Bible is full of men and women with far more interesting fates. By the time we reached the chemist's on the corner of the promenade what I found most interesting had been said: unknown, mysterious and enigmatic, he only makes one appearance, to greet Abraham in the heat and dust of the afternoon, in the middle of the road beyond which the Negev desert now stretches. Abraham is on his way back from battle, though the point is not that, I said heatedly, but what is said and done at that moment by Melchisedech, the archetype of all magi and shamans.

By now we were standing on the café terrace, which in those days, despite the warm weather, was bound to be empty, because the official season hadn't started yet. Suddenly Mateusz glanced at his watch and cried: "What a nightmare! How ghastly, I'm late – you grab a table, I'll be back from the station in an instant!" And off he ran, across the little square outside the church and vanished behind the post office.

Cherchez la femme!, I'll politely explain, rather than going into details. Maryna was furious with him for being late and for having had to wait five minutes for her lover. She had that sort of character – proud and imperious; so first they quarrelled on the platform, or at the taxi rank outside the station, and soon they were shouting about breaking up, saying never again, this was the last time, she'd get herself a hotel room, and he'd rather consort with some old hag of a model from the Academy than with such a virago, but all this, of course, was just a form of foreplay, and after a good ten minutes of loud remarks, exclamations and ultimatums they reached Mateusz's studio: he wielding her two suitcases, and she holding a bunch of lily-of-the-valley he'd managed to buy from a flower stall outside the station, and then, literally moments later, what usually happens between lovers after a long time apart must have happened.

I could tell they wouldn't turn up at the café for at least another two hours. I tried to imagine Maryna's gaze sweeping across the hardboard with the drawing of the three pillars of the Kabbalah: of mercy, severity and balance. Which one would she choose? However, as I sat over a weak coffee, my more serious thoughts were directed elsewhere. Do you remember that interior? In those days the Golden Beehive was divided into whole continents, separated by grey streams of tobacco smoke and invisible borders. Black-market money-changers, old ladies from the landed gentry, old men who fought for the Home Army, regulars at the races, pimps in the pay of the Security Service, their lovely, young novice whores, real and mythical artists, actors from the nearby theatre, petty swindlers and fraudsters, private business owners who had lost it all or got rich, the wealthier patients from the socialist sanatoria, students, distributors of the underground press, professors from the Academy, journalists who were either sober or drunk from dawn, merchant navy officers, ministry officials on business trips, provincial heroines – none of them can possibly have remembered the old name of the café dating from imperial times (when it was frequented by rentiers from Berlin, grain merchants from Drohobych and Polish aristo-crats from Ukraine), so quite without knowing it they were all keeping the spirit of this strange city alive, the emblem of which should be not a seagull with a fish in its beak, but a fallen, Secession-era angel, to teach us that as everything has already been and happened, and as everything is already behind us, the only thing to be done is to seize the moment and the opportunity: always avidly, without any scruples or consideration for so-called consideration. You may smile and think I'm exaggerating, but don't you remember how the Golden Beehive was like the atrium, the waiting room, the portal through which you had to pass to end up, once the sun had set, in the next, more decadent circle down, at "the Spat"?

So here's how it went at SPATiF – the acronym for the Actors' Club: Helmut had set up his double bass by the wall next to the drum kit, there were already lots of people, and there was a crush at the bar, into which the Engineer had wriggled his way like an eel; he probably knew everyone there – I saw him drinking to the poet George Kanada, who immedi-ately drank to the poet Olo, who meanwhile was drinking to Arthur Rimbaud – who was not actually there in person, though his spirit hovered permanently above the bar – and also to the poet Kamro, who was physically present, but spiritually absent. I also caught a glimpse of Professor Śledź accompanied by some of his female students from the

Academy, two worn-out journalists – one from the *Voice* and the other from the *Daily*; as usual there were also some of those young ladies known as "idealists" looking for "strong impressions", Editor Trusz from the local television, Professor Grzebień from anatomy, the dancer Mazuro, the tenor Goszczyński, and over the chorus of shouts, orders and toasts Wojtek the barman reigned like a conductor, now raising, now reducing the tempo of this entire symphony.

I didn't know the percussionist, but as soon as he sent the first ripple across the cymbals with his brush, at once you could tell Helmut had a partner, not a bungler: quiet at first, as if just being tapped out casually, the beat almost instantly put us all into a trance; needless to say, the conversation did not die down, but that wasn't the point at all: the idea was to set the air swinging, and along with it, gradually, systematically, bodies and minds, glasses, bottles, chairs, pictures, chandeliers, coat stands, french window panes, floorboards, nails, table tops, mirrors and urinals, and once that had happened, Helmut slowly got off his bar stool, stood behind the double bass and plucked at a string, just one, then a second: a low sound, modulated by the musician's palm against the fingerboard, literally pervaded everything, to reign supreme over the whole room, in symbiosis with the beat of the percussion from the very first bar.

Just then I noticed some commotion by the metal-plated door: Ksawery the bouncer had just let a new group of guests inside, including Mateusz, who waved to me, and Maryna, who was scanning the room as if to make sure she'd be recognised; and of course she was – famous from the cinema, her face at once drew a lot of stares.

"What a nightmare," Mateusz whispered in my ear. "Ghastly – I had to run and fetch the glazier, can you imagine? On a Saturday afternoon? In a country like this?"

But he wasn't at all downcast. He introduced me to Maryna, then to Doctor Lewada from the Medical Academy, Jan Wybrański, who was a physicist, the painter Siemaszko, and to Antoni Berdo, whose lectures I remembered from my first year of philology. Obviously, these introductions did not involve giving surnames, titles, specialities and employment, but perhaps you can guess why I am describing them so precisely: yes, they're going to form the canvas for this chronicle, though at the time neither I, much less they could have known, nor could Mateusz, that about fifteen years later we'd be meeting on a theatre stage at a table covered in a white cloth, in front of a camera lens.

"Maryna and I picked them up from the Beehive," said Mateusz, having to shout over the percussion solo. "Great that you've come!"

"I waited two hours!" I replied just as loud. "Then I walked along the beach!"

Helmut, who was back from the toilet, let the percussionist have a break while he took the lead: the tune on the double bass changed from a lyrical *staccato* into a *poco allegretto*, then an *allegro*, and finally an *allegro vivace*, only to turn into an *allegro furioso* and to keep going at that pace for a good quarter of an hour. By now we were all crowded into a corner, sitting at a small round table.

"Want a smoke?" Siemaszko asked me, taking some tobacco out of a small tin. "This is a thousand times better than that foul stuff," he said, pointing at the glasses, "that's real white man's shit. Do you know how the Scythians did it? They had a small, triangular tent" – at this point he took out some cigarette papers – "heated up some stones inside it, then tossed cannabis seeds onto them. Full steam ahead! And the Zulus? Well," he giggled, gluing down his roll-up, "first they cover a handful of leaves with manure, then earth, ignite it" – he gave me a light – "and poke a hole in it to inhale through, as they lie there on mother Earth! What a mystical coitus! But the Persians are best, because they invented the galjan. So what if Muhammad Shah gave it the death penalty? Or Napoleon? He ordered the cafés where just a single smoker was caught to be walled up."

"Probably not in Paris," said Doctor Lewada, overhearing Siemaszko's last sentence, "I've never read a word about that!"

"Well, of course not – in Egypt, not the Place de la Concorde!" cried Siemaszko.

"And what's a galjan?" put in the physicist.

"A narghile, a water pipe," replied Mateusz. "There weren't any cafés on the Place de la Concorde, just a guillotine! Under Robespierre it did about a hundred heads a day!"

"That's an exaggeration." Berdo, who had been quiet until now, put down his glass of gin. "About a dozen at most. Conservative propaganda!"

"So perhaps the concentration camps are conservative propaganda too?" said Doctor Lewada, almost standing up from the sofa.

Berdo's reply was drowned out by the clatter of a new wave of percussion improvisation. Professor Śledź's student was performing a belly dance on the bar top. Naked, except for a pair of army boots, a general's cap and a frivolous velvet ribbon round her neck, she was shaking her shapely breasts like an odalisque in a silent film from the twenties.

While Maryna talked to Berdo, Mateusz came and sat on my side of the table and asked why Melchisedech had blessed bread and wine in particular. I replied that of all the possible explanations known to me the one that speaks to me directly is this: the most sacred things are bound to be the simplest. Anyone who comes walking across the desert will understand that at once.

At the bar there was a momentary confusion: in an effort to jump up on the counter, the poet Olo had grabbed the dancer by an army boot which had remained in his hands; the girl had lost her balance and come crashing down, but luckily had been caught in the sober arms of Editor Trusz just before falling to the floor.

"Fucking hell," screamed the Engineer, "what a *salto mortale*, you commie hack, I'm gonna beat the shit out of you!"

One swift, extremely neat and accurate punch on the chin deprived the Engineer of the right to say more. The editor straightened his tie, and as if the whole incident weren't worth further concern, ordered a beer from the barman. The bouncer and his helper had to exert themselves: first they escorted the Engineer to the door, then they had to pick up the now dormant Olo from under the bar and put him in the alcove: maybe you remember, that's what the little side room with a sofa and two small tables was called. Helmut wasn't playing now, but Przybysław Diak had turned up with a new swarm of customers straight from the jazz club; minutes later he'd been invited to play, and had started up a dialogue with the percussionist on his saxophone.

"If that's the case," said Mateusz, "then Jesus' farewell to his disciples shouldn't have taken place in a chamber at all, but in the desert. Bread and wine," he repeated, "in the desert. But what on earth are we talking about? And why? It's absurd! Pure paranoia!"

"Of course," Berdo cut in, when Maryna had heard out his nebulous monologue and eagerly turned to Doctor Lewada, "this is the worst of all possible worlds! But if it was only a fraction worse, it couldn't exist at all!"

I already had the source of this quotation on the tip of my tongue. Antoni Berdo, doctor of humanities, had only read one philosophy book: a selection of epigrams by Arthur Schopenhauer, chosen and translated by Jan Garewicz: that was where he got all his wisdom and stock phrases for every occasion.

"You talk like a philosopher," I said, "but in practice it doesn't prove to be true at all."

I saw him go pale and clench his teeth: my answer came from the same source.

"Bread and wine," repeated Mateusz. "We're talking about something simple, not some clever sophistry."

"You've been to my lectures," said Berdo, staring hard at me, "and that's to your credit. Now I remember your face."

Przybysław Diak and the percussionist had finished their short concert. Behind the bar, Wojtek put on some psychedelic rock and the middle of the room filled up with couples.

"There's nothing wrong with living in need," we heard Doctor Lewada say, leaning over Maryna, "but I'm sure you'll agree there's really no need to live in need."

On the dance floor Wybrański and Siemaszko were dancing with the so-called idealists. Two young boys, nestling into a plush armchair, were kissing each other softly on the mouth, timidly, for the first time ever.

"Everyone wants the same thing," said Mateusz, tapping the ash out of his pipe, "but not everyone asks for the same thing. Or maybe they're not capable of it?"

So there was this too: the memorable staircase down, steep as a ladder. What else do I have to tell you? The local trains were no longer, or not yet running. Mateusz and Maryna disappeared, heading uphill towards his studio. Lewada, Wybrański, Berdo and Siemaszko stayed at the club. I had no money for a taxi, so I set off along the seashore towards Jelitkowo, to catch the first tram at dawn, so I thought. But instead of tramping steadily along the loose sand, I kept rising up in the air a couple of feet and then falling down again, becoming painfully aware of the force of gravity. The cannabis wasn't doing my inner ear much good, and to go any further was out of the question, so I found an upside-down boat, crawled under it, and although it stank of fish, tar, ether and cat piss, I lay my exhausted body straight on the sand. I didn't have any dreams. In the morning, shivering with cold, I heard the foghorn from the New Port. The bay, the beach, the city, perhaps the whole world too, were plunged in thick, white cotton wool. There was no one waiting for me with bread and wine.

CHAPTER III

or how it came to a difficult cricothyrotomy and why the best people always have to be in exile; it will also be about Monsignore's stay in hospital

THE ONLY THING DOCTOR LEWADA really liked about Pohańcza was the view from his surgery. Even on grey, hopeless days, the great stretch of meadows ending in a distant mane of forest gave him a vague sense of freedom. If the health centre's windows (the surgery was essentially the entire health centre) had looked out on the other side of this corrugated iron barracks, put up in the late 1960s, then instead of rolling countryside Lewada would have had a daily view of his whole life here.

In short, it was the view of a village street lined in former farmhands' housing that led from a defunct distillery to a church on a small hill. Naturally, the church was still active. Further on, in a weed-choked park, the ruins of a Junker's mansion loomed ominously. It had burned down so long ago that none of the locals could remember what it used to look like. The legend persisted that just before the Red Army invaded the former owners hid some treasure in the neighbourhood. In the late 1980s, when Lewada wasn't yet in Pohańcza, teams of treasure hunters had searched the ponds, the river bend, park and cellars. Instead of an Amber Chamber or a chest full of Jewish gold they had dug up a German corpse in an SS uniform. Throughout the communist era the large barns, stables, pigsties and granaries that had once formed the estate of the von Kotwitz family had belonged to a state-owned farm modestly named "The Future". Now they didn't belong to anyone: empty and pillaged of everything of any sort of value, they looked like the set for a film by Tarkovsky or Szulkin.

And so the doctor was spared this view during working hours, and sometimes that alone was enough to put him in a good mood. Especially if summer cumulus clouds were scudding past his window, or the sun were illuminating a large stretch of snowdrifts. Whenever it was rotten weather the doctor liked to remind himself of a phrase he had memorised from the *Egyptian Book of the Dead*: "There is nothing bad in any place where you abide."

You can guess Pohańcza was not his dream location, and yet for the locals, who after a few months of his practice came to respect and admire the doctor, his presence was the source of endless gossip. Some said he had botched an operation in the city, or that he'd run away from his debts, and there were others who claimed he had fled the Mafia, whose doctor he had been. As he kept himself to himself and wasn't a drinker, they found him all the more intriguing. He rarely went to church, but the old priest Father Jaźwiński spoke very highly of the doctor; anyone who had revived the practice here after five years during which the health centre door had remained shut could not be a bad person.

Let that suffice as an introduction. On the day I'm going to describe, Doctor Lewada got up at seven as usual, performed his ablutions and listened to the radio as he drank a cup of coffee.

"Today's bomb blast," said Superintendent Glinka in the studio, "cannot be compared with the earlier ones. Those bombs," he coughed, "went off in the alcohol sections at hypermarkets, and although they caused the owners big losses, no one was injured. They all exploded at night. But now," the superintendent cleared his throat, "we have a situation of a different quality, because the small all-night shop on Conrad Street has been literally blown apart, with its customers and staff inside! We are still trying to identify the victims and gather evidence."

As usual, various experts were there to make know-it-all remarks on air: after the superintendent came a Professor Jabłoński, who had predicted a situation of this kind. The all-night shops selling alcohol should have been closed down long ago, and as the government had failed to do so, despite a number of proposals – from the National League, for instance – someone had decided to give it a helping hand. Then Marek Norski, representing the aforementioned League, was invited to speak, but he was of a different view:

"Indeed," he said, "we have been calling for a solution for years, but what's happening now looks like the revenge of the Muslims."

"Do you mean to say the Muslims are blowing up alcohol shops?" asked the journalist.

By now the studio was near boiling point. Doctor Lewada changed channel to Music Best where a Bee Gees hit, "How Love Was True", was playing. He remembered it from his high-school years: the girl he had danced with at a party had blue eyes and a white school blouse. As he slammed the door of his health service flat behind him, Lewada remembered something else too: a night at the Actors' Club over twenty years ago. First Mateusz and Paweł had argued about a passage from Saint John, as if they couldn't find a better place or time! He thought it was over the fact that John never mentions the Eucharist, but only the washing of the feet, whereas the other three Evangelists cover the blessing of the bread and wine in some detail. But why were they arguing so fiercely, and why about that in particular? Lewada couldn't remember. But he hadn't forgotten the face of the famous actress: she had left before him with Mateusz, accompanied by Paweł. Lewada himself had ended up in the early hours at a flat on Conrad Street, above the grocery shop. In those days it wasn't open at night, nor did it sell alcohol. It was his first marital infidelity – two "enthusiasts" (or maybe they were called "idealists" in those days?), Magda and Ewa, had made love with him as if they'd all known each other for years.

Magda was a student nurse and Ewa was a manicurist at the Grand Hotel – he had jabbered nonsense, saying he was an artist looking for new, "strong impressions". In those days that sort of thing was called a "yarn", and later the word "scam" took over, but now, as he entered his surgery in the village health centre at Pohańcza, Doctor Lewada had no doubt that the only word, the only phrase to describe all that bravado, all that sex, that entire morning, was the common, brazen and impudent *hubris* of youth.

His memory of the Actors' Club was no accident. Among the memos, notepads and prescriptions on the desk in his surgery lay a letter from Mateusz he had received a month ago. Why did the photo shoot have to be held in a theatre? That was explicable: on a small stage, at a long table the photographer could get them all in easily without any technical hitches. But why did Mateusz want to paint that sort of picture? And why on earth did he want to have his friends from the old days as models?

The radio in the surgery was talking about the bomb blast on every local and national channel: nine people had been killed, three staff, five customers and one accidental passer-by. Doctor Ibrahim ibn Talib from the Free University was slowly and patiently explaining that the small number of Muslims in our country had nothing to do with this campaign. Although the Koran forbids drinking, the local believers do drink alcohol on the quiet, hence the simple conclusion that the attacks are the work of a madman or the result of a fight between rival wholesalers. On the other hand, in its latest statement the National League's Security Committee was blaming the liberals for it all, even if the attacks could be the work of Muslims.

Meanwhile the doctor checked his schedule, which he had copied into his diary the day before as usual. Eight-thirty – Mrs Janiak: excised boil, check-up, change dressing. Ten past nine – the organist: severe asthma, needs new salbutamol inhaler. Ten – the Pietruszkowa girl: suspected TB, be sure to send to hospital for X-rays. Then what?

Then he was to get in the car and drive a hundred and seventy-three kilometres to the city he had left for Pohańcza seven years ago. Park at the Coal Market, pay for a ticket at the machine, go into the theatre and ask at the box office where the photo shoot was taking place.

Must I add how very much Doctor Lewada was looking forward to this meeting?

Mrs Janiak came for her appointment punctually. He remembered her from the first year of his job at Pohańcza: every evening she used to stand outside the Rural Cooperative among the drunken village men and ask: "Isn't me old man back yet? D'yer 'appen to see where me old man's gone?"

" 'E's gone to the war," they'd say, laughing at her, and sometimes they gave her a swig of alcohol. One day her husband had boarded a bus and never come back. She was bringing up four children. The wound from the excised boil was healing well. The doctor changed the dressing and gave her some vitamins.

"For the kids," he said, "take them!"

The organist wouldn't stop complaining.

"Have I done the Lord God wrong? Tell me, Mister Doctor – why am I suffering so?"

The doctor had to check his pulse and blood pressure, and listen to his lungs and bronchial tubes through the stethoscope. The organist was extremely pleased with the steroid inhaler that Doctor Lewada had wangled from the county hospital.

"You are a man of God," he said in parting. "If there's ever a need, I'll play you a mass for free."

The doctor was not at all gratified to know that.

It was already after ten, but Mrs Pietruszkowa and her daughter had not turned up. The doctor switched off the radio, because he couldn't bear listening to the virtually identical comments non-stop. The theory that the media cause the disasters they then live by and feed on for a day, a week, a month, a year (why go on) – however absurd – seemed to be getting confirmation now. As this thought crossed his mind, he glanced out of the window and froze: two men were coming across the meadow at a rapid pace, plainly heading for the health centre, and carrying a third. In fact they were doing their best to run, but the grass was almost up to their knees, effectively hampering their efforts. They must have come out of the woods, and if so – thought the doctor, trying to prepare himself for a specific injury – they were woodcutters. A crushed foot? Skull? Shinbone? You could expect anything of forestry workers: Lewada had once removed an axe from a man's back, stemmed the haemorrhage from a handless arm, and searched in the grass for three fingers cut off by a mechanical saw. So without further reflection he moved a narrow couch away from the wall and into the middle of the surgery, and got some bandages, plasters, iodine and medical spirit ready. But when he glanced out of the window again he realised his first diagnosis was mistaken. It wasn't the woodcutters, but the Oczko twins, carrying their younger brother Michał across the meadow. He liked them: alike as two peas in a pod, in summer they worked on building sites, and in winter they sometimes did basketry. They didn't drink. At the Voluntary Fire Brigade fêtes one of them played the trumpet, the other the trombone. They provided for their old mother and the brother they were now carrying.

"What's happened?" cried Lewada through the wide open window. "Did he faint? Get hit on the head?"

Perhaps the twins were too tired, or maybe too shocked – either way, they didn't shout an answer, so the doctor ran down the corridor and into the vestibule to open the door for them. It was only in this sort of situation – and he had several each year – that he regretted being all on his own here, with no nurse or even a paramedic.

One glance at Michał Oczko and the doctor could see the boy was suffocating. In the surgery at last, as they laid him on the couch, wiping the sweat from their faces, the twins gasped in chorus: "Bee sting!"

The boy had a short, fat neck, which made it much harder to determine the size of the swelling. The doctor reached into a glass cabinet for some hydrocortisone. The one immediate decision he had to make was the dose, and how to administer the injection – intravenously or into the muscle. He chose the second option and injected two ampoules of the drug into the boy's arm. The wheezing coming from his airways was getting louder, his pale face had gone purple, and his body was shaking with convulsions. The doctor remembered he still had some adrenalin that should work much faster: he gave him a whole ampoule, into the muscle too. But it was no help at all. The boy's face was almost dark blue by now, and the wheezing was getting weaker. The doctor remembered all the incredible stories he had heard as a student: someone had performed a cricothyrotomy with a pair of scissors on a moving train, someone else had had to use a kitchen knife at a party. There was just one scalpel in the cabinet, from antediluvian times.

"Lay him on the floor. On the floor," he repeated the instruction. "There's no time to lose!"

As they watched the doctor unwrap the scalpel from its paraffin-stained tissue paper and then sit astride the boy's ribcage, the twins shifted from foot to foot in unison. With his left thumb and left index finger he did his best to feel and hold the boy's Adam's apple, pulling the skin taut. At the mid-point between the edge of the Adam's apple and the upper reach of the cricoid cartilage he made the incision, shouting: "For God's sake, find a tube in the cabinet, bloody well do as I say, I need a tube, now!"

The layer of flesh he had cut open, in other words the tissue of the neck, let out a long, high-pitched whistle. If Professor Grodzki had been here he would have given the operation top marks. The twins, who clearly had to move in tandem in this sort of situation, immediately rushed to the cabinet, but instead of opening the little glass doors and just reaching for a plastic drain, they overturned the whole thing. The crash of broken glass that rang out made the doctor furious, but there was no time for reprimands: in the debris of broken containers, vials, pills and bandages, among the sticky pools of iodine diluted in salicylic alcohol, he found a plastic tube, trimmed it with the scalpel, rinsed it at the sink, wetted it in hydrogen peroxide and stuck it in the slit in the boy's neck.

Michał Oczko was gradually starting to breathe steadily again, his pulse was returning to normal, and he had opened his eyes. The twins lifted him onto the couch, and then – of their own accord – started to clean up by sweeping the floor.

"Have you gone mad?!" said Doctor Lewada, noticing that only now had his hands begun to tremble with nerves. "Are you crazy? Get him into the car and take him to the hospital. Right now!!"

"But…" the twins began in chorus, "we ain't got the Fiat!"

"We left it in the woods," said the first one, "because we got a bloody flat tyre!"

"And before we seen it, that bee come and stung Michał!" added the second.

While waiting in vain for a connection to the county hospital – "Please wait for the operator" – Lewada nodded as he took in the following information: the Oczkos' tiny Fiat 126 was standing immobilised in a clearing, because the spare wheel, which they had managed to get out of the boot, had a flat tyre too. Carrying Michał almost two kilometres, they had been lucky to make it in time before he choked to death. Now it would take them at least two hours to get to the clearing, fetch the wheel, bring it back from town fixed and put it on the car.

The doctor finally got through to the admissions desk, where they matter-of-factly refused to send an ambulance. One was out of order and the other had been called to a heart attack.

"All right, we'll go in my car," said the doctor, handing the keys to the nearest twin. "Sit him in the back – he's got to have his head tilted the whole time, like this" – he demonstrated – "so his neck doesn't squash the tube. I'll just nip back to my flat. Off we go!"

But that day nothing could happen normally. The boy was so weak they had to unfold an old army stretcher and carry him to the car, and once the doctor had locked the health centre and rushed to his flat, it turned out he'd left the keys in his surgery. Finally, as he stood in front of the mirror in the poky little bathroom, three things occurred to him all at once. He wouldn't have time to shave, but he would have time – as Mateusz had asked him in the letter – to put on a white shirt with no tie and a dark jacket, and if he didn't want to be late for the photo shoot, he certainly wouldn't have time to take the twins there and back again. He began with that as he turned the key in the ignition.

"You can come back on the bus." He checked in the rear-view mirror to see if they were supporting their brother's head properly. "I've got an appointment afterwards."

They took this news in silence. There was something touching about the bear-like eagerness of their efforts to carry out the doctor's instructions. One of them had his arms around Michał so he wouldn't slump. The other one was propping the boy's nape on his forearm while at the same time holding his chin up. Only once they had passed the mansion park, as the old Renault started bouncing on the cobbled bend, did Doctor Lewada finally stop his hands from shaking. The operation had been a success, but truth be told, as he cut the fattened, swollen cartilage with the scalpel he wasn't sure if he was getting the right spot, or if he was using too much force. Professor Grodzki, who had demonstrated a cricothyrotomy in the old dissecting room on the neck of a sixty-year-old woman, had kept saying: "What counts are speed and precision! Precision, my dear fellows! Like this you can damage the larynx! And like this you can sever the artery!" Lewada remembered how his eyelids kept closing at the time. All night he had been on call in the emergency department, then they had written the Solidarity declaration at the student hostel, then he'd had to go to a lecture, and finally to the dissecting room.

Perhaps that was when he and Hanna had their first quarrel. All he had wanted to do was sleep, and she couldn't understand how he could be quite so very tired, why she alone had to take care of the child – her diploma was no less important than his Solidarity. As he changed gear at the slip road onto the asphalt highway, he reckoned they had both been right. And where was that little girl now, the patter of whose tiny bare feet had moved him so much at the time? His daughter Krystyna wrote to him regularly, about once a month, sending long letters and photographs of his growing grandchildren. As he only had the old kind of modem in Pohańcza, sometimes they blocked the mailbox in his computer. He was pleased she had a successful life as a microbiology professor at Yale. He never answered the question of why he remained in such a dreadful hole, where they still believed in witchcraft and demons. He never took her up on her invitation: almost every time she wrote she offered to help him get a visa and a good job. She couldn't understand his passion for self-torment – that's what she called it.

As the car crossed the bridge, from where they could see the church tower and the meandering river that had powered the von Kotwitz sawmills and water mills for centuries, Doctor Lewada felt a dreadful, almost strangling anxiety. His daughter was absolutely right. Since he had first holed up here – just for a while of course, and only with the aim of regaining some sort of psychological equilibrium – too many years had gone by. Real life was happening somewhere else. Here from time to time he had a minor consolation – long cross-country skiing expeditions in winter, fishing, riding his bike across the sort of wilderness he wouldn't even find in the Bieszczady mountains these days. But were the moments of good, profound solitude worth their price? Which was obvious marginalisation: once you'd fallen out of the system, going back to a good position seemed impossible. What hospital would give him a job nowadays? To set up his own surgery he'd have to work in Pohańcza for fifteen years without spending any money. And as for going to Ireland, Wales, Sweden or Spain, as so many young doctors were doing – he was too tired for that by now.

The feeling that he was trapped in a crystal ball being carried along by the waves in an unknown direction and that he would never get out of it suddenly came over the doctor with massive, almost physical force. In fact, somewhere at the bottom of his consciousness lurked the hope that today's outing – meeting up with his old friends, and maybe supper at a pub – would bring a sudden, unexpected turn in his monotonous, downhill life, but on the other hand he knew perfectly well that miracles don't happen. Especially to people like him, who, if they sometimes fell on their backs, usually broke their noses in the process. There was one more minor problem: he had told his son Mikołaj about his appointment, and gently asked if he could stay the night at his place. Mikołaj had agreed, though reluctantly; for years their relationship had been sub-Arctic. So at the end of a pleasant afternoon his son's chilliness lay ahead of him, but to call off the appointment – if he was to get there at all – would have been even worse.

A container lorry with German number plates overtook them, almost pushing the car into a ditch. As he drove off the verge and back onto the road, the doctor switched on the radio.

Yet another twenty-four-hour alcohol shop had been blown up in his native city. Shortly after ten, a powerful blast had ripped apart a small outlet not far from the beach. Why there exactly? Why in the daytime? Was this the start of a new series of explosions? Gang warfare? Or really the work of Muslims?, the journalists were asking on every radio station.

Even the Music Best channel had interrupted its non-stop, bland, babbling stream of hits to repeat the police announcements. Superintendent Glinka confirmed that a letter that had come from a madman might have a connection with the blasts: "I won't overturn this sentence," it said, "because they're selling the righteous for silver and the poor for a pair of sandals."

This quote – Glinka had called on the expertise of the church press office to identify it – came from the Book of Amos, chapter two, verse six, and as such would seem to exclude any Muslim culprits, who if they had been involved, would have used a verse from the Koran. Nevertheless, people had been throwing stones at the mosque on Polanki Street, and the one under construction at the centre of the Old City, opposite Saint Nicholas' church, had been set on fire by someone hurling Molotov cocktails at it.

"We saved almost all of it," the fire chief shouted into the microphone. "The fire's out now! The bottle just hit the fence, there's no cause for panic, ladies and gentlemen!"

The next expert, who was the non-aligned and unknown Professor Roztoka, maintained that the quote could be a smokescreen: the Muslims, especially the educated ones, know the Bible too and could have used it for obvious reasons.

Doctor Ibrahim ibn Talib of the Free University was firmly opposed to this idea.

"It's plainly a lunatic, not a Muslim," he said in a soft, strange, slightly drawling accent. "Besides which, allow me to quote Pascal: a man never commits evil as completely and unwaveringly as when he does it out of religious conviction!"

Doctor Lewada pushed an old Dire Straits tape into the cassette player. The song "Money for Nothing" always had a calming effect on him.

Only a little later did he realise that the twins were talking about a wine bottle that had started it all, out there in the clearing, where the three brothers had been picking mushrooms. It was lying there empty, drained dry, waiting for someone to drive over it, and that was how they had got their flat tyre. Just before the bee had stung Michał, they'd gone to take a look at the broken bottle. None of the locals could have dropped it there – the label had a picture of a priest on it and the word "Monsignore"; no one round here drank such expensive beverages or sold them in any of the shops. So maybe the bee flew out of the crushed Monsignore bottle in a fury and stung their Michał, the twins were wondering. A bee didn't normally sting a man in the woods, well, unless it was provoked.

Monsignore, thought the doctor, well I never!

It was in the first year after he had been reinstated at work. Professor Wojtaszkowa, who two years earlier had sacked him on Communist Party orders, was now his immediate superior. The Party no longer existed, yet Professor Wojtaszkowa had been promoted to head of the hospital. She never implied that the conversation they'd had then, when she'd said "Why don't you go abroad to cause trouble, there's nothing for you here, here we get on with our work, we can soon arrange a passport" had any significance today, in the free country Poland now was. She had behaved decently, affably even, though whenever Doctor Lewada had had to say something at a senior staff meeting, she never looked him straight in the eye. That day, when Father Monsignore had turned up on his ward, Doctor Lewada was on call. Summoned to the isolation room, he was surprised to find the patient had been brought in without going through admissions. In a silk, saffron-coloured dressing gown and sky-blue pyjamas, white socks and black slippers, Monsignore looked different from in the pulpit or in the hundreds of photographs distributed at his parish kiosk. In them his chest was bulging with medals and decorations, while here in the isolation room he looked like a tired, but smiling and amiable gentleman of leisure. However, that was not what Doctor Lewada found surprising. Father Monsignore was sitting on the bed, and next to him sat Wojtaszkowa, on a wicker chair by the bedside table. There was an open bottle of Hennessy and two glasses full of the golden-brown liquid on the table top, which was laid with a white cloth.

"They complain about me driving a Mercedes," said Monsignore, picking up a glass in two fine, ring-bedecked fingers, "but what I say is, I just can't abide poor quality!"

As she clinked glasses with the priest, the professor sniggered. "Quite right too – those journalists are such riff-raff!"

And then they noticed Lewada standing in the doorway.

Monsignore just blinked, swallowed his brandy, licked his lips, put down the glass and looked at the doctor inquiringly.

Professor Wojtaszkowa did not finish her drink, but with the glass in her hand she gave Lewada an irritated look.

"I can see I was called at the wrong time," said the doctor, making a slight bow.

"Of course you've come at the wrong time," she replied. "You always do."

This remark threw the doctor off balance. What could it mean, if not an allusion to his work during martial law? He hadn't done much, but when demonstrations were due to be held in the Old City on the anniversaries of military action against striking workers that had ended in tragedy, he and a colleague had been on call in a specially appointed apartment. Instead of going to the hospital, where the security police were on the lookout, the wounded demonstrators came to them. One day someone had informed on them and they had spent some time in prison. Tried by the magistrates' court, they were found guilty of conducting medical practice without the appropriate permission and conditions, paid a fine and lost their jobs. They had been sent to the aid committee at Father Monsignore's parish, but had given up on ever being received. A young lad had offered them a food parcel that they had refused.

On his way back to the isolation room an hour later, Doctor Lewada had remembered one more detail of the parish waiting room: from a huge portrait Father Monsignore looked down on the applicants dressed in a white, papal cassock and a bishop's calotte. Or maybe his memory was wrong? Maybe the cassock was a bishop's purple and the calotte was white? From behind the closed door came the low, deep voice of Professor Wojtaszkowa, accompanied by short, almost monosyllabic remarks from Monsignore: "Quite so!" "Oh no!" "Surely!" As soon as the doctor knocked the conversation broke off. The Professor and the priest were laughing loudly and without restraint. He could smell tobacco smoke. Although no one had said "Please come in," Lewada opened the door a little and asked: "Am I needed yet?"

"Who called you, Doctor?" Wojtaszkowa was clearly in a good mood. "The Father perhaps?" she addressed Monsignore, who shrugged. "You see – always at the wrong time! Always!"

"You called me via the ward sister exactly an hour and fifteen minutes ago!" thundered Doctor Lewada, so that his words sent a booming echo down the corridor. "I'll put that in my report, and please don't summon me here again!"

As he drove up to the admissions department at the county hospital, Doctor Lewada remembered that all his subsequent problems, which had resulted in him leaving the hospital and the city, and going to live in Pohańcza – that whole sequence of events, here at the end of which he was now taking the boy he had saved to the intensive care unit – had started right then, from the remark he had bellowed in the corridor after slamming shut the door of the isolation room: "Birds of a feather flock together!"

Not that Professor Wojtaszkowa or Father Monsignore had done any harm to his career. Naturally, that would have been too simple and probably not all that possible. And yet from that moment on a faintly hostile atmosphere had surrounded him. He had not noticed it immediately, but a year after that incident when the number of his duty shifts was reduced, then he was no longer allowed to operate, and finally, as part of a reorganisation, the only full-scale job he had been offered was at the outpatients' clinic, he knew his winning streak was coming to an end. No one ever reproached him – it was never about anything, yet decisions that were more and more unfavourable to him were always being made behind his back. Just as if Professor Wojtaszkowa, who had retired by now, or Father Monsignore, who had started attending the city's first, newly established private clinic, had come after him step by step.

Maybe he hadn't been able to adapt to the new times? When he published an article in a popular newspaper about the corruption of the pharmaceutical firms, the new head of the hospital had summoned him for a chat. When he protested against a plan to privatise and divide off part of it for a commercial services zone, his contract hadn't been extended until the very last day before it ran out. His old colleagues had all gone abroad long ago, and the new ones were as silent as if they'd been bewitched. In fact he was isolated, embittered and undermined. That must have been why, when a well-known politician called Kamil Urski was brought to the outpatients' clinic, he had received him politely, but asked: "Would you please refrain from chewing gum while you're talking to me?"

Urski had then said: "I can bloody well chew what I like when I like," to which Doctor Lewada had replied, as calmly as could be: "And I can bloody well ask you to fuck off out of here this instant and close the door behind you!"

For refusing to perform a procedure – such was the formal accusation – he had lost his job. Not even the Solidarity union that he himself had founded years ago stood up for him. At the time he was already living alone, in a rented studio flat, and had no savings – where could he have got any? For a while he was employed at the railway workers' clinic, and when that was closed down he worked for the ambulance service as a paramedic. One day he read a feature about Pohańcza in the weekly *Polityka*. His predecessor, Doctor S., was an out-and-out alcoholic and had hung himself from an oak tree opposite the entrance to the health centre, which no one could take over after that – not because of the suicide, but thanks to a piece of bureaucratic professionalism: for a good few years the post had disappeared entirely from the ministry distribution lists and statistics. It simply didn't exist, just as a person doesn't exist if he hasn't got a national insurance number, a personal identity number or an address. The first time Doctor Lewada stepped inside his surgery, the whole place – floor, cabinets, couch, shelves, windowsills and desk – was covered in an inch-thick layer of dust, and it was full of cobwebs, mould and mouse droppings.

Is that enough for this chapter? I tap away at the keys, then I e-mail it to you and I never know what you'll say. When for instance you reply that the ending of the previous chapter, "There was no one waiting for me with bread and wine", is all right, I have a problem. I'd like to finish this one with an equally short sentence. But Doctor Lewada is still a hundred and fifty kilometres from his destination; he's only just driving away from the county hospital, after talking to Doctor Markowski to make sure Michał Oczko will get an oxygen mask, a drip, glucose and vitamins at once. At the next viaduct he'll accelerate and illegally overtake an old lorry. The road is horribly crowded. The motorway that was supposed to have been built ten years ago is still waiting for the politicians' consent, but they've got more important things to worry about. However, that's not what the doctor is thinking about. He is a realist, and he is fully aware that at an average speed of about forty-eight kilometres an hour he'll be late for the photo shoot. He doesn't feel anxious about it. If there's confusion reigning in the city because of the terrorist attacks he certainly won't be the only one to arrive late. What do the police always do in situations where they're utterly helpless? They block the streets and control the cars, even though it wasn't them that exploded in the night and early morning in his native city. Yes, now, as he breaks the law again to overtake an inter-city bus, Doctor Lewada is thinking about the wine with the Monsignore label. On the printed picture the priest is wearing the Order of the White Eagle, the Polonia Restituta medal and God knows what other decorations. This lucrative business, outside the control of the tax office, is – *ad maiorem Dei gloriam* – a brilliant commercial idea. But once again, that is not what is occupying the doctor's thoughts. He has never known the cut of anyone's purse. If Father Monsignore increases alcohol consumption in this way, what does Rome or the Vatican have to say about it? No one has ever given an answer to that question. Briefly Doctor Lewada wonders if the bombs planted in the alcohol shops could have anything to do with the Monsignore brand wine. It's a weak lead, though of course, if he were the superintendent, he'd give immediate orders for it to be checked. If it turned out shops that didn't sell Monsignore wine were flying into the air, the circumstantial evidence would be tangible.

But that's a dead end, thinks Lewada, as he stops the car at a level crossing. The millionaire priest surely doesn't have to clutch at straws.

Once he's over the crossing, the doctor stops the car on the hard shoulder and urinates under a tree. Just then he has a brainwave: the bomb blasts are not the work of Muslim or Christian fundamentalists – that's nonsense. They're being organised by someone who loved to drink, but can't do it any more. A dry religious order – a non-drinking alcoholic who's longing for a drink. I leave him with this thought, or rather intuition, as he gets back into his Renault and rejoins the traffic. But now read on.

CHAPTER IV

*will be about how a certain Uryniewicz founded an
exclusive brothel in our city, where a professor of physics
learned some ancient Greek words; and also about a
discussion with Mateusz on the difference between the
Greek and the Hebrew understanding of the word
"virgin"; finally the Engineer will appear; but before
that some views of Jerusalem*

FROM JAFFA TO JERUSALEM is about fifty kilometres as the
crow flies. In the days of René de Chateaubriand the pilgrims
making this journey on horseback or by camel needed two
days and an armed escort paid in advance. Attacks and
robberies were the order of the day, the power of the Pashas
was weak and corrupted, and gangs and Bedouin tribes held
the highway in check.

There was certainly an element of enduring local tradition
about it: an anonymous Roman scribe from the time of Herod
wrote that the stretch of road from Jericho to Jerusalem –
which on our scale of measurements was no longer than
thirty-eight kilometres – was full of bandits who waylaid
travellers in the many caves and chasms of the Judean Desert.

René de Chateaubriand, however, travelled from Jaffa via

Ramla – there he changed horses, rested, and headed onwards. In his description he mentions that he entered the sacred city through the Pilgrim's Gate, beside the Tower of David. A little earlier he notes that the desert they had to cross between Ramla and Jerusalem "still emanates the greatness of the Creator and the terror of death".

The French aristocrat made his journey in 1806, and so about two hundred years separate us from his time there. "In those days Jerusalem was almost entirely forgotten," he writes. "The age of scepticism had lost its memory of the cradle of our religion."

Even greater forgetfulness – or rather isolation, perhaps – is reflected in a lithograph by the Scottish artist David Roberts, produced a dozen or so years after Chateaubriand's journey. Even the air in this view has a desert-yellow tinge, and the city – not very large and as if perching on the top of a rocky outcrop – looks lost among the sombre, lofty chains of desert mountains that surround it. I don't know if David Roberts read Chateaubriand's account of his journey, but as he sketched the panorama of Jerusalem from the top of the Mount of Olives, he must have been aware that the city was marginal, provincial, a Turkish garrison town with at least three times fewer citizens than in Jesus' day. In 1844 the city was inhabited by seven thousand one hundred and twenty Jews, five thousand one hundred Muslims and three thousand nine hundred Christians. According to a contemporary census, that makes sixteen thousand one hundred and twenty citizens. Not until 1931 would the population come close to the number of people that filled the narrow alleyways as well as the squares before the Temple and the Antonia Fortress in the days of procurator Pontius Pilate. By then, a total of ninety thousand people were living in Jerusalem. Curiously, in that same year – for the first and last time in the history of the city – the number of Christians and Muslims was just about equal at nineteen and a half thousand each, while the number of Jews was growing the fastest and there were then more than fifty-one thousand of them. Naturally, David Roberts cannot foresee that, because the Russian pogroms, Doctor Herzl's Zionism and the Aliyah from Europe are still in the future. Perhaps with his sketchpad spread on his knees and a crayon in his hand David Roberts is imagining the Frenchman riding on horseback through the Jaffa Gate into the old city (Chateaubriand mistakenly called it the Pilgrim's Gate) or, as he gazes down at the garden and church of Gethsemane (which is later missing from his drawing), maybe he is wondering at exactly which point Jesus crossed the brook of Cedron as He and His disciples came down from the Last Supper chamber? To tell the truth, the Briton is aware of the fact that most of the rural paths around the city have not changed here for millennia, such as the one from Bethphage, the village from where a donkey was brought to Jesus. And so the path from Mount Zion, down which the Apostles came in the morning from the Last Supper chamber, singing a hymn, may be the same one on which David Roberts can now see two Arab women heading towards the city; he does not put them in his drawing either, or in the lithograph later on.

However, I would love to ask David Roberts, who had the chance to see the sacred city reduced to the size of a shell, what he thought of the views painted by the Old Masters – those who had to imagine Jerusalem as they painted scenes from the Gospels, but who never actually saw it, of course.

So this is how I envisage it: it's the afternoon, it's blazing hot, and there is the sacred city, which David Roberts is looking at, the dazzling whiteness of its walls, and the towers of minarets and churches that seem to hang in the air like a mirage, without touching the desert rock of Zion or Mount Moriah. After putting his equipment away in a wooden case, the Scot comes down a narrow stony path from the Mount of Olives, along the wall of the Jewish cemetery towards the brook of Cedron. Why did Antonello da Messina put the widespread, almost idyllic waters of a bay in the background of his extremely expressive scene, wonders Roberts. Was he thinking of the Mediterranean Sea near Jaffa? Surely not, thinks Roberts as he passes an Arab riding a donkey – so what waters, what sea, what bay did he want to show us behind the dying Jesus and the two frantically contorted bodies of the thieves? In Andrea Solario's painting, recalls Roberts, briefly raising his hat to wipe the sweat from his brow, there are no criminals being crucified with Jesus, but in the background there is an entire port, with ships, barges, and a whole set of relevant buildings. Michele da Verona had an even bolder approach to the port theme, thinks Roberts, as he crosses a wooden bridge over the almost dried-up brook of Cedron; in his picture Jerusalem looks like a big maritime polis, whose political and commercial life depend not on camel caravans across the desert but the traffic of arriving ships. And what about Bellini? He used the familiar Euganean Hills near Venice to create a distant background for Jesus praying in Gethsemane. Now David Roberts stops before the wall of the Muslim cemetery situated nearest to the Golden Gate. It is walled in, but the Messiah, who is to come down from the Temple hill and pass this way to the Mount of Olives, will demolish the wall, enclosed by the Turks, just in case.

I should leave David Roberts in this very spot with his questions. He is a well read artist and he knows that in depicting the Crucifixion or the scene in the Garden of Gethsemane the Italian Masters wanted to see them against the background of their own cities, or places familiar to them from their travels. I do not know if the Scot has read Vasari, but even without reading this monumental work he knows very well that this was how the Old Masters aimed to bring the drama of the Cross closer, as if saying to their audience, look, this happened everywhere, in your city too. And yet, thinks Roberts, it happened here, a mile from the spot where I am standing – on the side of a gloomy quarry, with a couple of stunted sycamores in the background and a view of the sombre walls of the Roman fortress. So what then is art? A synthetic fraud? Or aesthetic decorum? Pierced by Longinus' spear, Jesus dies in convulsions, with a charming view of a port in the background. Isn't it a scandal? thinks the Scot. Maybe that is exactly why the view of Jerusalem by David Roberts is so severe and ascetic, I wonder, as I leave him on the road down to the Jaffa Gate – the same gate through which René de Chateaubriand entered the sacred city. It was right there, as I walked into the old city beyond the walls, that I once bought a poster with a reproduction of Roberts' panorama.

In the dream I described to you at the beginning of this chronicle, the lower part of the city was actually by the sea. Why was that? Where did I get that from? After all, I hadn't studied the works of the Old Masters then, yet in my dream I made a journey from somewhere on the Mount of Olives across Cedron, and then the old city, all the way to the port district, which Jerusalem doesn't have. Maybe there's an archetype in there that Doctor Jung would have something to say about? Is it that the city in the mountains would like to have a view of the bay, and the city on the bay would like to have some mountains and deserts, at least in the background?

Such, more or less, was Jan Wybrański's awakening. Wrapped in a towel, he was standing by the bed, in which a young woman was still sleeping, gazing from the apartment window at a very familiar view of the port canal, with a small motorboat coming along it. But something wasn't right about the landscape: why, on the other side of the green ribbon of water, instead of the familiar red-brick Hanseatic-style granaries, was there a chain of snow-capped mountain tops? Now, as usual, the professor began to feel annoyed with himself; he couldn't find his glasses, nor – let us add without the slightest reproof – could he remember exactly what had happened before he fell asleep. Of course he had drunk some alcohol and had sex with the girl – that was why he had his own apartment within this shrine, with its own separate entrance – but it was a long time since he had had such an ominous gap in his memory. What was the prostitute's name? Hora? Sophia? Had he got her from the Leonardo Room, where the generally reticent, haughty Uryniewicz sat on a curule chair, discreetly conducting the traffic of guests? Or, as he liked best of all, had he plugged his laptop into the local network and chosen himself a companion from the multimedia presentation? All this was nothing compared with the sudden memory that in defiance of the principles to which he tried to be true, he had taken a snort of cocaine. From whom? Out of the clouds, his slowly returning memory drew the face of Chief Inspector Zawiślny: so he must have been downstairs in the Leonardo Room, and there, at the bar – no doubt discussing the rugby results, the decline in morals, the by-election or something of the kind – he had accepted the powdered offering. It was a bad omen. And a sobering one too. But the Chief Inspector, an addict himself, must have done it with some purpose, and although of course plain old entrapment did not come into play at Uryniewicz's establishment, the hook was now embedded for once and for all.

Wybrański found his glasses on the carpet next to the bed. The mystery of the mountains that had sprung up on the far side of the port canal proved simple: hanging on three of the granaries undergoing renovation was a huge advertising banner with a view of the snowy Alps and the legend: WE MAKE THE IMPOSSIBLE ACHIEVABLE. Below, in the right-hand corner, where some cattle were grazing on an Alpine meadow, there was a company logo, "F&F", in elegant, rather old-fashioned lettering.

"The incompetent fools," thought Professor Jan Wybrański, "from a distance the letters look as if the cows have shitted them out!"

But that wasn't what held his attention now. From opposite directions two rowing crews were coming down the canal – two five-man teams with coxes. As their prows came even, then a second later one boat shielded the other from view, and almost immediately after each of them went sailing on in its own direction, the Professor had a strange sense of déjà vu.

How many years ago had he been standing on the boulevard by the Rhine, watching the cargo-laden barges gliding up and down the river? The *Concordia*, flying a Dutch flag, was passing a vessel called *Suzanne Maria*, on which a French tricolour was fluttering. The final words of the lecture he had given at the local academy – "The extremely odd way of looking at the world that the number dictates to us, ladies and gentlemen, arises from the fact that from its point of view all things are the same, yet they are not the same thing" – rewarded with thunderous applause from the audience, were still keeping him company on that walk, as, either standing on the boulevard or moving slowly onwards, he watched the succession of river boats gliding up and down the Rhine like a motorway. That was when, for the first time in his life, he had had a sense of the completely random nature of the time and place he happened to be in. He had sat down at the nearest café, ordered a glass of red wine and, as he gazed at the meadows stretching away on the other side of the river, had thought about an alternative incarnation: if he had been born, brought up, educated and employed here, would he have been a completely different person? He knew it was nonsense, but he couldn't deny himself the pleasure of imagining the family apartment in one of the affluent, three-storey Düsseldorf houses, whose bay windows overlooked the Rhine. So who was his father? He was first violin in the philharmonic orchestra, and every evening, or rather afternoon before going to the concert, he filled the drawing room with his latest exercises. Passages by Brahms, Beethoven or Wieniawski were as much a part of his childhood as the smell of the Christmas tree, the Sunday cake or chicken soup. And what about his mother? She worked at the Heine Museum and, quoting his poetry, often joked that she would swap the black shawl she had inherited from her mother for the one in the museum display case that had once belonged to Klara Schumann. Just then an excursion boat from Amsterdam docked at the embankment. With the charming name *De Zonnenbloem*, it was brilliantly lit from inside. Behind the large panoramic windows he could see a spacious lounge, a dining room and perhaps a hospital room, because most of the passengers were lying on made-up beds in their pyjamas; some of them were even connected to drips, and only a few – in wheelchairs – had left the midship once the gangway was lowered. The sight of this luxury hospice did not make the professor feel depressed.

On the contrary, at the time he felt a sort of joyful, Nietzschean will to power, which though not specifically, was already distinctly pushing its way to the surface like a forceful underground spring.

On his way back to the hotel, Professor Jan Wybrański passed the graceless Kaufhof building erected in the Jugendstil style, and stopped on a bridge to gaze in the falling dusk at the lamplight reflected in the mirror of the water. On the edge of the lawn stood a blue trailer with a yellow sign advertising a building firm called "Heine". For the first time in his life the professor took a prostitute back to the hotel – an expensive, luxury one. But it wasn't the joy of discovering things that had been previously inaccessible to him in the sphere of sex that gave him such a euphoric sense of power and freedom that evening in Düsseldorf. Instead it was the memorable sentence that someone had written in a not yet perfected style of graffiti on the building firm's trailer: "The greatest pleasure is being able to choose pleasure".

Next day, on the train to Frankfurt, he already knew great changes were coming in his life.

If I were to take advantage of this chronicle and stop the passage of time for a moment to say a little more about the two Jan Wybrańskis, the old one and the present one, I would be happy to dust down the hackneyed, but visually appealing image of the guardian angel. Invisible, he follows the professor as he pushes his luggage trolley through the labyrinth of Frankfurt airport, and with truly angelic concern shields his face with his wing. Why? Not in the least for the sake of yesterday's basically trivial adventure with the prostitute at the hotel. Pahalias – for so, not without reason, the eminent physicist's guardian angel might be called – can see two lines converging in his charge's not too distant future: success and addiction. From now on they will form the inseparable twine of his fate. And they joined together right there, in Düsseldorf, as the result of a message he happened to read by chance, which gave him the inspiration for some brilliant ventures, as well as the spasm of bliss which, tied for ever to that first moment, would make him a compulsive sexoholic.

It is early morning, and as he looks out at the sun-drenched canal, where the rowing crews have just passed each other, Jan Wybrański returns to reality. Beyond the line of the water rise the towers of the Gothic churches and the pinnacles of the Old City's harbour gates. On this side, a black Lexus is driving up to the narrow forecourt outside Uryniewicz's establishment, escorted by two unmarked police VW Ventos. It's a sign that something has happened in the city, because it is usually only the Lexus that comes for Chief Inspector Zawiślny if he happens to stay here until morning. The man who offered him a snort of coke yesterday is now walking briskly towards the black limousine with a spring in his step, talking on his mobile phone. The hair thinning on the crown of his head makes a natural tonsure, which gives Wybrański the amusing thought that it wasn't a police officer he was talking to at the bar in the Leonardo Room, but an excommunicated former priest.

But why excommunicated and why former? The professor

is chortling to himself under the shower now, because he has never seen anything like that at Uryniewicz's establishment; for Wybrański at least Uryniewicz had proved a real man of the moment.

How many times, as head and owner of Festus & Felix, the company he founded as soon as he returned from Düsseldorf, how many times, he thinks, as he soaps his athletic body, did he have to sneak along, with his collar turned up and his cap pulled down, to the door of those common brothels, which in the new language of freshly restored democracy took on the genteel name of escort agencies? Venus, Isaura, Alexis, the Havana Club – just summoning up those names stirs unpleasant associations in the professor's memory. He will never forget the two shots fired at close range into the temple of a grey-haired man who seemed very genial and chatty. The thug in a balaclava had left the bar and nonchalantly sauntered off, and next day the papers had reported on the execution of a Mafia boss in the city. Another time a demolition gang had invaded the Isaura after midnight: although their baseball bats did not bash any of the customers, the crunch of trampled glass, bottles of alcohol breaking, furniture being smashed and the screams of the terrified girls could be heard very well in every room, including the one where, *post coitum*, Wybrański himself had been polishing his Russian with a hairdresser from Kaliningrad.

As he rinses off the rest of the soap suds and shower gel under a luxurious stream of warm water, his final visit to

Doctor Ponke has come to mind. How many of them were there? More than twenty, for sure.

"You are an extraordinary case," the sexologist had said, spreading his arms like Pontius Pilate, "because I refuse, nor as a doctor am I allowed to say it's hopeless. After three unsuccessful courses of therapy I can only prescribe drugs. However, lowering the libido will not stop you from being compulsive. It could even," here Doctor Ponke had paused for a moment, "cause the compulsion to increase. And that is even more dangerous in your situation."

He had put special emphasis on the last two words of this statement. But what did he mean? The patient's psycho-physiological state, or his public and social position? Surely both, considering Festus & Felix had just gained a place among the top hundred European companies.

"Or maybe," the sexologist had said, removing his glasses and wiping them with a soft cloth, "you'll go back to the university?"

Now, in the spacious bathroom, as Jan Wybrański removes the stubble from the soapy skin of his left cheek with even strokes of the razor, remembering the doctor's remark no longer prompts a fit of laughter or even quiet amusement. How does the motto on the wall in the Leonardo Room go? You never go up the same river twice, thinks the professor. No, it's not that; he clearly remembers spelling out some Greek letters to make a single word – *helios*, and then another one – *neos*, so it must be something to do with the sun; oh, yes – he recalls a conversation at the bar with a foreigner who was thrilled with the idea that here in the north, in a room built according to an authentic design by Leonardo da Vinci for a bordello in Pavia, it says on the wall – not in Italian, not in Latin, or German, but in ancient Greek – "the sun rises every day".

Colloquially it was called Cepac, or the CPAC, which stood for the Centre for Promoting Ancient Culture. It had all been Uryniewicz's idea. Tall, thin and ugly rather than despicable – thanks to his comical, dainty little ears – he was hated for the role he had played in the final days of the communist regime; as a clever, canny and influential member of the military junta, not long before the dictatorship fell he had bought up three gutted granaries on Corn Island, where a few years later he had built central Europe's most expensive bawdy house, a celebrated venue for the new elite.

While shaving his right cheek, Professor Wybrański comes to the conclusion that these days Cepac's discreetly issued slogan, "Three Times Yes – Pleasure, Property and Openness", could successfully substitute for a political party manifesto. Pleasure requires no commentary. Property – offered to the wealthiest, like him – meant an apartment for his own exclusive use on an annual contract. Openness was a strategy calculated for his media image: in television and press interviews, without hiding his face or his name, in his typically arrogant way Uryniewicz would state: "I sell my customers openly what others sell on the sly. I teach culture, respect and tolerance, and I pay my taxes to the state budget."

When two commercial television channels had presented

an ancient banquet held in a partitioned area of Cepac on a reality show, no question in parliament, article in the nationalist Catholic press or protest by Danish feminists could stop Cepac's winning streak. Only the extremely left-wing *People's Gazette* had sued Uryniewicz for insulting the unemployed by calling them wimps and beggars. According to unconfirmed rumours, the lawsuit was dismissed when he sponsored ten trips to Majorca for readers of the newspaper. Not long after, *Global Express* discovered that the editors of the *People's Gazette* had made use of eight of them. The former propaganda minister's erotic enterprise was an extremely classy operation.

As he is having all these thoughts, dressed and refreshed by now, Professor Wybrański regrets he hasn't time for a chat over breakfast today.

First he loved working out the meaning of their ancient Greek names, invented not just to sound scholarly but also funny – you had to give Uryniewicz credit for that. Hadn't he once felt aroused at the mere sound of the word Adikia, meaning nothing more or less than immorality? Hypomone – meaning tenacious – really was tireless when it came to oral practices. Kleis had a little gold key round her neck and a pair of handcuffs jingling above her left ankle. Anaideia had an insolent look and a manner to go with it. Peristera looked sixteen years old, and there really was something dove-like about her. Neither the banal Phota – meaning light – nor Sophia had left any particular impressions in the professor's memory, whereas the taciturn, gloomy Skotos – darkness – or the lascivious – even by the standards of this establishment –

Moichieia – adultery – made him shudder every time he
thought of them. Maybe because these two hetaerae had
tempted him to use the catalogue? First, wearing a blindfold,
he had picked up the volume called *Bdelygma tes eremoseos* –
literally, "the abomination of desolation" – and opened it at
random, then from among hundreds of reproductions of
black-figure vases, reliefs and frescoes, to find his evening or
all-night destiny. What other names could he remember from
the past few months? Doxa, Dryma, Charis, Elpis, Epangelia,
Pleroma, Epithymia, Sindon, and Pleonexia – respectively
Glory, Acrid, Mercy, Hope, Promise, Full Moon, Desire,
Bedlinen and Avarice. Yes, they were prepared for it:
Wybrański will never forget how much he laughed at Metafora
– combining "fero", "I carry", and "meta", "between"; thus
"carrying something between the thighs" – or Parabola – from
"paraballo", "I lie beside" – hè never could have imagined that
the common meaning of these words, when transferred into
an order of erotic names, could provide so many amusing and
inventive situations.

Once the classical philology theme was at an end and the
waiter he called on the intercom had quickly and silently
entered his apartment with the breakfast trolley, Epangelia or
Hora loved to hear the professor's theories (or at least they
were extremely good at faking it).

"How much longer will the sun last?"

He handed her some crispy rolls.

"The reserves of nuclear fuel will run out in about five
billion years," he said, stirring his coffee. "But before it dies

out, its final explosion will literally blow away our entire planetary system. Can you imagine that?"

And when the girl nodded appreciatively, he changed the subject to something even harder to understand.

"Have you ever heard of anti-matter?" he said, topping up her glass of fruit juice. "Do you know what it's made of? An anti-particle is the twin of an ordinary particle, except that it has the opposite electrical charge. If one gram of anti-particle were to collide with a gram of particle, the energy released would be equal to an explosion of roughly forty kilotons of TNT! The Americans have been working on it for over a decade now. The point is that to capture an anti-particle and prepare it for a collision, you have to do it at a temperature lower than zero point five degrees on the Kelvin scale – so far it can't be done, but the first person to do it will be the master of an inexhaustible supply of energy. Do you get it? Inexhaustible! Oil will just be for the camels again!"

But, as I have said, that day Professor Wybrański had no time to teach a free course in general knowledge about matter. He loved doing it, because to some extent it was a substitute for the lectures he used to give at the university, which he had left after founding the company.

He came out of the bathroom and did up his tie at a large pier glass.

"If I heard rightly," he said to the prostitute who had just awoken, "your name is Athanasis. But what does it mean? You didn't say. Or maybe you did – I can't remember."

"A-thanasis. It means Im-mortal."

"Really?" The professor was amused. "So I spent the night with an Immortal. Shall we meet again?"

The girl shrugged. The top-floor customers who had apartments here generally sought novelty each time. Wybrański tossed a roll of banknotes onto the bedside table for her – though she had been paid in advance – and as he left with his laptop case over his shoulder, he added that he had already ordered breakfast for her, but downstairs in the restaurant, not up here.

In the noiseless lift he thought of Samuel Pickwick. Why couldn't he live like him? Mr Pickwick was never in a hurry. When for instance he smelled a delicious aroma of roast meat at an inn, he took a room there, invited his friends and sampled the qualities of the local cuisine to the full. No stress. And endless conversations that produced nothing but *joie de vivre*. If now – he thought, as he walked across the underground car park where his olive-green Saab and driver were waiting for him – he were to sell his shares in the company and invest the profits well, he could be Samuel Pickwick for the rest of his life or for all eternity. But is there nothing more to life than peace and quiet and a well cooked roast? As Wybrański got into the car, his mobile phone started ringing, while Zdzisław, the driver, briefed him on the day's agenda, as established the night before.

"First to see the gardener with your wife. Then a board meeting. Then lunch with a certain Engineer, and finally a photo shoot at the theatre. Dinner with two representatives of Jannes & Jambres Corporation." At this point Zdzisław looked at his notes and continued: "You asked to have this meeting underlined in red, boss, with the comment 'informer'."

Wybrański glanced at his notebook and was surprised to see that yesterday, next to this item – J&J – he had written a Latin proverb, which must have been meant to express his attitude to this day: *Cotidie est deterior posterior dies*. Where had he first heard it? Who was it by? Every new day is worse than the one before, he thought, that's obvious if you're dealing with Jannes & Jambres. But was there any alternative? The man he paid so handsomely had recently passed him some disturbing news from their boardroom. All these meetings, talks about joint ventures and offers – even the merger proposal – were aimed at swallowing up his company. If he were on the stock exchange, as Antoniewicz had once advised him, the confrontation with J&J would have been much more to his advantage. On the other hand, by not being on the stock exchange, he kept full control and freedom of movement, not to mention discretion about turnover, net income and all that, which would have to be made public knowledge if his were a quoted company. On yet another hand – because there is always a third side to every problem – as he was trying to win the biggest contract ever to be concluded in the city since the arrival of Saint Wojciech in his boat to found the place, he had to talk to J&J. In spite of all, he was too weak to go it alone. So he'd have to enter the lion's cage, give it some food and emerge unharmed, slamming the bars shut behind him – merely having taken a purse of golden sand from between the monster's paws. Those were roughly Jan Wybrański's thoughts related to the Latin proverb, which he would never have written in his notebook if not for his problems with the rival firm. Ultimately, he thought, as he closed the notebook, I'll only have to deal with it later on.

"What's the Free University?" he quizzed the driver as he heard the mild voice of Doctor Ibrahim ibn Talib coming from the radio. "I've never heard of it."

"He's been saying all morning it wasn't the Muslims who caused the alcohol-shop carnage."

"I heard that. I'm asking about the Free University. Do you know anything about it? And switch off the radio. They've never got any in-depth information, just too much speculation. Redundancy. Know what that is?"

Zdzisław smiled, because he heard that sort of question, followed by a definition, several times a week from his boss, and promptly answered:

"Redundancy? Well, boss, it typifies a message containing more information than necessary to convey its content."

He glanced at Wybrański's face in the rear-view mirror. As ever, first the professor was surprised by the accuracy of his reply, and then a split second later he remembered they had had this conversation before. But in these situations he never showed any impatience. On the contrary, he nodded and gestured as if to say: "Oh yes, I've forgotten again."

"The Free University," the driver continued, "is not a free university at all. They teach the Koran there. And the jihad. It has been going for three months, next to the mosque they're building. Anyway, the opening will be delayed now." There was a hint of satisfaction in his voice.

"If it's already up and running," said Wybrański, as he wrote a text to his wife, "why is it called the Free University? In any case a madrasah is not a university. Why doesn't anyone ever call a thing by its name? Especially journalists?"

"Because that's how the system works, boss," replied the driver instantly.

"What system? What are you on about?" His morning greeting to his wife had floated away on the ether to the Olympic estate. "What system's that?"

"The one that means nothing gets called by its name here."

They were just driving off the island onto one of the city's main arteries. Or rather they were trying to – the tailback into the city centre was over three kilometres long, and the line of cars at a standstill did not bode at all well.

"About an hour to the junction," predicted Zdzisław, "then it might not be much better. Assuming they let us in here."

Before they managed to move off the drawbridge into the right lane of Kaczyński Avenue a quarter of an hour went by. Professor Wybrański felt no pangs of conscience, but the fact that he would be at least an hour and a half late getting home was irritating. His wife, Zofia, accepted his way of life, but only under certain conditions. Firstly, she received the annual income of a board member of Festus & Felix paid into her personal bank account without any obligation to work. Secondly, twice a year they went on holiday together. Thirdly, they also went to parties, concerts and private views together. Fourthly, every Sunday Professor Wybrański accompanied his wife to High Mass at Father Monsignore's parish and took communion with her. Fifthly, at least once a week he was supposed to go shopping with her. Sixthly – if he were ever to break these conditions flagrantly or receive one of those paid women at home, desecrating their domestic harmony – there would be an instant divorce, without publicity; the money that would be due to Zofia had already been deposited for this purpose in a suitable bank. Mutually agreed, signed and filed with two separate solicitors and a family notary, all this could have implied a humiliating defeat for the professor and a triumph for his calculating wife.

In fact, the situation was different. These two people simply couldn't live without each other, like two players who cannot finish a game of chess, not for lack of will or ability, but just because they cannot imagine anyone else on the other side of the chessboard. If Professor Wybrański were hopelessly addicted to alcohol or gambling, or even worse, the powder the Chief Inspector had offered him last night, matters might have taken a different turn. Luckily, compulsive sexoholism, which Zofia regarded as an illness, and which the professor himself felt to be the irrational, Nietzschean, essential driving force behind his success (something Doctor Ponke had played a major role in helping him to realise), allowed them to continue their marriage. So what if they didn't sleep together? Only once, when he heard the quiet but audible purr of an electric motor through a gap in the door between their bedrooms, had he felt pity and a vague sense of remorse.

In the next fifteen minutes the car did not advance more than twenty-five metres. There was a long snake of trams queuing on the tracks, with people getting out of them and walking into the city centre along the edge of the roadway. Horns were blaring. From a distance came the wail of fire engine sirens and the rumble of a helicopter.

"All we need are some fucking bangers going off and we'd get top marks for military studies," groaned Zdzisław, then immediately added: "Sorry, boss."

But the professor, who really couldn't stand swearing, was miles away in his thoughts by now: he could see himself as a nine-year-old boy on the bank of a slowly moving river. He was with his brothers Franek and Karol, catching crabs. They took a whole bucketful home for their mother to cook. As they walked past the ruins of the von Kotwitz mansion, rising out of a thicket of elder, bird cherry, juniper, birch, broom and viburnum like a steamship abandoned in the jungle, they told each other stories about the old Junker, Baron Adolf von Kotwitz. Just the name itself implied that he must have been one of Hitler's secret cousins. Of course he was. At night he would creep out of the dungeons and wander round his old barns, fields, weirs, orchards, woods, open land and peat bogs.

"Are there any Jews here?" he would shout. "Until at least one Jew forgives me I cannot leave here for Germany! Not for a thousand years!"

And because – even on moonlit nights – he was always answered by the silence of the woods and meadows, on his way back to the dungeons *Euer Hochwohlgeboren* Baron Adolf von Kotwitz would attack little Polish boys. Once he sucked the blood out of Popik, the drunken farm manager, who fell asleep under a hawthorn bush. Once he cut the throat of a wedding chef. Another time he just bit Kołas, the tractor driver. All covered in scabs, wearing a tattered tailcoat and a top hat the birds had made holes in, *Euer Hochwohlgeboren* was the terror of the local villages. Neither the Security Service nor the local priests and their Catholic incense were any use against the German devil. He could escape any sort of trap or exorcism. And certainly, although the boys could not have known it, the inscrutable verdict of History or Providence was a permanent element in this unsolicited land, to where their father and mother had been brought in ox carts straight from Belarussian Lithuania.

Jan Wybrański could smell the scent of that meadow. It was dense with the resinous ingredients of blooming grasses, herbs and flowers. Clover, thyme, savory, stocks, camomile and mint mingled with the reeds on the riverbank and the odour of wet sand to create such a specific blend (somewhere at the bottom lurked a smell of pine trees too, carried from the forest on gentle gusts of wind) that even now, a few decades on from his indigent childhood, they brought a moment of pure happiness back to mind.

When was it? Probably in June, because that was when the haymaking began. They got up before five. His mother had made them sandwiches, tea in an old vodka bottle and apples. Why did he remember that exact moment? It was the only time when his father was sober and approachable, and sang so beautifully. The accordion player took the lead, while his father, in the line of harvesters by now, picked up the tune in his strong, clear voice. There were more than thirty men, standing in a loose rank, and then suddenly all thirty scythes made the first sweep, then the next, then another.

He had never forgotten that moment, which had a sort of indefinable, ancient sublimity about it. As his father worked the scythe like death, the swathes of grass meekly lay down before his blade, and the other workers copied his movements. The sweet smell of grass wafted around them as the women and children followed with rakes, gathering the fresh, damp hay into stacks. In those days there were lots of horses in Pohańcza and just one broken Soviet tractor. But in the evening, as they sat down to supper by the light of an oil lamp, the spell of the shining morning had broken. By now his father was as usual tipsy, nagging his mother about any old trifle. The boys had to eat in silence, then they said their prayers – Our Father, Hail Mary, Angel of God – kneeling before the holy picture by their parents' bed. In their tiny little room next door there was another one hanging on the wall too, but his mother thought the one in the big room had greater power, so the evening prayers had to be said before it. As if Jesus and the twelve apostles called the three children to witness every evening that their mother was innocent. Because she always was.

His father used to go out for some air. Only in a snowstorm or extremely foul weather did he abandon this habit, in which case he drank a glass or two of hooch and went to bed, and the house was calm. But usually he came back from getting his fresh air well after midnight. Roaring drunk, with deep, incurable anger towards the entire world, he would berate their mother with a list of all the betrayals she had committed during their engagement. The catalogue of Kaziks, Stasieks, Barteks, Janeks, Jędrzejs and Anteks sounded like a litany to the Sacred Heart of Jesus, and then came the thrashing. Sometimes, but rarely, their mother managed to defend herself. Usually after all the banging, hitting, cursing and shouting they could hear their father's monstrous, bestial snoring, and their mother's soft, inconsolable sobbing.

One winter night, after one of these scenes, in the darkness of their little room Franek said: "We've got to kill him."

Karol didn't reply, maybe because he was the oldest, and if he put in a word they would have to do it.

But after a long pause Jan, the youngest of the three, replied: "Yes, he's worse than *Euer Hochwohlgeboren* Baron Adolf von Kotwitz."

Now, as he gazed through the window of the air-conditioned Saab at a large advertisement for his firm covering several floors of an ugly skyscraper from the 1960s (again he was bothered by the letters F&F flying from under the tails of some Alpine cows), there was one thing Jan Wybrański could not establish: how did they know that German term, meaning "His Highborn Lordship"? There wasn't a soul in Pohańcza who could have uttered a single sentence in that language. It was rather different at the New Port, where they moved to when his father got a job as a carpenter at the Lenin Shipyard.

"We're up the creek, boss," said Zdzisław, who had a receiver in his left ear to listen to the radio. "Another bomb's gone off! The whole city centre's blocked! Can't go forwards or backwards – we're stuck for two hours! Do you want to listen?"

"No," he replied curtly. "I have to make a call."

The short conference with his wife had a businesslike tone. The idea of her coming down the hill from the Olympic estate to the gardener's in her own car and them meeting there for the shopping appointment obviously fell flat. Like a giant octopus, the gridlock was already choking the city's main arteries, all the way back to the inner suburbs. The Chinese rose seedlings from Holland would just have to wait for a better day. She would stay at home. He'd get to the office somehow.

"You haven't got a clean shirt," said Zofia.

"The board meeting will be cancelled," he explained, "I've got an informal lunch, and I'm sure they can lend me something at the theatre."

"Is it the premiere today?" This time he could hear a note of impatience in her voice. "You never said a word. Or maybe," she paused, "you just…"

"No," he interrupted, "I'm not up to anything. Mateusz – you remember him, don't you? – is going to paint a picture. A big one, yes. So he needs models. Twelve of us. He invited his friends. His old friends. Didn't I tell you? So they're going to sit us on the empty stage, at a table, and take photos. All together, and each separately. And that's the whole farrago. How should I know why he wants to paint it? Maybe because it's out of fashion? Judas," he laughed, "me as Judas. No, I've no objection to that. OK, so let's keep in touch, bye," he signed off, irritated.

Not by Zofia's suspicion of scheming, or the fact that she didn't know about the wardrobe stuffed with shirts, suits and underwear at his apartment on Corn Island. He realised that once again he had made a slip of the tongue, or to be precise he had used a phrase from the past, which he had avoided like wildfire for years, ever since burning all the bridges leading to and from Pohańcza. It felt disastrous, instead of saying: "And that's the whole fandango", as he'd wanted, to have said: "and that's the whole farrago".

Wybrański's analytical mind immediately found the paths that had led him to use the phrase he found so embarrassing. If he hadn't talked to his wife about the meeting at the theatre, where he was supposed to appear – only temporarily and deliberately, but still – as one of the twelve apostles, the image from childhood would have sunk back into the depths of his memory. But yes, because of the conversation, once again he could see the big room in the farmhands' block, where above his parents' bed, Jesus, with his fingers curled round the stem of a golden chalice, was raising His eyes to the invisible Father. A mysterious light shone from the chalice as little Jan stands there looking up to stare into His Face and whispers the words he hears every Sunday in church, which he knows by heart now – *"Benedixit deditque discipulis suis, dicens: Accipite, et bibite ex eo omnes. Hic est enim Calix Sanguinis mei, novi et aeterni testamenti: mysterium fidei"*. He knew exactly what it meant: "He blessed his disciples and gave it to them, saying: 'Take it and drink from it, every one of you. For this is the Chalice of my Blood, of a new and eternal covenant, the mystery of faith'." It's dreadful, and there's nothing little Jan can do about it, but every time the priest gets to the words "et bibite ex eo omnes" he sees his father under the old oak tree next to the carpenter's shop, where summer, spring and autumn, as soon as work is over, he and his mates start drinking from a single bottle that circulates from mouth to mouth. If one of them has had enough and excuses himself from the round, the rest of them yell: "Everyone drinks from it, everyone drinks from it, only Judases don't drink!", and then the renegade overcomes his momentary weakness and rejoins the community, which today, as he remembers those scenes, Professor Wybrański would not hesitate to call sacramental and masculine.

He tried to run as far as possible in his thoughts, but the smell of the incense he waved as an altar-boy in Pohańcza was like a memory-trapping drug; he could smell it here and now, in the air-conditioned Saab stuck in the traffic two kilometres from the city centre. Out of the blue he found he was imagining himself as an altar-boy at Father Monsignore's church: in a fine lacy surplice with the priest's monogram embroidered in gold thread at the bottom, he swings the heavy censer and a cloud of grey smoke shrouds everything for the moment: the national flags, the police uniforms, the soldiers, the city guard, the firemen, scouts and war veterans, as well as the figures of councillors, judges, prosecutors, presidents of union groups, pensioners' groups and Radio Maria groups, and finally the ordinary people packing this beautiful mediaeval church to bursting. The cloud falls, and suddenly, by the side nave, where Father Monsignore once hung a sign saying: "The Jews killed the Lord Jesus and they persecute us too" – which always had fresh flowers under it – Jan the altar-boy sees his adult self, pushing his way through the dense crowd to the confessional. Zofia, sitting in her usual place in the third row, just behind the retired district Party secretary, is worried; the preface is about to end, then it'll be the transubstantiation, and her husband isn't here. He always said confession during the sermon, quickly and briefly, got his absolution and came back to her just in time, so what can have happened now? Does the fact that today, Sunday, he came home literally an hour before they left for church have any significance? She tries glancing to the side, but it wouldn't be right to look behind her, especially in view of the local television cameras, so she cannot see what little Jan can see from the altar: he sees himself, the adult Jan Wybrański, leaving the confessional box empty-handed. He was too late – plainly and simply, the curate has already hung up his stole and is heading for the altar to celebrate the Eucharist. Slightly put out, Professor Wybrański hesitates, as if wanting to leave the church, then finally moves forwards; the little bells ring, everyone kneels for the transubstantiation of the bread and waits for the transubstantiation of the wine to follow, and as Father Monsignore picks up a golden chalice and utters the words of Jesus – "take it and drink from it, every one of you" – the adult Jan Wybrański finally reaches the pew and kneels beside Zofia. Jan the altar-boy cannot take his eyes off him: now Jan the adult approaches Jan the boy, opens his mouth, receives the Body of Christ and says "Amen". Below Father Monsignore's hand as it reaches for the next communion wafer, and above the paten that Jan the altar-boy is holding, the gazes of his former and present self cross paths for a moment.

"Bloody hell, I must have a smoke," said Jan Wybrański in a stifled voice. "I can't stand it!"

Zdzisław glanced in the rear-view mirror. The boss didn't have that sort of fit. Never. He rarely smoked a cigar, and he never let anyone smoke in the car, not even when they'd fetched the former premier from the airport or a current junior minister. Without a word he handed the professor his cigarette case and a lighter, and turned up the air conditioning. They drove another two and a half metres and stopped again, for God knows how long.

It was the first and last quarrel he'd had with his wife since they had made their arrangement. He said he'd had enough of pushing his way through the crowd, the curate's stupid cautions and finally the stares of the obsessively devout old ladies who recognised his face as he left the confessional.

"People at our level have the right to some discretion, after all," he said, in an effort to force a change of church on his wife. "Can't we go to mass somewhere else? There are so many places of worship! With no war veterans, military, or police!"

But his wife was unbending. She adored the patriotic, truly Catholic atmosphere of Father Monsignore's parish. For her the man was not just a hero of the struggle for liberty, Solidarity, honesty, purity and morality – he had something in him the other priests and bishops didn't have: he could thrill the congregation with a single well-aimed slogan just as well as with his piety. Last and finally: he was the Holy Father's teacher. This was reliably proved by a picture in the book distributed at the parish, signed "Father Monsignore – the Pope's chaplain". Indeed, in the photograph Father Monsignore was clasping the hand of Saint Peter's successor.

The only answer he could give to these arguments was that he would go to confession in the middle of the week, or maybe on a Friday, but not during mass and not at Father Monsignore's church. From then on he took communion without making his confession at all, though he believed that Zofia believed he performed the sacrament of penance at the Dominican church, then at the Cystercian, then at the Community of the Resurrection, in the middle of the day, between lunch and a meeting. God – as he wanted to see Him and as the church presented Him – was something he had not believed in for ages, not since the days when they had moved from Pohańcza to the New Port.

In a quite simple way, all these reflections and images from the past made Wybrański feel annoyed with Mateusz. As he had agreed and solemnly promised to take part in the photo shoot, he couldn't really refuse. But he felt increasing distaste for the image of himself in the role of an apostle, and his old friend's whole idea was starting to bother him. For Professor Wybrański was one of those people who believe that in our world you only have to ask a man if God exists and you ruthlessly deprive him of the chance to give any sort of reply to a question put like that. And if so, why on earth get into that particular subject? Quite another thing if the painting – whatever it is like and whenever it is painted – gave an answer. But there wasn't one. Mateusz wasn't going to be the exception, and even if he created a brilliant work of art, the situation would remain the same. So why add a new fiction to a chain of fictions?

Like Doctor Lewada that day, but a couple of hours later, Jan Wybrański remembered that crazy night at the Actors' Club over twenty years ago. He had danced with Maryna. Comparing that thirty-year-old woman with the one he had seen a few years ago in the screen version of a national epic, where she played one of the main roles, would not in the least have discouraged him from asking her to dance again nowadays. She was still beautiful. That night, when he had escorted her back to the table, in the terrible din Mateusz and Paweł were discussing virginity, or rather the virginity of the Holy Mother of God. All these years on he couldn't have recreated their points of view – whether they coincided or conflicted – but his brilliant mathematical memory enabled him to fish the essence of their debate from the depths of his mind: the Hebrew word *alma*, which Isaiah used in heralding the coming of the Messiah, meant – as everywhere else in the Bible – a young woman of irreproachable repute. Nothing more or less. If Isaiah had prophesied that the Messiah would be born of a virgin, he would have used a completely different word, *b'tula*. Only in the Greek translation of Isaiah, roughly two centuries before the birth of Jesus, was Isaiah's *alma* replaced by the Homeric *parthenos*, meaning a virgin. So the Evangelists already had a word and a concept ready for them, which in only a few hundred years would become dogma, of such a powerful kind, that the very thought that the story could be different – occurring to anyone with a Catholic upbringing – seemed a shocking crime of heresy, apostasy or blasphemy worthy of death by stoning.

Who did the talking and to whom? More Mateusz to Paweł or Paweł to Mateusz? They must have read about it in some religious studies philological journal, for sure, but why were they so keen to discuss that particular point in a club buzzing with jazz, sex and alcohol? Oh, and dope too – now he remembered Siemaszko's joints and his lecture on the Scythians and the Zulus – of course, they were carried away on the wings of EEE: erudition, euphoria and empathy. But they hadn't disproved or settled anything. It was typical of the state induced by saturating the organism in $C_{21}H_{30}O_2$, or monohydroxyl phenol, but anyway, Wybrański went on thinking, if they hadn't been so stoned, if they had kept more of the Apolline spirit instead of the Dionysian, they would certainly have reached the only possible conclusion: Isaiah's prophecy could not have referred to Jesus. Nothing emerged from this obvious truth but the fact that the first community of Christians in Jerusalem were completely wrong to invoke that prophecy. Though on the other hand, if Jesus read and commented on the scroll of Isaiah in the synagogue as a rabbi – albeit a different extract, not the bit about Himself – was He providing a telling clue, or was it just a coincidence caused by the calendar of readings? And what was the calendar of readings like in those days? This final question could certainly be answered, he reckoned, by reading a few books, but all the others were like steep paths of reasoning leading straight to aporia.

He certainly didn't regard this as a quality exclusive to religious issues. As a brilliant physicist he knew all too well that to any simple question, such as "What is chaos in occurrences of turbulence?", there were all sorts of totally conflicting answers.

One thing was for sure: Mateusz already had this idea in mind then, and at today's photo shoot he would clearly want to answer a few simple questions. Who would he make into Judas? Why did he want to paint the Last Supper? How did he imagine the face of Christ? Perhaps if he hadn't left the Actors' Club early that night and had seen doctor of humanities Antoni Berdo fondling those two boys on the sofa and roaring to their amusement: "Behold my servants, whom I uphold, in whom my soul delighteth!" he would have chosen the Last Judgement instead.

Just once the evangelical scene, in which Jan Wybrański's

soul did not delight, had amazed and enthralled him. It was in Edinburgh, where he was on a business trip for the then newly founded Festus & Felix. Among lots of deadly boring pictures in the Scottish National Gallery, he found Poussin's painting mysteriously captivating. Judas has turned his back on the rest and is leaving, as if exiting stage left. In a moment he will be gone, but he is already outside the circle of weak light cast by three lamps burning on a chandelier to illuminate the Master and his disciples. In fact the diffuse light is only falling on Judas' back, while his face is entering the realm of darkness. He had been arrested by this image, and had instantly thought of their move to the New Port. In the dense autumn fog he and his brothers had carried some sticks of furniture up to the second floor of the old tenement block. Before they had finished their mother had banged in a nail above the bed and hung up a print – that one of the Last Supper. But the Jesus of Pohańcza was no kinder to them in the big city. Their mother slaved away on shifts at a tea packer's, growing more and more introverted, silent and absent. By then their father had stopped working at the shipyard, after being sacked for drunkenness and a fight with the foreman. Karol had run away to sea as a sailor; occasionally he sent a postcard with an exotic stamp. Franek had sat out his first sentence at the detention centre for breaking into the local shop. He had stolen some cigarettes, two kilos of sugar and five bottles of vodka.

That afternoon the young Jan had come home earlier than usual. His stomach ached with hunger, but he was bursting with pride; he had won the maths Olympiad, he had come first in the whole country, and in his patent leather briefcase he had a diploma and a letter confirming a place at university after high-school graduation. He rushed straight into the kitchen, where there was nothing to eat but a small chunk of bread and margarine. As he was putting the kettle on for tea, he realised his father was at home. There was a groaning noise coming from his parents' bedroom – his father was demanding a washbowl. "Let him puke and lie in his own filth," – that was Jan's immediate reaction. But on second thoughts he took a bowl and a rag from under the sink and went into the bedroom; he didn't want his mother to have to clean up again. His father was in the first throes of a fit of retching. Two or three seconds more and he would vomit on the bedclothes before getting his head over the side of the bed. Later on, Jan had never been able to tell if he took the decision while still in the kitchen (probably not, or he wouldn't have taken the bowl with him), in the bedroom doorway, or at the bedside as he gazed at the puffy, purple face of the man who was worse than *Euer Hochwohlgeboren* Baron Adolf von Kotwitz, Hitler's secret cousin.

As his father lay there on his back, he covered his entire face with the rag, pressed a pillow on top and waited. What was dreadful was not his convulsions, kicking legs or pincer-like arms that instinctively tried to dissuade his son from making this sacrifice, but the stink of gushing puke as, like a volcano with no outlet, it went back down his father's throat and windpipe, leaking here and there from under the rag in narrow streams. Jan did not have the makings of a detective, yet once his father was showing the final signs of life, some infallible instinct led him to turn him face down on the pillow and then tug away the rag so the last bit of vomit soiled the pillow case and the sheet. When the ambulance he called by phone arrived half an hour later, followed by a police officer, no one was in any doubt that the deceased's final drinking spree had not done him any good. As he stood before Poussin's painting it all came back to him vividly: his parents' bedroom was in semi-darkness, the curtains were drawn, and when it was all over, as he turned to leave, he could not help feeling a pair of eyes fixed on his back from behind the Last Supper table, as if just this once Jesus had stopped looking upwards and was staring at him, Jan, winner of the national maths Olympiad. But he hadn't turned to look. He had spent at least fifteen minutes soaking the rag in the sink, and had washed his trousers and shirt sleeves too. Only once he was dressed again had he knocked at the neighbours' door and asked if he could use their phone.

"Haven't you got your mobile, boss?" said Zdzisław, looking hesitantly into the rear-view mirror. "Isn't it working? You want mine?"

Professor Wybrański nodded, but when the driver handed him his phone he seemed completely confused.

"What's this?" he asked.

"But you said 'May I use your phone?', didn't you?"

"I said nothing of the kind."

"OK, boss." Zdzisław reached out a hand to take back the

mobile. "No problem."

They drove another five metres, but Wybrański felt he should say something.

"I'm tired. I've never felt so exhausted in my life. It's all so utterly pointless." He gazed out of the car window. "I wish I were already in my grave. I wish I could just think about nothing. Nothing at all. Get it? A great big nothing. Complete lack of awareness. Like before we were born."

Zdzisław never got into debate with his employer. And although highly surprised by this last declaration, all he said was: "Right, boss, of course."

Don't you think I should leave them on Kaczyński Avenue now, like Doctor Lewada in the roadside copse? I have a right to be tired too, and Jan Wybrański has really worn me out. And I can guess your reply: "How do you know all that? You weren't in Pohańcza where Doctor Lewada drove from, or in Wybrański's air-conditioned Saab, much less at Uryniewicz's luxury establishment."

It's true. I am not an omniscient narrator. But as I haven't yet told you, I did use a recorder to tape conversations that were meant to lead to a book. I had meetings with all twelve of them, because that was the original plan. But the story never got written. As you already know, on the day the painting was unveiled, when the crowds gathered in Saint John's church to see it, the avant-gardists immediately destroyed it with acid. As I watched the faces of Lewada, Wybrański, Siemaszko, Berdo and the other eight becoming rapidly and fiercely distorted because of the harsh chemicals, it felt as if my work were being effaced just the same as their images and the entire enterprise.

What did I feel at the time? A real Bacchanalia of democracy. If Mateusz had painted his Last Supper on the concrete base of a bridge across the Vistula in graffiti style (of course there would be some speech balloons inscribed with the messages *Fuck Jesus, I'm the son of God; If I eat holy bread, I'll never end up dead...*), his success would have been huge and unquestioned. But as he referred to the Old Masters – if only to Roger van der Weyden and Memling – he was doomed to defeat from the start. None of the cabbalistic and gnostic elements floating around Rabbi Joshua ben Joseph in Mateusz's vision of the Last Supper could ever have aroused anybody's interest, because they were immediately coated in acid.

Mateusz had been taken from the church to hospital suffering from a heart attack. Amid the terrible chaos, as he was wheeled into the ambulance, I thought of Saint John's gospel again. Yes, many years earlier we had talked about it that memorable night at the Actors' Club: why exactly had the Master's favourite disciple, who wrote this gospel (or, as the experts would have it, told it to another John who wrote it down), so why did the man, who at any rate was closest to Jesus, not say a single word about the bread and wine? Wasn't establishing the Eucharist important? That's impossible – in Mark, Matthew and Luke it is the central moment of the Last Supper. John, however, saw the washing of the feet as more important, which in their turn the others do not mention. So where is the truth, we asked that night. We were talking about art, not theology. Poussin, whose painting Professor Wybrański admired in Edinburgh, was clearly inspired by Saint John. The three other gospels do not mention Judas leaving the table. Only John writes that the traitor left, finishing this famous passage with the sentence: "And it was night."

Perhaps Mateusz made a mistake? If he had followed Saint John to the letter, perhaps instead of spending several years on the painting he would have made a video installation in a single evening? Imagine a church full of people, twelve tramps drafted in from the station, and the artist using a basin, a sponge and a cloth to wash their cracked, festering, fungus-ridden feet. If to end with he had poured the water into twelve bottles, corked them and handed them out among the audience as works of art, the avant-gardists would have had nothing to coat in acid. Recorded on tape and played back *da capo* on monitors, the Supper according to Saint John would have toured one gallery after another. And what if the artist had drunk a swig of water from the basin after performing those ablutions? Or – to consider a rather shocking variant – poured it into a goblet labelled "The Holy Grail" and passed it around the assembled company, just to wet their lips?

In that case you'd probably say: "But then he wouldn't have been himself any more, not a painter but someone completely different – he'd have become just like all the rest, who do things like that on a mass scale…" You'd be right. As Moses ben Jacob Cordovero used to say, God is any kind of reality, but not every reality is God. The avant-gardists proclaim quite the opposite in relation to art. Since they accept it as being anything, they also accept anything as art. The only thing they don't accept is whatever doesn't come from them. They make full use of cult followers and the holy inquisition, but I don't want to go any further down that road because it doesn't belong in the chronicle I am sending you in episodes, and I'd like to finish this one with David Roberts: we left him on the dusty road, on the other side of the brook of Cedron, the side nearer the city, on the road that since the 1967 war bears the name of Melchizedek. Soon he will come to the foot of Mount Zion and then turn along a not very deep, shady gorge, with the walls of the old city to his right the whole time.

He is not a biblical scholar, just a draughtsman, but he has prepared for this journey very carefully. And so he knows that the building on the summit of Zion, which he cannot see from here, but which he is now in the act of passing, like an invisible parallel at sea, he knows that this inconspicuous stone house, where the body of King David lies on the ground floor, long since turned to dust, is not really the site of the Last Supper, that *anagaion mega estromenon, hetoimon* – "a large upper room, furnished and prepared", as mentioned by Mark, is not the location of that farewell, that blessing, that mystery, because it was only recognised as such in the seventh century after the death of the Messiah, under the patriarch Sophronius. Throughout the preceding centuries it was claimed that the Passover supper took place in one of the caves in the Cedron valley, on Golgotha, or at the site where later the Church of the Holy Sepulchre was built. These versions are supported by the sixth century *Jerusalem Breviary*.

David Roberts does not regard this information as of fundamental importance: wherever it happened, it happened somewhere in the near vicinity, at roughly the same time of year – the day before yesterday when he arrived in Jerusalem was the start of the month of Nissan. Now he is trying to unearth from memory the various representations of the Last Supper that he has seen with his own eyes or in copies. None of them corresponds to what he imagines. He came to Jerusalem after a long expedition to Egypt and Syria, he knows what the chambers in inns, caravanserais, better and worse trading posts and posting houses look like, and he knows that despite the passage of time it is these rooms that are more like the *anagaion mega* mentioned by Mark and Luke than the breathtaking vistas of Ghirlandaio or Veronese, painted with Renaissance panache, a splendour of brightly coloured robes, a courtly display and true respect for decorum.

How should it be expressed? The greyness of the dust that the wind from the desert brings here always and everywhere, mixed with the white and the bile yellow of the stones used to build everything here, all plunged in the unnatural light of oil lamps (they give a quite different glow than candles) produces a particular shade of ochre with a narrow, monochrome spectrum. None of the colourful orgies of Perugino, Titian or Signorelli, bright blue, red, yellow, white and green – these are fantastical combinations, but in this land an *anagaion mega* was nothing like a Roman villa, if even just a poky, rented *cubiculum* with no decorations at all and the minimum number of fittings.

David Roberts stops for a while, with Zion rising behind him by now, and a straight section of road ahead at the foot of the walls leading to the Jaffa Gate, and the Tower of David visible in the vista. This view will be one of the finest in his book. Now he regrets that he did not follow Governor Achmet Aga's advice and take a porter with an ass. His case full of drawing equipment is heavy, the leather strap is cutting into his shoulder, his shirt is sticking to his body and sweat is streaming from under his hat. The cool mountain air of Jerusalem has been driven far out to sea by a sticky gust of desert wind that is only a mild harbinger of the summer heat to come.

Only Mark and Luke mention a man bearing a pitcher of water. Two disciples were supposed to have been sent out after him, to reach the location for the supper and make arrangements for Passover with the landlord. *Estromenon, hetoimon*: furnished and prepared. Mark was the son of the owner of the house. When Jesus came down at sunrise with the disciples, over Cedron to Gethsemane, the guards guided by Judas knocked at that door first of all. Only afterwards did they set off into the valley. Mark wanted to get there first. He ran at breakneck speed in his nightshirt, taking short cuts, desperate to warn Jesus. He was in time, but that didn't change anything. David Roberts cannot remember where he learned this detail that isn't actually in the Gospels, but that seems as real as what he has seen and is now looking at: the stones on the path down the Mount of Olives, or the acanthuses growing in between the bare rocks of the Hinon valley.

As he moves onwards, his thoughts return to Goya's painting. He saw it during his travels in Spain, at Santa Cueva in Cadiz. Although Jesus has a distinct halo, and the disciples lying nearest to the viewer are dressed in Spanish peasant breeches, this picture is the only one that corresponds to the Scot's mental image of the Last Supper. Everything in it, including the rough, bare walls in the corners of the room, is sparse and simple, as if accidental – the shabby couches, poor robes, the barely visible and apparently incomplete tableware. The scene of blessing the bread (though perhaps the wine too – that cannot be confirmed) is steeped in exactly the sort of light that, as David Roberts knows well by now, is the only kind that could have filled the *anagaion mega*. The disciples are lying about in a rather slovenly way. One of them, clearly overcome by wine, is asleep, resting his head on the table, which is as low as a footstool. Painting a last supper like that one, thinks Roberts as he remembers his impressions at Santa Cueva, in ultra-Catholic Spain, dripping with gold, the Baroque, the hypocrisy of the clergy and the tears of the general populace, was an act of courage, mad determination or extremely profound intuition. Because it wasn't insanity or even less stupidity.

The Scottish cobbler's son, who throughout his time at the art academy had an apprenticeship with an interior decorator called Gavin Beugo, and later worked for a travelling theatre, moves onwards. A short, sudden gust of desert wind tugs at the burnouses of the sheikhs riding by along the road. David Roberts squints, shields his face with a batiste handkerchief marked with his monogram and hopes that in thirty minutes from now, when he reaches the Church of the Holy Sepulchre, he will still have time to make at least one preliminary sketch.

Meanwhile, as Professor Jan Wybrański finally passes the last, now broken lights before our city's major intersection, he remembers the Latin verse of a psalm: "*ita desiderat anima me ad te, Deus*", meaning "so my soul pants for you, O God", which he used to sing in response as an altar-boy. He is extremely sorry there's no Latin in church any more. After all, the language in which we address God should be ceremonial. That would give at least one guarantee: we would swear, lie, blaspheme, cast slander, fawn on harlots and solicit support for ragtag politicians in a different language from this festive one, reserved for pure matters. And in his thoughts he adds the beginning of the phrase: "*Quemadmodum desiderat cervus, ad fontes aquarum*", meaning "As the deer pants for streams of water". He closes his eyes. He sees crystal-clear, rushing mountain streams. He repeats like a mantra, *ad fontes aquarum*, for streams of water, *ad fontes*, for streams, and it brings him a sort of temporary relief.

As he tucks his batiste handkerchief into the pocket of his travelling coat, David Roberts is also thinking about languages. According to his naively adopted belief, it was along the road he is now walking that the dancing David brought the Ark from Kiriath-Jearim. In the desert the Ark rested in the Tabernacle of Meeting, made of sealskin. Roberts has heard this word in Arabic during a stop on the very shore of the Red Sea: *tuhas* – it means a sea cow. In Hebrew, they explained to him, the same sea cow, or seal, is *tahash*. Just as *"Salem Aleikum"* is *"Sholem Aleihem"*, thought the Scot, smiling to himself and walking a little faster. Now what will you say to that?

CHAPTER V

will mainly be about a difficult exam preceding Antoni Julian Berdo's conversion, and also about a certain Bosniak lover

THE PIERCING PAIN IN HIS FOOT, wrist and doubled-up body seemed unbearable. If not for his fear of the stick held by the guard who was slowly pacing the two rows of stocks, occasionally striking one of the prisoners on the head or the back, if not for his terror at this new, extra dose of pain, he would have screamed out loud to relieve his suffering. If only he could see again. But by the Gate of Charisios, also called the Adrianople, he had ended up too near an exploding bomb. He remembered a deafening whistle, followed by darkness. Once he had been dragged to the stocks, he regretted that none of the janissaries had stabbed him with a dagger. To be wounded, chained into a hunched position, and on top of that blind meant the worst thing possible.

He had lost his bearings – he, who used to know every

stone of the sacred *polis* and could make his way blindfolded –
as people liked to say over a glass of wine – from Phanarion,
for example, along the Valens Aqueduct into any narrow,
winding little street in the Venetian quarter, or the even more
remote Genoese quarter at the foot of the Acropolis; he, who
by the smell of a bakery, a well or a fruit stall could recognise
not just a district of the city, not just a street, but even a
specific section of it; he, who breathed to the rhythm of this
city, just as a child in its mother's womb lives by her pulse and
breathing – now he was unable to identify the location of the
wooden stocks to which he had been chained with a hundred
other slaves. A vague hypothesis led him to believe they had
been driven somewhere to the south, so they might be near
the Golden Gate in the neighbourhood of Saint John Studion,
but they might just as well be anywhere else: in the northern
part of the city, for example, near Saint John the Baptist, close
to the Golden Horn. Here or there, the sea was roaring nearby,
and that was a sign that soon they would load them onto ships
and carry them away to one of the markets in desert-bound
Timbuktu or rich Isfahan.

He had also lost his sense of time. A night, a day and a
night may have passed since the moment when, already
chained to the stocks, the brand had been burned onto his
arm. It was probably after the second night that another man
had been chained to the stocks beside him. Once a day they
were given a handful of dried, worm-eaten dates and a sip of
water served from a small wooden pail on a stinking sponge.
They urinated and defecated underfoot. If not for the rain that

now, as the sun was going down, had begun to fall in copious streams, the stench and stinging flies would have increased their suffering many times over. The water was cleansing their tormented bodies, quenching their gasping throats, and its constant roar made strictly forbidden conversation possible, muffling more than just a whisper, because the guards had taken shelter in a nearby portico. They must have had a cauldron of hot food on a fire there. A strong odour of falafels pervaded the poor wretches' nostrils with such intensity that some of them began to vomit with hunger.

"I am Milan Duškov," whispered the new man beside him, "from the town of Kikinda in Vojvodina. What about you?" Indeed, his Greek was marked by a Slavonic accent.

"Antony of Trabzond," he replied with the greatest effort, overcoming the pain in his throat, where a splinter of arrow was still stuck.

"Ah, Trabzond," the Serb rejoiced. "Apparently your ruler has already sent ships to rescue us. He is bringing Armenians, Georgians, Bulgarians and even Russians. Are you his courier?"

"John IV," he slowly wheezed, "will do nothing to fight Mehmed. He has one leaky battleship. And a hundred eunuchs for his entire army. I was born here. My father came from Trabzond. He was a merchant. And I became a soldier."

In this final remark the Serb could sense bitterness. The monks and the soldiers were in the worst situation. Those who hadn't been killed in the victors' first fury were going into slavery for ever. The merchants were needed by the new rulers. As usual.

"I am a soldier too," replied the Serb after a short pause. "I escaped from the Sultan's camp. I fought on your side."

He did not reply, because he could no longer speak. The other man took that as a reproach.

"Our despot Djuradj Branković," he slowly explained, "is a vassal of Mehmed, who conquered us before you. Haven't you heard that?"

"Yes," he whispered at last, "I have."

"At the Sultan's demand he had to send us here. One hundred and seventy-eight horsemen. But we hate the Turks. That's why I escaped to your side. I was at the Holy Roman Gate when they found the Emperor."

The Serb's declaration moved him greatly.

"Did you see him with your own eyes?" he whispered.

"I was near him through the final hours. Very near."

The rain had changed into a real cloudburst. Strong gusts of wind coming in from Anatolia were literally shifting a wall of water now in one, now the other direction. But Milan Duškov went on telling his story without stopping in a lowered tone, and his declaration had something of a lofty epic poem about it, though the subtleties of the aorist tense and the refinements of Greek syntax were evidently alien to him.

He had made his way to the city two days before it was stormed, telling the sentries that he was a Serb from Branković's cavalry. Indeed, they had no doubts. Afterwards, once inside the gate, he was interrogated in the presence of an officer. He quoted a remark that made a huge impression on them: "Better to die fighting than to live in shame." They did not know that it was uttered sixty-four years earlier by Prince Lazar Hrebljanović to his troops before the Battle of Kosovo. He was surprised to be assigned to Constantine's personal guard. A deserter is always a deserter, even when he swells the ranks. That day they had all borne up bravely, until Giustiniani was wounded. The Emperor asked him not to leave the field of battle, but Giustiniani had no strength left, he was staggering on his feet and finally made for his own people, back to the Genoese ship. That was the beginning of the end. The Genoese lost heart, and janissaries swarmed in the breach in the gate made by the Turkish artillery.

"Is there any man among you who will run me through with his sword?" cried the Emperor. "Take courage, and do not surrender me to dishonour!"

But no one was brave enough to carry out the king's wishes.

The Emperor cast off his robes, and in the simple clothing of a soldier plied his sword at the Holy Roman Gate. He killed many. But just as many rose up immediately behind them. Stabbed in the side by a spear, and at once cut down by a janissary, he fell dead, like hundreds of others, and was soon buried under a heap of corpses. When Mehmed entered the city, he immediately ordered a search for the body of Constantine. Someone must have reported that he was fighting by this and no other gate. He was recognised by his boots. Only the king wore shoes with a double-headed eagle on the tops. His head was cut off and taken to Mehmed, who asked the Megadux Lucas Notaras, who had not been killed: "Is this the head of your master?" "Yes," replied the Megadux, "that is the head of my emperor." Stuck on a lance, it was paraded before all the troops. Then for half a day it hung on a column in the Augusteon. Next Mehmed ordered it to be skinned and stuffed with straw, then announced that it would be taken on a tour of the countries of Mohammed, starting with Egypt, to show that the Turks would never withdraw from Europe. That was how the last emperor Constantine XI Paleologos Dragaš, who refused to flee from besieged Constantinople, met his end. His body was thrown into a ditch for the dogs to eat. Isaiah was not wrong when he said that all your good deeds shall be like a bloody rag.

Disguised as a petty tradesman, Milan Duškov had wandered about Phaleron. He saw what always happens in conquered cities – rape, robbery, people begging for mercy, children impaled on pikes, monks placing their heads beneath swords and axes. Outside a Venetian bakery one of Branković's cavalry patrols had recognised him.

"Your king never disowned his mother," he concluded. "That was why to the surname Paleologos he always added the Serbian Dragaš, as if in memory of the Battle of Kosovo."

The rain had stopped. The guards were slowly and reluctantly returning to the stocks. Someone was struck with a stick and cried out in Italian: "God have mercy on us!" But God was silent, just as if the Temple of Hagia Sophia were a hotbed of crime and not prayer, and as if He now favoured the victors, not the vanquished.

They were unchained from the stocks and lined up for transport onto the ship. He felt that as a blind man he would either immediately be killed or sent to the galleys. And there he would die, in filth and humiliation, after several years of terrible labour. The fear was paralysing. He felt a deep pang in his heart. He heard the wail of the muezzin and woke to find his pyjamas drenched in sweat. But it was not the summons to *salat al fagr*, the morning prayer – it was his mobile phone, carefully set to buzz as usual. Antoni Julian Berdo was gradually returning to reality, digesting scraps of images from his dream.

Why Constantinople? Paleologos Dragaš? His cut-off head, skinned and stuffed with straw, in Cairo, Bukhara, Samarkand, Isfahan and Damascus? That was the first thing he imagined after waking up as he went to the toilet: a small, dried skull with a miserable tuft of hair, finally thrown on some rubbish heap in a desert city where camels shat and dogs were burned. Once it had been full of Platonic ideas, the sayings of Heraclitus, the subtleties of Nicaea and the complexities of the Florentine Union, taxes in the Despotate of Morea and nurturing the alliance with Trabzond. When at last some minor bey, aga or vizier had decided to throw it out, there was nothing inside but a few grains of sand. Not even maggots – just sand, and nothing more.

He did not have a reverent attitude to Byzantium. On the contrary, the corruption, nepotism, dynastic murders, attacks on weaker parties and compromises with the stronger all belonged to a tradition he knew very well, not just from books

about Byzantium, but also from the third, Orthodox Rome –
Russia, which from Ivan the Terrible to Stalin's grandsons had
performed these practices to perfection.

So why was he so concerned about the skull of
Constantine XI Paleologos Dragaš, thrown on a rubbish heap
after years on display? If Mehmed had ordered a Christian
burial for his enemy would it have been different?

But it couldn't have been different. As he shook off the
last drops of urine, Antoni Julian Berdo thought of the Al-
Jazeera television channel. The severed heads of hostages,
including journalists, charity workers and politicians, were
shown to the cameras still dripping with blood, their eyes
wide open, like the fetishes of the French Revolution, proving
that the show was still going on and might never end. Those
who claim that as they can't conquer us, the Muslims want at
least to intimidate, and above all humiliate us, are right. That
was Berdo's conclusion as he left the toilet with an empty
bladder.

By the way, how many years had his country fought
against Turkey? After washing his hands and putting some
bread in the toaster he did a quick calculation, which came to
him easily, though he wasn't a historian. Władysław III of
Varna was killed on the tenth of November 1444. And then
Jan III Sobieski routed the Turkish army at the Battle of
Vienna on the twelfth of September 1683. Between these two
dates no more nor less than two hundred and thirty-nine years
went by. The participation of some of our volunteers at the
Battle of Kosovo in 1389 did not fundamentally extend this

era, which in round figures – thought Berdo, as he spread cottage cheese and honey on his toast – lasted a quarter of a millennium. Rather a long time, undoubtedly.

Oh yes, honey. A pot of honey. Who told the story about it? It wasn't the lady who taught history, who only knew how to talk about the oppressed peasants. Why had the Sultan kept the king's severed head for years and years in a jar of honey? Thanks to this original Turkish preserving method, did Władysław of Varna's eyes continue to shine and keep their colour? And if the Sultan kept taking the young king's head out of the pot again and again to savour his victory, didn't the flies come swarming?

Through a haze that morning was coming back to him: he and his mother had got off the train after an all-night journey, and immediately set off across Krakow to Wawel Hill. He remembered the pigeons and the puddles on Kanonicza Street. And then those incredible, oriental treasures kept in the Royal Castle: the Vizier's tent, the horses' caparisons, the armour, yatagan swords, bows, shields, ornate jewel cases, rubies, emeralds, topazes and long robes – all captured at the Battle of Vienna.

"He said he'd turn Saint Peter's Cathedral into a stable."

Shortly he had realised who his mother was talking about – the Grand Vizier Kara Mustafa. But it was abstract, remote, hard to understand. Only in the cathedral, at the tombs of the Polish kings, had the story of Władysław's head in the pot of honey made a strong impression on him. Over his second piece of toast – with the same dose of honey and cottage cheese – Antoni Berdo remembered that Prince Lazar Hrebljanović, taken prisoner after his defeat at the Battle of Kosovo, was beheaded. None of the general sources he knew – he wasn't a specialist on the subject – said anything about a pot of honey. But anyone who wrote about the battle was bound to mention the Greeks and the Genoese who, handsomely paid by Murad, tipped the scale of victory in favour of the Muslims.

Matters are never as simple as they should be, thought Berdo, as he put down his mug of coffee next to the computer and started up the local morning news service. In 1683 a large number of Hungarians set off for Vienna with the Turks because they wanted to throw off the Habsburg yoke. No one who knew just a little European history can have any illusions – for many peoples the Habsburgs were no better than the Osmans. The Venetians did not come to Constantine XI's aid because they didn't want to spoil their existing and future trading relations with Mehmed. A few hundred years later, when Venice was occupied by Austrian troops, finally putting an end to the Most Serene Republic, no one declared war on them for this reason. Maybe it was because of all these thoughts that Berdo reacted extremely calmly to the news of the bomb attacks.

The only thing that occurred to him as he looked at the photos of the young people in balaclavas throwing Molotov cocktails at the new mosque was whether he would get to his exam today. And whether it would actually happen, seeing the Free University was located in the building adjoining the mosque. So he called Ibrahim ibn Talib's contact number on his mobile, and to his amazement soon heard his calm, equable voice: "Hello?"

"This is Berdo," he introduced himself matter-of-factly. "Is our meeting today still on?"

After a brief pause Ibrahim ibn Talib replied in a dignified tone: "There is no reason for it not to take place, Professor. Mr Hatamani will be expecting you without fail in the Azure Hall at the agreed time."

Did any of his students or university colleagues speak such refined Polish? No, not even Żelazny, the lecturer who had resisted the vulgarisation of the language the longest (in fact, the watershed had been not the now long forgotten presidency of Wałęsa, but the more recent tenure of the phenomenal Kaczyński twins), which made people joke at faculty staff meetings that he spoke like the brave insurgent nobles in Eliza Orzeszkowa's nineteenth-century novels, not even he would have still used such a refined phrase as "will be expecting you without fail", or "there is no reason for it not to take place". He would have said: "will be waiting for you", and "Well, of course it is."

Was it a trick? Or just the special talent of the man who went by the pseudonym Ibrahim ibn Talib? He thought the former was unlikely, but he couldn't discount the latter.

It all began a long time ago, a few years after the war ended in now non-existent Yugoslavia. The small charter plane carrying twenty-five Pilgrims of Truth should have made its emergency landing in Budapest, but for obscure reasons the pilot had announced that the break in the journey would happen at Sarajevo. At about seven in the evening they had descended the narrow stairway to a waiting bus. Mr Tiszpak's efficiency was admirable. In a few minutes, using two phones and three local dialects, he had arranged high-speed VIP immigration clearance (though none of the pilgrims was a diplomat), a hotel and an evening tour of the city with a guide.

"Have you any suggestions?" he had asked Berdo, almost in a whisper.

"No," he had replied just as discreetly. "My programme is over. There might be a sacred mountain here, but not locally. At least mentioned in the Bible. But I can't think of one. What about you?"

Tiszpak shrugged. It wasn't really part of his duties. If it were a matter of providing three helicopters, a supply of champagne or a home cinema kit in the desert he'd have set about the task at once. He regarded Berdo with respect, because the rituals he performed were so well liked that despite the exorbitant prices their charters enjoyed huge popularity and were booked up six months in advance.

Once they were through immigration, as the minibus was rushing into the city centre, after a silence Berdo told Tiszpak: "I'm not going on the city tour. I'll eat at the hotel and go to bed. I'm tired."

"Of course," said Mr Tiszpak. "*Ex*cellent."

That "*ex*cellent" of his, in which he always exaggerated the "ex", had annoyed Berdo for a while now. But as everyone, or almost everyone in this trade had their favourite phrase or nervous tic, he merely limited himself to calling Mr Tiszpak "Mr *Ex*cellent" in his thoughts. So later on, when Mr *Ex*cellent had assembled the whole group – maybe not of pilgrims any more – in the hotel lobby to accompany them on a tour of the city and supper, refreshed by a quick shower and a change of shirt and shoes, Berdo slipped past into the bar, where he calmly ordered a double Scotch on the rocks.

He had reasons to feel pleased. From an idea he didn't actually believe in, that he had suggested to Jan Wybrański two years earlier over dinner as a joke, or rather a fantasy on the theme of "what else Festus & Felix could do", from a project he had simply pulled out of the air, which might not really fit the bill, a profitable, but very limited activity by the company's standards, the thriving, highly prosperous "Pilgrims of Truth" had been born. Everything he had said at the time in an ironical, derisive way about the need for spiritual light, the energy of sacred places, the crucial role of a guru who introduces an unusual atmosphere and administers a painless dose of meditation using convenient new rituals, all this – reinforced with a prohibitive price and advertising exclusively reliant on information scattered here and there about the inaccessibility of this exceptional form of travel to the origins – had prompted an avalanche of interest. After the first Pilgrimage of Truth, for which the participants had to pay almost five thousand dollars each, instead of running the next one, Berdo had responded to Wybrański's urgent request to work on recruiting and training suitable gurus. For here lay the key to their success.

Knowledge, appearance, the right tone of voice, a languid way of moving and reacting, and some sort of eccentricity (the most welcome was pure vegetarianism combined with a not too blatant fondness for numerology and cabbalistic associations) had to be enriched with a whole range of suitable gimmicks, quotes, behaviour and habits, adapted to each specific place. The guru earned twice as much as the group's courier, but that was fair: he knew when – just before the summit – to take off his sandals and walk the last thirty metres barefoot, when to bend over and pick a blade of grass, split it in four and cast them north, south, east and west, when to wash his face in a stream, dip his feet in the sea, or sit down in a grotto and say nothing, give no explanation, but explain the silence during transcendental meditation.

It wasn't easy. The guru had to be middle-aged, and had to remain detached from the pilgrims throughout (they were supposed to court his attention, not the other way around), but he was not allowed to put them off or discourage them in any way. Addictions were out of the question, and additionally an asexual aura was required: anyone who watched the guru should always be under the impression that at every second of his existence he, or at least part of his being, was elsewhere, not where the rest of them happened to be.

At the outset, two of Berdo's colleagues from the Psychology Institute were meant to help him select candidates, but they turned out to be idiots. All they were capable of was setting the next target and describing behavioural features. But what was needed here was profound intuition.

"I'm looking for brilliant born conmen, not professionals," he had screamed at them.

They had parted ways. Ultimately, once Berdo had done six months of backbreaking work, the PoT programme had seven spiritual leaders at its disposal. They travelled the first route together, where he tested their acquired and innate skills. Later it was his favourite itinerary, which he was reluctant to yield to others: the ten sacred mountains. They started from Jerusalem (the Temple Mount, Calvary and the Mount of Olives), and ended in eastern Turkey on the slopes of Ararat. In between they visited Sinai, Tabor, Hermon, Carmel, the Mount of Beatitudes and Mount Nebo, where Moses died. To Berdo's amazement, the best guru turned out to be not Felicjan, the excommunicated priest (let's say three plus out of five), but the DJ Popo Cooler from the seaside Viva Club (definitely top marks). Also very good was Patrycja, though he had had to fight with her categorically to give up wearing shorts and tight T-shirts entirely. Soon after, Berdo had elaborated some other itineraries, variants and mutations, on the trail of: the Holy Grail, the Megaliths, the Albigensians, the Pyramids, the Templars, Artemis, Apollo, Asclepius, the Labyrinths, the Kabbalists, the Alchemists, the Conquistadors, the Vikings, the Druids and the Shamans.

"You are a genius," Wybrański praised him a year on. "Our customers are founding an Eleusis society. This is already much more than just some charter holidays and tours. Do you realise we're selling something that isn't material?"

Berdo was far from enthusiastic.

"Just like the Church and its eternal life," he had said at the time. "Cheques that bounce."

"Oh no," laughed Wybrański. "That's my speciality. But let's get down to business." He lit a cigar. "I've sold a hundred thousand copies of the first issue of our magazine, called *Eleusis*. Eleven zlotys a copy. Think of that – I never imagined anything like this could come of all your bullshit."

Berdo did not let his disappointment show. After all, he was working – having taken unpaid leave from the university – as a spiritual guide for the Pilgrims of Truth. He liked it, he wasn't complaining, he had been to Yucatán, Siberia and Scandinavia, yet he was expecting Wybrański to offer him more. But he did not. Whenever one of the gurus dropped out of the business, he looked for a successor, trained them and tested them out, without getting any remuneration. He had a terrible employment contract and could drop out of the game at any time. Wybrański had not invited him to co-edit the magazine.

"Why not?" he thought, as he ordered another double Scotch on the rocks.

He never had a proper answer to that sort of question. Maybe the only answer was that, in spite of all, the success of the PoT project was marginal in terms of the profits Wybrański's firm made. But if so, he thought, as he took a swig of whisky, shouldn't I try to find my own place?

He wasn't hungry, but he was a little tipsy now. The loudspeaker above the bar was pouring out Balkan music, with lots of quavers and semiquavers. Berdo paid and headed for the lift. As he was passing the reception desk he caught sight of dozens of little leaflets. He never picked them up. The items on offer – such as the hotel gym or recipes for the local cuisine – did not interest him. And yet, automatically, he took one of the colourful rectangles, and once in the lift he read in English: "The thrilling dance of the dervishes. Every Friday at Suleiman's Hall. Admission free. Charges only for photographs and video recordings." It was Friday today. In his room he put on a jacket, and with the leaflet in his hand, went downstairs and ordered a taxi.

"Do you know what we went through here?" The driver was one of the talkative kind. "The Serbs hammered us for months, from the hills, over there, the city was closed off, and we couldn't keep up with burying the corpses! Europe? Who cared if one thousand five hundred people were being killed in Sarajevo every week? Who cared? Like here – look, outside the bakery – fifty people were killed by a mortar while queuing for bread, only then did the politicians start talking! You get? For bread, fifty people! And what had we done to them? Nothing. Why did they want to kill us all? Because the Bosniaks are Muslims. Traitors. *Jebi ich majku!*" The driver shifted about in his seat. "The Croats are no better! To them we're left-over Turks, Slavs who gave in to the foreign power of Mohammed. *Jebi ich majku,*" he repeated the obscene curse, "*do krve jebi!*"

Antoni Berdo felt abashed and said nothing. Briefly he imagined being a Warsaw taxi driver who knows German, taking a German from the airport to his hotel.

"Do you know," he says to Helmut out of the blue, "right

outside that building over there your compatriots shot some Poles in revenge for the resistance movement? And do you know that to prevent them from shouting patriotic slogans their mouths were plastered shut before they were executed?" Helmut tells him to stop, screaming that it's a scandal and he won't pay, gets out and takes his luggage.

And what would happen in Lviv? This time Antoni Berdo is the passenger, travelling from the railway station to the Hotel Georges. "You're a Pole?" says the taxi driver. "Do you know that in 1918 your compatriots shot our insurgents right outside that house over there?"

Antoni Berdo doesn't want to hear all that any more. Serbs against Bosniaks, Bosniaks against Croats, Croats against Serbs, Poles against Ukrainians, Ukrainians against Poles and Russians against Poles and Ukrainians, and up to a certain time as well as from a certain time always against the Germans. Only the Slovaks and Czechs had managed a velvet split, though before that happened Father Tiso's regime had sent thousands of Jews straight to the gas chambers, with a Catholic blessing and prayer, the Czechs had taken revenge on the Germans, and there'd been no end of mob rule in the Sudetenland for two whole years. Earlier the Germans in their turn had shot the Czechs at their discretion. Where, by whom and how would all these scores be settled? And what about the French, who could have changed the course of the war at its very start, but didn't want to die for Danzig, or Gdańsk, because it was a Polish, Slavonic, eastern squabble, wasn't it? But at once Berdo reckons he hadn't wanted to die for Sarajevo either. Did that mean he was politically a Frenchman? For the French, the Russians are solely and always innocent. The Russian writer Eddie Limonov had let himself be filmed in the Sarajevo hills, using a machine gun to blast away at the city, at the Muslims, and blithely remarking: "There'll be less of this shit in Europe!" And then there were the humanitarian raids on Belgrade by American planes. Did they really have to call them that?

Antoni Berdo can tell that all these thoughts are muddled and make no sense. The taxi driver has reached his destination and is telling him to pay – thirty-five euros. Although the price is inflated, Berdo gives him forty, and as the driver seems rather reluctant, he gets out without demanding his change. He can't see the river yet, but he can hear the roar of the water and smell the typical odour of a mountain stream. A path leads downhill past a few small cottages, whose gardens, irregular, or maybe just neglected, are turning into boggy thickets. For a moment he thinks he has ended up in the wrong place, but some noises behind him – the cheerful conversation of some Americans, from which it emerges that they too are eager to see some ethnic attractions – confirm that he should keep going. A long shed, standing sideways on to the water right above the river, which is not very wide or fast flowing, must be Suleiman's Hall. It looks like an old sawmill warehouse, or an abandoned paper mill depot.

Inside, it is divided into two unequal parts by a curtain and lit by weak light bulbs, and there is quite a crush of people. In the smaller area, for the audience, there are only a few empty seats left. Berdo perches at the end of a wooden bench in the third row. The Americans will have to stand at the back. The compère, who suddenly appears in front of the curtain, is wearing a white shirt, striped trousers held up by braces that are too loose, and an inside-out waistcoat; the whole time while he's speaking he doesn't take his hands out of his trouser pockets or the smouldering roll-up from the corner of his mouth. In fact it is hard to understand what he's talking about. It's probably that those who want to take photos mustn't use a flash, and that fees for filming will be collected on the way out. And that this is actually a ritual, like a religious one, so no one should sing or shout. They can smoke and applaud at the end. Finally he disappears behind the curtain, from where for the time being a slow, as yet tentative rhythm of drums, flutes and pipes can be heard.

Antoni Julian Berdo knows what to expect of the performance. The dervishes' white robes and red fezzes will whirl faster and faster to the bewildering rhythm of the music. The sing-song chorus, *La ilaha illa Ilah*, will be repeated four hundred, perhaps even five hundred times, until the members of the brotherhood are united in mystical ecstasy. Like this they will achieve a Third Reality inaccessible to mortals, which contains everything, all the power of existence. As in the Gospel of Thomas, where it says: "Blessed is he who will stand at the beginning – he will know the end, and he will not taste death." For one moment in their ecstasy the dancing dervishes will be beyond life and death: the moment they suddenly stop, when the music breaks off, they will find themselves in a stream of light, like a narrow crevice in the mountains, that will show them the true fabric of existence.

As a large circle of some fifty dancers emerged from the darkness, Berdo thought there was something improper about it; it seemed crude to be watching something that wasn't meant for public display but was in essence a mystery. On the other hand, as the show was free, at least it aimed to have a purpose – like a mass anyone can attend without being a Christian, to see the most critical moment, the transubstantiation.

His doubts evaporated when his gaze picked a young dancer out of the circle. Berdo could not take his eyes off him; in spite of the long white robe and the red fez, in spite of the rotations he was performing, the gentle bending of his torso and the perfect tilting of his head in time with the ever faster music, there could be no doubt he was watching the ideal of beauty dancing the Sema: a classical youth, whose total perfection he had admired so often in Greek sculptures. Yet this was no effeminate ephebe, sculpted by Kritios. As Berdo's expert eye divested the dancer of his robe, the shudder that ran through him confirmed his intuition: here before him was the ancient model, the victorious athlete, known for over two and a half thousand years as the kouros. By contrast with the ephebe, so full of lovely roundness that could never go beyond the canon of human beauty, the kouros, taller than a man, broad shouldered, with a narrow waist and a stream of thick curling hair flowing down his back towards powerful, extremely shapely buttocks, came straight from the world of the ancient gods. Such at least was Berdo's impression of the young, whirling dancer, who could never have guessed that simply by comparing him to a Greek statue in his imagination a foreigner in the audience was bordering on ecstasy himself.

Foreseeing the bitter feeling he would have as he left this place and set off for his lonely bed at the hotel, to spite himself he repeated a remark from the fifth volume of Goethe's autobiography: "Every bird has its decoy." How could he at least get close to him, so that he could ask a banal question and hear the sound of his speech, feel the aura of his warmed-up body and gaze into the abyss of his two shining eyes? Feverishly he thought up various versions of this situation, but none of them seemed possible. He could not even dream of going back stage; he could certainly wait outside the building, but only to catch a glimpse of him in a group of about a dozen men heading for the city on foot, or rather in a bus laid on for them. Here a bit of sharp practice could come into play: he could go with them on the excuse of not knowing the city, or any other pretext, but even if they took him, what could he possibly do inside the vehicle – what if, as a foreigner, without a working knowledge of their language, he was barely tolerated, if not regarded as a suspicious intruder?

Dizzy with desire, Berdo almost missed the final moment, when the music suddenly broke off and the dancers froze on the spot for a few seconds. Applause rang out in the darkness, first tentative, then thunderous, and when the lights came on again, all he and the rest of the audience could see was the drawn curtain.

Feeling crushed, he was one of the first people to leave the shed, and then he turned off the narrow path to the water's edge. He stood on a rock and stared into the dark flowing current as he listened to the noises from the nearby road. Taxis were slowly driving up, a coach appeared, and loud remarks, in a mixture of Spanish, English, French, Italian, Norwegian and local words, accompanied the slamming of doors and the purring of running engines.

Homo festivus, thought Berdo, as he flung a white pebble into the water, nothing more nor less: not *homo faber*, not *erectus*, not *religiosus*, not *sapiens* or even *sovieticus*, but for ever and always *homo festivus*.

When he walked uphill to the roadside, he saw just one taxi still waiting there. The light was on inside, and the driver was standing by the open door, smoking a cigarette. As soon as he spotted the approaching passenger he threw the dog-end to the gravel and trod on it. But Berdo did not hurry; instead he slowed his pace, as if undecided. Then, on the same side of the road, from opposite, he saw his dancer walking towards the taxi at a rapid pace. Without the fez and white robe, in a blue shirt loose over jeans, and with a small rucksack slung over his shoulder he looked different from on stage. Their glances met by the open door of the car, and although no clear sign was given, long years of experience seemed to whisper to Berdo that they were both followers of the same religion – mightier, superior to all the Books and all the imams, rabbis, bishops and shamans put together. A religion that had been severely persecuted in Europe until recently, and had only emerged from the catacombs in the past few decades, not without sacrifices and hardships. A religion whose secret followers could also be found within the corps of the clergy of all possible mono- and polytheistic groups, in short, a religion to which the future of this world undoubtedly belonged. But what if his intuition were misleading him this time? This sort of situation had happened before – once, in Marrakesh, he had almost paid with his life for a similar mistake. So just in case he said cautiously, slowly and clearly, so that the driver could hear:

"I'm going to my hotel. I can drop you off on the way. Even if it's in the opposite direction. I'm not in a hurry."

Without a word, the dancer nodded and got into the back seat first, and when Berdo sat down next to him, at a seemly distance, he cast the driver a resonant word that Berdo couldn't catch, probably the name of a street or a district. It wasn't towards the city centre; on the contrary, they were passing fewer and fewer cottages with gardens. Some of them, bombed out by the Serbs, still had ominous-looking skeleton chimneys.

The car turned into a side road, cautiously rolled across a small bridge and then drove along a tributary of the river. The water went roaring down the rapids, and Berdo could hear it surging along through the open window; as he stared into the gathering darkness, suddenly he noticed the black contours of a rocky mountainside, surprisingly close, into whose solid mass they were simply disappearing along a metalled road as narrow as a crevice. Suddenly they were on the other side of it.

The driver stopped outside a low walled building. As soon as Berdo took a breath to say something that might suggest he desired company tonight, he felt the touch of a hand on his knee – very brief, but firm enough to fire his imagination, or at least for him to pay the fare without a word, get out of the car and go after the dancer.

Meanwhile, he had disappeared. The taxi drove away, and Berdo stood staring all around him as if in a hypnotic trance. This place looked like a very deep cauldron bored out of the cliff. It took him a few minutes to realise he was standing at the bottom of a disused quarry. Some rusty conveyor belts, rock-crushing machinery, and some small but probably deep excavations full of very still water shining like a mirror – all this lay in total silence, beneath the strong, whitish light of the moon, like a set for an unfamiliar film.

A light came on in the building. Berdo headed towards it and pushed the half-open door. Inside it smelled of must, vegetables and antiquity. It was not encouraging. But when he heard his first sentence (though in fact it may have been a single word), everything in there seemed beautiful and fantastical. The unmade bed, the office units and the moth-eaten kilim on the wall – none of it seemed too shabby or worn-out now.

They drank rakia from some small shot glasses. And they made love as he never could have dreamed was possible, without saying a word. His name was Mihajlo – that much he revealed between embraces. He was an expert lover, and whatever Berdo did not even dare to suggest with a touch, a hand signal or a body movement, the dancer guessed and at once effected with a quite perverse, as if studied pleasure.

"I'm the watchman here," he told him at last. "What about you?"

"It's unimportant," whispered Berdo. "Can we meet tomorrow? The day after?"

With his arms around Berdo's neck, Mihajlo didn't answer. Finally he said: "Don't come here in the daytime. But in the evening, after sunset, yes, do come."

Then they lay beside each other for a long time in silence. Somewhere outside a stream was bubbling. Mihajlo started talking about a motorbike, an old machine from the Yugoslav era that for lack of a certain part was languishing in the barracks where the workers used to get changed. The tiny missing piece couldn't be found anywhere now, so Drago had been planning to make it on his lathe, but typical Drago – all talk and no action, and then they'd broken up over a pointless, stupid quarrel. As for Stefan, he had promised to buy him a completely new motorbike. But Mihajlo had broken up with Stefan even sooner than with Drago, and that was because of his fondness for too young boys. He always wanted to bring them here, to which Mihajlo simply hadn't agreed, and when Stefan still came here one day with an eleven-year-old gypsy boy in that tank-like BMW of his with the darkened windows, Mihajlo hadn't let them in.

Then, at Berdo's request, he spoke about the mystical dance. But reluctantly, in short sentences, with distinct effort. The Sema is a whirl, in which the seven heavens and the

Earth, and everything to be found on it, glorify God. At the most critical moment there is nothing in existence that does not declare His absolute praise. Like the atoms that never stop spinning in water, stone, wood, air and our human bodies. The Sema is an imitation of this miracle of motion, nothing more. Mihajlo had joined the brotherhood of dancers the year after the war – it would never have occurred to him before. He had never taken the various stories about spiritual elevation seriously. But the first time he tried it, he felt that lift, and became a member of the brotherhood, because what happens to a man during the dance cannot be compared with anything.

At dawn Berdo left the disused quarry and walked to the highway, where he was to find a bus stop. A cold, misty breeze was blowing from the mountains. With every step he took downhill towards the city it grew warmer and sunnier. Only as he boarded the city bus did he switch on his mobile phone. There were seven identical messages from Mr Tiszpak demanding an immediate reply: "Where are you? The plane is ready. Please contact me urgently!"

Berdo answered: "I'm staying here a few days. Don't wait for me. Be in touch via the office. A.J. Berdo."

Mr Tiszpak knew perfectly well that if anything had happened to him, according to instructions the text would have been signed just "Berdo". Like this, thanks to two letters he was free of any more questions and could be almost certain that once he finally reached the hotel, the Pilgrims of Truth and Mr *Ex*-cellent Tiszpak would already be on board a charter plane, flying back to their homeland.

And so it was. At the reception desk he found a message on F&F company paper: "In that case please call me on your return, good luck."

It's a good thing he didn't write "have a nice day", thought Berdo, glancing over the sheet of paper at the young receptionist – that would be in true *Ex*-cellent-Tiszpak style.

What is there to do in a foreign city you've landed in by accident, when all day, afternoon and evening is sheer anticipation of the night to come? Berdo extended his room reservation indefinitely. He set the alarm and slept for three hours solid. Then, after a long, purposeful bath, he ordered breakfast and ate it in his room.

He had never been one of those effeminate narcissists who are morbidly oversensitive about themselves, and cannot go a single day without a trip to the sauna, the hairdresser or the masseur. Nevertheless, once outside, he went to a beauty salon to have his nails done. During the pedicure, as he stared at the nape of the pretty young girl who looked to him like a Serb, he could not stop thinking about Mihajlo.

"Why do you live on your own in the middle of nowhere?" he had asked him before leaving.

At first he was silent for quite a while, then finally he said: "Once there was a Sufi, to whom an angel appeared, and he asked the angel: 'What is the best remedy for the heart?' Without a second thought the herald replied: 'Little contact with people'."

Now, as he wandered the city idly and aimlessly, Berdo told himself this parable again. It was ideally suited for the next meditation with the Pilgrims of Truth. It would work just as well by the ocean shore as at the top of the next sacred mountain. But did he want to go on with that job? And did he want to work at all? Their parting the night before had been strange. Berdo had discreetly dropped two rolled-up banknotes on the bedside table, each of a hundred euros. But as Mihajlo showed him to the door, he felt a hand pushing them back into his trouser pocket.

"The Sufi teaches," came the metallic sound of the dancer's voice, "that only he who rescues himself by honest means and who occupies a pure place shall be saved." Then he added in a whisper: "Remember, after sunset."

What did he mean when he spoke about rescue? Not the Sufi, of course, but Mihajlo? Perhaps he just parroted all sorts of mantras he had heard at meetings of the brotherhood? That was too crude a conjecture. Berdo was a good judge of people. His lover hadn't been a watchman at a disused quarry all his life – on the contrary, he was from the educated class, though he preferred to keep quiet about it. He hadn't really said anything about himself, apart from the motorbike story. Only now as he sat at a little table in a café garden did Berdo imagine his predecessors. Drago could have been a mechanic, the good-for-nothing type, maybe even a member of the same brotherhood. It was impossible to think that of Stefan, who must have been a dealer for the drugs mafia that relies on similar types the world over.

Jesus Christ, thought Berdo as he knocked back a shot of rakia, what am I getting myself into?

Indeed, it wasn't exactly a situation he had often experi-enced. A short session in a hotel room, paid for in advance. A weekend trip to a club in Amsterdam. Or a week's holiday in the mountains with a waiter he'd met by the sea. Deep-down, his instincts told him he should go back to the hotel and hurry to the airport, leaving behind for ever the memory of just one, extraordinary night. And yet the promise – the virtual certainty – of once again enjoying a more intense pleasure than he had ever felt before immediately dismissed all his anxiety. He wasn't young, and he knew this sort of fulfilment and affection would probably never come his way again, not even if he had as much money as Festus & Felix at his disposal, or even more.

A motorcyclist drove past the café, and just then Berdo had an inspiration. At the corner of the street outside the hotel – as he had noticed several times – there was a shop selling two-wheelers. He paid, and went straight over there, and fifteen minutes later he was talking to a salesman about a new Honda. He had trouble making the payment. They didn't accept credit cards here, and he could only withdraw the equivalent of seven hundred euros a day from the ATM – not enough to buy an XRV 750 Africa Twin then and there.

At the hotel he soon got information on all the foreign banks in the city centre. Unfortunately Barclays – where he had a secret account that couldn't be accessed by our tax department – didn't have a branch in this city. On the way to Raiffeisen, he reminded himself of the rules for using the company's emergency accounts. Festus & Felix only allowed a few employees to withdraw cash during Pilgrimages of Truth, and only in extraordinary circumstances. Berdo was one of those few. And the circumstances were extraordinary.

An hour later, he rode into the hotel parking lot on the brand new Honda, and collected his parking receipt; in the hall, when he asked for his room key with the helmet under his arm, the young receptionist glanced at him with distinct curiosity. But Berdo didn't notice. On the wings of euphoria, without waiting for the lift he ran up the stairs to the second floor. Once in his room, he tried on the helmet again and studied himself in the mirror. With the dark visor screening his face he looked like an alien, or the master of ceremonies from one of Lautréamont's cruellest scenes.

Berdo closed the computer. His stream of reminiscences had been interrupted by the comments of internet users: "I'd like to put up a monument to Osama because he's a real national hero, best of all facing the monument to King Jan Sobieski," wrote Voo doo. According to someone called Tiny Tot: "The explosions in the city are probably sponsored by Father Monsignore, because the wine with his mug on the label is doing badly, the usual scheiss." Whereas Beatka said: "I don't give a shit, the muslims can go to Auschwitz, the Jews to Israel, the Poles to a party and the Russkies to work!" D-liter meanwhile declared: "i don't feel sorry for those deelers of you-know-what origin who get the Polish Nashun pissed in those all-night shops. Blowing them up's too good for them. You gotta send them to the camps allez zusamenn."

"Democracy," muttered Berdo, scattering some dry food

into Heraclitus' bowl, "gives the same vote to reasonable people and imbeciles alike. Is that really all right? And is that what we meant? Come on, tell me!"

The cat dipped his nose into the heap of brown biscuits and crunched them happily. As he stroked his back, Berdo added: "After all, you yourself said democracy was a bad thing, because most people are fools, and wise men are extremely thin on the ground! Isn't that so? Or have I got it wrong?"

For a moment Heraclitus stopped eating and looked straight in his master's eyes. The only way he could have answered a question like that was with another quotation from his namesake: "Pigs prefer filth to clean water", or "Asses prefer straw to gold", but in his feline wisdom he plainly realised that today such a riposte would only have brought chaos and confusion into their mutual home. So he didn't even purr, but just nonchalantly went on with his breakfast.

Berdo went into the bathroom. Under the shower his memories of Sarajevo came back to him again: vivid, powerful images of several days of happiness, that came upon him so unexpectedly. At first Mihajlo had refused to accept the motorbike, though his eyes had lit up at the sight of it. It had all happened like something in a surreal novel: each evening he had started up the Honda and ridden it to the quarry, then gone back to the hotel at dawn. He had slept off the night hours, then wandered aimlessly about town, waiting impatiently for dusk again, and anxiously asking himself how long this could go on for.

On the penultimate night Mihajlo had agreed that Berdo would leave the motorbike for him when he departed. But neither of them had said a word about when that would be.

Now, as he dried his body with a towel, he made himself remember every detail of what had happened with masochistic precision.

As usual, he had ridden right up to the cottage with the lights off. The echo bouncing off the vertical walls of the quarry went on carrying the whine of the dying engine a few seconds longer. He took off the helmet and went inside. Mihajlo was lying in bed with his head tilted back. His throat had been cut. The bedclothes, floor and wall were splattered in blood. For some time Berdo held his lover by the wrist and gazed into his wide open eyes, as if expecting to find a final spark of life in them. But the body was cold. The murder must have been committed at least an hour earlier. Without moving from the spot, Berdo looked around for the murder weapon within his range of vision. And that was when he smelled that odour wafting in from the entrance on a gust of mountain wind: the smell of sweat, rakia, cheap tobacco and a well-oiled weapon. A man with a Kalashnikov slung over his shoulder, barrel pointing downwards, was standing in the doorway, staring at Berdo.

"I didn't do it," Berdo replied to the question that hadn't been asked.

"If it wasn't you or me, then who?"

The man's voice was dry, toneless and unemotional.

He was wearing an army shirt with no insignia, black

jeans and extremely worn-out trainers.

"I don't know," said Berdo, watching closely as the other man relit a burned-out cigarette with a plastic lighter, "but we should inform the police."

"Are you sure you really want to do that?"

Berdo didn't answer. The man came right inside, looked around him without much interest, and pointed the rifle at Berdo.

"Passport!" He gestured towards the bedside table with the Kalashnikov. "Put it there and stand against the wall. But slowly."

He spent a long time leafing through the passport, as if trying to memorise not just the owner's name, date and place of birth, and the place of issue, but also the stamps from all the border crossings and visas that filled page after page.

Finally he said: "Get out and stand by the bike!"

Berdo carried out the order, only realising once he was outside that he hadn't taken the helmet with him. But it was already on the armed man's head.

"Keys," he said, tossing Berdo's passport to the ground. "Put the papers here, on the seat."

Berdo took a key ring out of his trouser pocket with two keys, for the ignition and the immobiliser, and the motorbike's temporary registration document from his jacket pocket. He put it all on the Honda's concave seat and stepped back a few paces.

Before starting up the engine and hanging the Kalashnikov back on his shoulder, the man said: "You can get out of here. But quickly."

And so it was.

Berdo switched on the small radio in the bathroom.

The familiar sound of Chief Inspector Zawiślny's voice was reporting that the situation in the city was more or less under control. A few extremists, who had thrown Molotov cocktails at the new mosque, had been arrested. In the case of the blasts at the all-night off-licences, various hypotheses were being investigated and the circle of suspects was getting narrower. Unfortunately, the gridlock caused by the blockade would continue to paralyse traffic in the city centre for some time to come. Anything suspicious could be reported on a special infoline, 777 777 777, though of course the public were asked to exercise responsibility. Stupid hoaxes and informing on neighbours could be followed up and fined in due course.

An advertisement for Twingo Power cut short the Chief Inspector's statement. Then Momo the DJ gabbled away about the need for tolerance, and put on a hip hop hit by some kids from an estate in the New Port: "Street riot! Street riot! Keep your issues quiet!", which had been terrifically popular a year ago, when the soccer fans had pulverised a police division after the Arka versus Lechia match and smashed up half the district adjoining the stadium while they were about it. Normally Berdo would have switched off this racket, but standing at the mirror with soapy cheeks and his razor in his hand, firstly he was waiting for a news update, and secondly, he couldn't put off the task of shaving any longer.

He remembered that awful night in the hotel after a two-hour walk in the dark. He hadn't been afraid of arrest, interrogation or scandal – if it had come to that. Oddly he was sure that by tossing his passport to his feet the man with the Kalashnikov was giving him the guarantee of a safe getaway. But why? Did he have anything to do with Mihajlo's murder? Maybe he had turned up by accident? Or maybe he had been following their trysts all those nights? Had he found the body, then waited for Berdo, and improvised requisitioning the motorbike? He could just as well have been a random thug of the sort the war here must have produced by the dozen. But in that case he would have shot him without batting an eyelid. Why hadn't he taken his money?

Only on the flight home, after changing planes in Budapest, had the agonised Berdo realised that out of Mihajlo's muddled remarks a story to do with that place had emerged. Inactive throughout the years when Sarajevo was under siege, the quarry had been bought straight after the war by a Belgian-Dutch company. But they hadn't been able to get any mining going, because part of the city administration, or maybe the district authorities too, had demanded that a plaque be set into the wall there – a memorial plaque. During the war the Serbs had shot prisoners there – people caught trying to get through the blockade. The company had refused, apparently because of intervention by the Serbs. There was a stalemate, but although he himself wondered why, Mihajlo did receive his salary regularly. He didn't have much to guard, because everything that could have been stolen had disappeared long ago. His family home had been blown up by two heavy artillery shells in the first week of the siege – with his mother and sister inside.

But as he smoothed cream on his cheeks, Berdo wasn't thinking about Mihajlo any more. He was pondering the irrational sequence of events that, while seeming to be over and done with in one part of the world, had found their continuation in a completely different place, many years later, like in novels about mummies brought back from Egypt. As he had got out of the plane in his home city after that terrible journey, could he have imagined that a few years on he would be reading in the local news about the construction of a new mosque at the very heart of the mediaeval Hanseatic Old City? Could he have foreseen that he would receive a long and serious letter of invitation, and then be off to the Free University for an interview and a reconnoitre? And that he would instantly gain employment there – with an excellent salary – as a lecturer specialising in local cultural tradition? That his every word, comment and digression would be assiduously noted down, not only by the growing number of immigrants, but also by the local neophytes? And that finally, one day he would be asked to come to the university office by a man named Ibrahim ibn Talib, who spoke very good Polish, and who would offer him the chance to talk to the Mufti? De facto that meant an invitation to convert. The man who wore that name like a badly cut shirt had politely stressed that under no circumstances was that a condition for Berdo's further employment.

"We are highly satisfied with you," he had said, glancing out of the window at the Gothic tower of Saint Nicholas' church. "We never so much as dreamed of finding someone like you here. And that is exactly why we are proposing that you should become one of us. It is not an exam. The Mufti will ask about the fundamental truths of the faith. Then you will make your statement. I have been authorised to assure you that from then on all our universities will be open to you. The whole world," he went on, without taking his eyes off the window for a second, "from Dubai to America. Your knowledge of the psychology of this civilisation is priceless."

"Circumcision?" Berdo had asked dryly.

The man with the assumed name Ibrahim ibn Talib clearly had some difficulty stifling an outburst of laughter.

"We are not Jews. That is not something we require!"

He had a feeling he'd seen this man somewhere before. Especially his voice – and Berdo was sensitive to voices – seemed not unfamiliar. But he must have been imagining it. Until this conversation he had only noticed him once, when he had sat in the third row of the lecture hall, hanging on Berdo's every word – at the time he had been explaining the psychological conditioning of pagan criticism of early Christianity. He had moved on to talk about the third-century philosopher Porphyry's text *Against the Christians*, quoting an extract that even the Calvinists find offensive, although they reject the divine nature of the Eucharist, and that says: "It is not just horrifying and shocking, but it goes beyond all manner of abomination – to gain eternal life by consuming human flesh and drinking fraternal blood – is it not altogether monstrous?", at which point the man with the name Ibrahim ibn Talib had jotted something down in a small notebook he took from the pocket of his loose, shiny silk jacket.

Could he have predicted then, as they went outside together after their conversation into a street full of German tourists, that in another year or so he would decide to take the exam? And that today, in the telephone receiver, he would hear the incredible sentence: "There is no reason for it not to take place, Professor. Mr Hatamani will be expecting you without fail in the Azure Hall at the agreed time."

"The ineluctable modality of the visible," he remembered a quotation from *Ulysses* as he was doing up his tie. But who said that phrase? Bloom to Molly? No, nonsense. Dedalus to Bloom? Unlikely. So it was probably Dedalus on his own, yes, definitely Dedalus on his own, walking along by the snot-green, Irish sea. Most precisely so.

It was an astonishing feeling. Berdo had no scruples – social, academic, and least of all religious – about making such a change in his life. In view of his fundamental atheism, though he never actually flaunted it, filling in the form for one religion or another seemed an act of no significance – but one that also opened up new opportunities. And yet, as he went out of the front door and glanced up at the Baroque towers of the Arsenal, erected here almost five centuries ago by the Dutch, he felt immense regret, because of that phrase from *Ulysses* he had just remembered. As if the conversation with the Mufti was to be a sort of *auto da fé*, during which he would have to renounce this very book and no other, promise never to read it again, to remove it from the bookshelf at home and never once mention it to his students.

Of course he realised it was an absurd assumption, but as he couldn't stop thinking about it, maybe it did express some genuine anxiety, or even a real threat? But no, he calmed himself as he bought a newspaper. Mufti Hatamani, of whom he had heard a lot, applied a completely new policy. Inculturation – that was the technical term for it. Clever – you can profess this religion, while keeping all – well, almost all your old customs. A bit like the Jesuits in Paraguay. Here, smiling to himself, Berdo had to slow down, because a city guard patrol had blocked half the width of the roadway and was directing cars and pedestrians down one side only. Just then his mobile phone rang.

"Antoni?" he heard Mateusz's trembling voice. "Are you alive?"

"I don't frequent all-night shops," he replied calmly. "I'm alive."

"It's a nightmare," groaned Mateusz into the receiver, "a nightmare. Do you know Franek won't be joining us?"

"Really? Why not?"

"Haven't you heard?"

"No, what?"

"He was at the shop on Conrad Street. He's in the Academy hospital, badly injured."

"If only he'd stopped drinking a few years ago, like me…"

"What the hell do you mean?" Mateusz was outraged. "He

was just walking past the place!"

"Even sadder," said Berdo. "What else?"

"I'm looking for a twelfth man. Can you think of anyone?"

Only now was Berdo surprised. After the exam he was meant to be going to the theatre for the photo shoot. The anger that came over him at his own forgetfulness spilled onto Mateusz.

"Am I an Evangelist? A prophet? Why can't you postpone the whole thing? Half the apostles won't get there! Do you think this is such a good day for it?"

Mateusz bellowed his message at the rate of a sports commentator: It's too late to change anything. The next possible date would be after the holidays. He had called everyone, and they had all confirmed they were coming. Lewada, Wybrański and Okiennicki were sure to be late, but they'd get there.

"So you're coming, right?" Mateusz concluded in a conciliatory tone.

"Yes, I'll be there." Now Berdo was outshouting a fire engine, which for some unknown reason was driving away from the fire with its siren on. "On condition you make me Judas!"

And without waiting for Mateusz to answer, he ended the call.

Must there always be quails and manna, thought Berdo, a prophet rising from the rocks, or a teacher who should have returned from the Father long ago, but hadn't done as he predicted?

Suddenly he thought of a suggestion he would put to Mateusz in front of them all on the stage. Wouldn't it be better to paint "The Last Conversation of Socrates"? Once Xanthippe has left the cell with their small son and the guard has removed his shackles, the philosopher rubs his aching leg and starts up a conversation with his pupils. "What a strange thing it is," he says, "this sensation which is popularly called pleasure!" Or the scene after the debate, when he picks up the chalice and says that now he will pray to the gods for a successful passage into the other world and, as Plato writes, "having said this, at a single draught and without the slightest difficulty" he drinks it dry.

At least there were no miracles there, thinks Berdo, turning the corner at Saint Mary's hippo-like red-brick cathedral, just questions and arguments. It's true they're not convincing, for what can there be on the other side of death? The dark side of our ego, a river of subconscious images, hopes and fears – nothing more. And yet the presence of the pupils and the Master, who swallows the fatal chalice in an Athenian jail, having first assured them in every possible way that the soul is immortal, has something noble about it. Because it is devoid of miracles, that event is purely and simply a duel between the mind and fate that affects everyone, a struggle with the nothingness that will envelop us after death, just as it enveloped us before our father's sperm met our mother's egg. A lamp once the wick has gone out feels the same as before it was lit.

As Berdo had left home too early and was literally two

steps away from the Free University building, now he was circling the cathedral like the Flying Dutchman, continuing to muse about the "Last Conversation". They were ad hoc thoughts, yet Berdo couldn't help remembering that in his cell the Master was surrounded by fourteen pupils, to whom he bequeathed his message – exactly the same number of people as the Minotaur demanded each year from the Athenians as his victims. It couldn't be a random coincidence – the fifteenth was Theseus, the liberator, just as the fifteenth person in the cell during the "Last Conversation" was Socrates. Theseus killed the monster and guided the people out of the murky Labyrinth. Whom and what did the Master rescue?

Excited by this unexpected association, Berdo walked even faster, deciding that this afternoon, once it was all over, he would re-read *Phaedo* extremely carefully, and look at a few dictionaries and articles too.

With exactly three minutes to go as he crossed the threshold of the Free University, he headed for the gateway with the arabesque mosaic reminiscent of the Alhambra. Once the policemen had let him through, he knocked three times at the stylised wooden door, and remembered one more sentence uttered by Socrates to his pupils as he died: "Many carry a wand, but only a few are inspired." And as the door opened, he thought of this one too – "I'd rather have a bath before death than leave it to the women to wash me."

Can we abandon him like this? In the passage between two worlds? Decided, and at the same time undecided? Confident, though never more full of doubt? Still pondering the words spoken during the last conversation, but already considering what Mr Hatamani would ask him about Qa'im al-Qiyam, Ruler of the Resurrection, who will return and announce his rebirth to the world?

I can tell you're getting impatient at this point, you're scrolling down my e-mail, because you're eager to study their conversation about the hidden imam of the Shiites, who after the seven cycles predicted by the Prophet will finally reveal his true Name to the world. But for now I'd prefer not to enter the Free University with Berdo as the door crashes shut behind him.

David Roberts, whom we left approaching the Jaffa Gate, requires far more attention now: in less than thirty minutes, in the afternoon light he will start to sketch the view of the Church of the Holy Sepulchre. But first he stops for a while in front of David's Tower – then much smaller than it is today, when almost a quarter of its height had been buried in desert sand. This time Roberts isn't thinking about the Bible, nor is he remembering the capture of Jerusalem from the Jebusites, roughly a thousand years before the birth of Christ. Gazing at the tower walls, where stones laid by the Romans, Greeks, Persians, Crusaders and Mamelukes form a unique chequerboard of eras, he recalls the start of his own journey to the Holy Land. On the eighth of February 1839, with Mr Pell and Mr Kinnear, dressed in Arab costumes, with a well-armed escort and servants, they set off from Cairo to the east. Their caravan numbers twenty-one loaded camels. Roberts is surprised how cool it is at dawn: until the sun is really warming the air and the sea of sand to a temperature of forty-plus degrees, he can almost feel a chill. Nineteen days later they will reach Aqaba on the Red Sea. It is there, by a campfire beneath a starry sky that Roberts will hear the Arab word *tuhas* meaning a seal, and will find out that the Hebrew name for this mammal is *tahash*, which will prompt him to conclude that the feuding nations are closely related. They will visit Petra, Mount Sinai, Bethlehem and Nazareth, which he will describe and sketch in his notebooks at first hand. Now, after entering the Jaffa Gate – where the pushy salesmen are already accosting him – he passes David's Tower on his right, goes down the narrow Suq El-Bazar, and turns left a few minutes later into an even narrower alleyway. He will pass the site of the old Pool of Hezechias and finally reach a square surrounded by ruins. It will take him a long time to find a suitable spot. The courtyard itself is cramped and crowded with noisy tradesmen touting potable water, dates, nuts and sugary sweetmeats in Arabic. He won't be able to get a good perspective there. Finally he finds the right point: it is a wide terrace, a sort of platform on top of some old stone walls that probably date from the Mameluke era.

In the foreground of the lithograph we can see three men dressed in Turkish costume. They are standing beside a small table, with the carafe from a hookah on it and two small boxes, probably for tobacco. At the moment immortalised by Roberts they are not smoking. One of them, captured in profile, is holding a long-stemmed pipe. The second has his back towards us. Just the third, leaning against a balustrade, is looking in the draughtsman's direction, as if detached for the time being from the conversation, to scrutinise what the strange man with the sketchbook on his knees is doing. A cushion and a small carpet laid next to the table attest that this is their permanent site for smoking the galjan.

Only in the middle ground, a little lower down on the left-hand side, can we see the crowded courtyard, two typical ogival portals, the church tower flattened by a fire in 1808, and in the background behind it the domes and towers of minarets. If it weren't for the crowd in the square, the Church of the Holy Sepulchre would look like a sad, deserted ruin in an eclectic style, not quite Romanesque, not quite Byzantine, and not quite Gothic. The shadows on the lithograph made from this sketch do not enable us to establish the exact position of the sun. Plainly Roberts was thinking about something else at the time, and it is highly probable to suppose he was wondering how strange it is that inside the church, which he had already visited the day before, all the holiest places were such short distances apart – the cell where Jesus spent the night before His execution; Golgotha, where the crime was committed; the anointment stone; and finally the tomb, from which after three days He rose again.

Therefore when He was brought from here onto His Via Dolorosa Jesus must have turned a circle along the alleyways of Jerusalem and come back here to His death, and finally to His tomb, donated by the good Joseph of Arimathea.

The main building in the sketch is already finished. As he shades in the figures of peddlers in the courtyard, David

Roberts thinks of a small book by an unknown author that his daughter gave him before his journey to Egypt, Syria and Palestine. Among all the other materials, maps, descriptions of customs and monuments, and advice about finances and hygiene, this publication is probably the one he remembers best. Its title was *False Messiahs*, but it wasn't about the miraculous healers, hypnotists and theosophists whose numbers are increasing in the current era, but some Jews, particularly those among the chosen race who, in defiance of common sense and logic, proclaimed themselves to be the Messiah, many centuries after the death of the Rabbi Joshua ben Joseph.

Wasn't the case of Abraham Abulafia an example of madness? To make his way to Rome in 1280 to convert Pope Nicholas III to Judaism? For this insolent, exceptionally incomprehensible proposition he was to have burned at the stake, and only the Pope's death saved Abulafia's life. As the Messiah he doggedly headed for Sicily, where however the numerous local peasants and the less numerous Jews refused to recognise him as the saviour of the world.

Another one to make the pilgrimage to Rome was Salomon Molcho, who arrived there from Portugal some three hundred years later. He spent thirty days by the Tiber with the beggars and the sick, announcing his coming in narrow little streets, low dives and brothels. Caught, accused and condemned, he could have escaped death by renouncing his own faith. He chose martyrdom, who knows whether or not on the basis of the same verse of Isaiah as Jesus. As he read the book, David Roberts was quite amazed to find that Salomon Molcho's clothing had ended up in Imperial Prague and is preserved there by the Jews as a relic to this day.

The one to gain the largest number of fanatical followers was Sabbatai Zvi. Maybe because he didn't travel to Rome? Imprisoned on the orders of the Sultan, he did not choose martyrdom. That verse of Isaiah did not apply to Sabbatai. He converted to Islam, and so did many of his followers, trailing after their Messiah into exile in Albania.

Now David Roberts is drawing a thin line to correct the parasol of palm leaves above the Turkish pipe smokers. Indeed, the crucial feature of being the Messiah, he muses, is to announce the date of a Great Change, the Coming of New Times.

According to Abraham Abulafia, the messianic era was to come in 1290. When he died a year later in Sicily, not a single rock so much as trembled. Salomon Molcho prophesied the coming of the kingdom in 1540. He died a martyr eight years earlier, but the date he designated brought no change to the world order either. Most curious of all, in view of the three sixes, was the year 1666, as prophesied by Sabbatai Zvi, but even then the messianic age did not follow. Only Salomon Molcho proved an actual prophet, at least in a certain limited sense of the word – he predicted the flooding of Rome of 1531, and the earthquake in Portugal a year later. Only Jesus said: "In a little while you will see me no more, and then after a little while you will see me." But what does a little while mean, when God uses that phrase? Making his way to the

Aethiopians for a feast, Poseidon remained there for several days. The measure of that time was defined by man: in Homer the gods, though immortal, measure time with the same hourglass as people. But what about Jesus? And the Father He was making His way to – for a little while? *Mikron* – the Greek word used by John – is present in all the languages of modern Europe for technical rather than Biblical reasons, meaning literally little, not much, very few. So almost at once the disciples asked: "What does He mean by 'a little while'?"

David Roberts puts the finished sketch into his portfolio. He decides to go downhill, to the square outside the Church of the Holy Sepulchre and to continue drawing: the number of peddlers has plainly decreased, there is a far better perspective, and the light, until the violet Jerusalem dusk sets in, is even better than a while ago: bright enough, and yet soft, not so contrasting. Years from now this second lithograph from outside Christianity's holiest site will end up – like all the others from this journey – in the Victoria and Albert Museum, where it remains to this day. Evidently Roberts recognised it as especially important, as it is the one that will grace the first volume of his album, *The Holy Land*, which will be famous in Europe.

After greeting the mildly surprised carpet sellers before whom he has swiftly set up his easel, he gets down to work. He will immortalise their unrolled goods spread out on the flagstones, some repair work using a ladder at a window on the first floor, the sleepy figures of Arabs and Turks resting against a wall, sitting almost motionless in the hot, late afternoon air. Both the portals look completely different than they did from a distance. The one on the right is walled in, like the Golden Gate giving straight onto the Mount of Olives, through which the Messiah has yet to pass on Judgement Day. In the left portal we can see a solid door fitted with ferrules – it is shut.

And now, just as David Roberts is putting dots on the coarse-grained paper that on the drawing and then the lithograph will form the bumps of the ferrules in the closed door of the Church of the Holy Sepulchre, I fancy pursuing a daydream of my own and describing an encounter that never actually took place.

As he worked his freshly sharpened pencil, he thought about his voyage up the Nile: three months spent on a hired felucca – with stops at caravanserais, sand-strewn temple gateways, villages by the river, avenues of sphinxes, oases, the sacred trees of the dervishes, flocks of flamingos taking off in flight, the idle bulk of crocodiles, the nocturnal screaming of jackals, the growling of lions, the shouts of camel drivers, storks wading among stands of papyrus, islands with temples, the beautiful, spiritual faces of the ferrymen, their evening prayers, all this in the blinding heat of sunny days, also the sunrises and sunsets that accompanied him daily from Cairo to Abu Simbel, and then back again, like a great performance by nature specially prepared for him, the child of the North he undoubtedly felt himself to be throughout the expedition.

It was in the first stage of the journey, when after spending the day sketching, he returned from Giza to the El Rashid hostelry in

Cairo, recommended to him by the British consul in Alexandria, Colonel Campbell. At that point he wasn't yet acclimatised; the sunset here is short, and when the orange disc vanishes beyond the desert horizon or behind the minarets, pitch-black darkness falls, only brightened a little later by the increasing brilliance of the stars. At just this moment, weary beyond words, he dismounted his camel; his guide-and-porter rolled into one never even thought of passing down his drawing kit from the third dromedary or getting off his own mount; all these complicated duties – untying the straps, arranging the packages, and carefully setting down the portfolio full of drawings – Roberts had to do himself, in total darkness, so maybe that was why, sweaty and mildly annoyed, as soon as he entered the El Rashid hall, loaded down like a camel himself, he put down his things on the floor, nodded to a servant to carry them to his room, then sat down at a small table and demanded some bread and wine. The room was empty – only in the very corner, near the open window, through which came the rattle of a gig arriving late, David Roberts saw a man: he was surely a European, a man of fashion and a traveller. Between two oil lamps, leaning not over a plate but an album, his face had a touch of the Far East about it, but Roberts had seen too many kinships of the kind in the drawing rooms of Edinburgh and London or among the French aristocracy to draw any conclusions from them. David Roberts does not have to watch the stranger a second longer to realise what he is busy doing: he is delicately rubbing the background of a newly completed drawing with a piece of tissue paper torn from a pocket book. Just like him, he must have spent the day making sketches, and now, at the hostelry after supper he is making minor corrections, fully aware no doubt that there is nothing more deceptive for a draughtsman than his memory.

Later, on the cataracts of the Nile, at the temple of Karnak or among the cliffs of Syrian Petra, as he recalls that unusual encounter David Roberts will never be able to answer his own question about where he found such an un-British, un-Scottish urge to approach the unknown artist. First, before being served the bread and wine he had demanded (appalling laziness was a feature of all the staff at the El Rashid hostelry), he swiftly went upstairs, chose three sketches by the light of a cresset, put them in a new folder and swiftly went back down, as if afraid the stranger would already have left. But he hadn't. Now as he passed by his table, Roberts indiscreetly cast an eye at the drawing on a page of the open pocket book. Even in the weak, flickering light of the two oil lamps he could appraise its perfect quality: the Nile, palm trees and pyramids on the other side of the river, the bulging sail of a felucca, and also the tiny human figures on the far bank – perhaps they were peasants driving oxen round the treadmill of a water pump – all this was brought together with perfect perspective, but also with lightness and panache.

"May I please ask you a question," he said in French, "as I can see you are just finishing?"

The other man was so absorbed in his occupation and his thoughts, and so little expecting to talk to anyone again today that he did not react at all. On hearing Roberts' remark, he cannot have taken it personally, though there was no one else in the El Rashid dining room apart from the two of them and the servant.

"Hello," said Roberts, switching into English. "May I please ask you a question? I think we follow the same passion and profession."

Only then, putting down his tissue paper and pencil, but without closing the album, did the stranger glance at David Roberts. Under a shapely brow and some locks of wavy hair his large, dark eyes were shining. In this light he looked like an Armenian.

"Indeed," he replied in fine, pure English, though with a rather strange accent, "are you sure of that? We can talk in the language of Racine too," he said, switching to French, "because you cannot possibly know my native tongue."

"A Greek," thought Roberts, "from Smyrna, Missolonghi or Athens. Or any of the thousand cities of the diaspora to which the Turkish slaughters have driven them." And to prove the issue was by no means foreign to him he said: "I am a Scot, a British subject. Like Lord Byron, I have always regarded your struggle as valid, just and heroic. The Osman Empire will soon fall. You must have seen that in Cairo, Alexandria, Damascus or even in Istanbul. Everywhere. It is a colossus on feet of clay. Your time will come."

As he said this, he raised the cup that had just been served him and addressed the stranger in Greek, not the modern version, which he didn't know, but an ancient formula.

"Kylix philotesias," he said – the cup of friendship, as he drank symbolically to the stranger.

The man laughed wholeheartedly.

"Do you take me for a Greek?"

"Indeed I do."

"I am a Pole." For some reason he made this particular remark in French, then returned to his pure, lucid English. "If you have ever heard of such a nation."

In fact, for Roberts this was even more curious. He knew very little about the Greeks, but he did know something specific, whereas he associated the Poles with a newspaper item from seven or eight years ago about some violent unrest in the snows far away. He would have been ashamed to admit that he didn't know how far Poland was from Saint Petersburg. Fortunately, the conversation advanced on less political lines.

"Yes," said Roberts, "Chopin, of course. But he rarely performed in public concert halls. He preferred palaces. But not everyone could go in to hear him there."

God knows what the Pole thinks about that, as the Scot invites him to his table. The servant hands him a clean glass, a tumbler of water and a dish on which to break the thin, flat bread and dip it in olive oil. Soon he comes back again with a full, uncorked bottle of Syrian wine. At Roberts' express demand he also brings and lights some candles, whose flame gives far stronger and more stable light than the oil lamps. Now at Roberts' invitation they show each other their sketches and exchange minor comments.

"As you are a poet," says the Scot at length, "and only do drawings for passing pleasure, how would you define what prompts you to write poetry? Is it inspiration? Or necessity?"

The Pole replies that both are involved, though it cannot be explained as simply as the moment when one reaches for a pencil or a brush. He also talks of the language of his nation, which, condemned to political nonentity like Greece, finds its only freedom and understanding in poetry.

At Roberts' request Słowacki reads out the one Polish sentence written in his album and instantly translates it into English. "In happiness they would have been good, but misery will change them into bad and harmful people. O God, what have You done?"

Roberts likes the exotic sound of the rustling consonants. After hearing the translation he says – as it is proper for him to say something – that such a sentence is worthy of the excellent talent that he has just met. Soon they will part with a sincere farewell. Next day the Scot is heading up the Nile, while the Pole is returning downstream.

Now as he finishes his sketch in the square outside the Church of the Holy Sepulchre, David Roberts remembers the closing words of their conversation. He could not have misheard: something was said about the Messiah. Not a specific person, but the Messiah nation, that is nailed to the cross, but will rise from the dead, bringing freedom to all others. However strange, not to say idiotic it sounded, he agreed that the poet was right and wished him a happy end to his journey, encouraging him to make frequent sketches of the views and monuments.

As he places his drawing in the portfolio and folds his portable easel, there is just one thing Roberts cannot remember: the poet with the sonorous name mentioned a specific date, maybe it was the coming of the Messianic era – at least for his nation – but, tired by the long day and mildly lulled by the wine (at the El Rashid it was served only to Christian travellers with the local pasha's permission), Roberts had not committed it to memory. Could this well-bred, elegant, highly educated poet have given the year 1978? And thus a date a hundred and thirty eight years from the present day? Abraham Abulafia, Salomon Molcho and Sabbatai Zvi gave dates within the range of their own lifetimes. The Polish poet, who did not in fact regard himself as a Messiah, but evidently saw his own nation in that role, had gone beyond, into the next century. I wonder what the world will look like

then, thinks David Roberts. London? Jerusalem? And finally his
unhappy Poland? And so he leaves the square outside the Church of
the Holy Sepulchre.

You know just as well as I do that this encounter never
actually took place, though according to the calculus of
probability we could infer a quite realistic chance of it having
occurred. Juliusz Słowacki went on a journey to Greece and
the Holy Land in August 1836. A year later, at the monastery
of Betheshban in the mountains of Lebanon he wrote his long
poem in prose *Anhelli*, in the spring. He sailed by felucca down
the Nile, saw the pyramids, and could have stopped at the El
Rashid hostelry. But by December 1838 he had reached
Florence. That same year, towards the end of September, a
steamer called in at the port of Alexandria with David Roberts
on board, who was only just at the start of his grand tour. In
December 1838, when Słowacki was already in Florence,
Roberts was on his way back from Abu Simbel in Nubia to
Cairo, with a hundred drawings and paintings. From there, in
February 1839 he set off for Syria and Palestine, to visit
Jerusalem at the beginning of the month of Nissan. When I
bought a long, scrolled-up poster at the Jaffa Gate showing his
panorama of the city, I never imagined that these two men,
such different kinds of artist, had passed each other in Egypt
by a hair's breadth. Nor did I know that I would take up this
chronicle, which from one, admittedly lengthy e-mail to you is
getting longer and longer. So back to business: let us now
return to Antoni Julian Berdo, who, as Ibrahim ibn Talib

escorts him to the Azure Hall at the Free University, is keenly wondering how to start this conversation in the rhetorical sense: with silence, a question, a statement or maybe an elliptical sentence.

However, he did not have to make any decisions. With an extremely polite gesture Mr Hatamani invited him to take a seat on the sofa, though he himself did not sit down. As he fed titbits to a pair of goldfinches in a cage he turned to face the visitor, smiled and asked: "Do you know that in my country there are still fire worshippers? And that for them Zoroaster, likewise Mithra, is the supreme image of God?"

Berdo did not know that.

So Hatamani continued: "The three kings, whom you know from the Gospels, were followers of that religion. The peoples of the East, more or less aware of it, while worshipping various other gods, were conscious that under the surface, deep-down, that was where the origin of the earliest origins lay. Just like in Jung, isn't it?"

Curious to find out what he would hear next, Berdo did not deny it.

"And so the Evangelist – I am thinking of Matthew, as the others don't write about it – decided to show that the oldest religion came in search of the youngest. He pays it tribute. He fosters esteem for it. Respect. In this sense Jesus continues the mission of more than just His own nation. Not everyone knows Isaiah. But at the mention of the Magi from the East everyone turns to the archetypal images. 'See, I am doing a new thing! Now it springs up; do you not perceive it?' "

Berdo was mildly shocked. He had been expecting anything, but not that Mr Hatamani would start the conversation with Mithra and Zoroaster, move on to the three kings, and then perform a pirouette with a quotation from Isaiah. In fact he could not quite place it just now, but naturally the tone of the phrase, its meaning and authorship were familiar to him.

Now the goldfinches were drinking from a small dish of water; Mr Hatamani sat down in an armchair facing Berdo and clapped his hands. In came Ibrahim ibn Talib with a drinks trolley, then put strong, excellent coffee, mineral water and some sweets resembling halva on the table. Before Berdo had had time to fill his coffee cup the assistant was gone.

"I have a confession to make," said Hatamani, adjusting the wide sleeves of his long grey-black robe. "I am the representative of an old nation. In short, I am a Persian. And here too, I view many issues from a totally different perspective. I don't wish to say a deeper one, because that might offend someone. Instead I shall say and repeat: a different perspective. Do you understand me?"

"Yes." Berdo had come to the conclusion that the less he said, the better. "Perfectly."

"Quite so," continued the cleric, after a sip of coffee, still holding the cup. "One of the reasons why I am here is to convince many people that Islam is not necessarily just the Arabs, and that the Arabs are not the whole of Islam. *Toutes proportions gardées*. You can imagine an old Roman senatorial family whose ancestors built their city in the days of the

Republic, and who in due course will adopt Christianity. Isn't that beautiful? To follow the spirit of the times. Not opportunistically, of course, but by understanding which way the underground current is flowing. Those are the mightiest sources, aren't they?"

"Surely," agreed Berdo. "Even mass culture can sense it."

"Especially mass culture," Hatamani willingly picked up the thread. "Naturally, the point is to have an influence on it. Not to prohibit, no, but to give it shape. Do normal parents hand their child a razor? Or feed them drugs? Yet that's often just how it looks. You have too much freedom, and so you die."

Hatamani spoke the last four words firmly, as if he were passing sentence, but without any satisfaction: more like a surgeon than a prosecutor. Just at that moment the bells rang out from the church towers of Saint Nicholas', Saint John's, Saint Elizabeth's, Saint Barbara's, Saint Joseph's, Saint Mary's cathedral and also Saints Peter and Paul's, so Mr Hatamani changed the subject.

"I took my doctorate at an Islamic university, of course, on the various conceptions and metamorphoses of the figure of Saoshyant. Do you know what I am talking about?"

"According to the religion of Mazdaism, and before that in Zarathustra, Saoshyant performs the function of saviour," said Berdo calmly. "Something like a Messiah. He will lead the people to the final battle with evil. Victorious, of course. One can find traces of this concept, or rather vision, in the Apocalypse of Saint John the Evangelist. And also among the Shiites."

"Excellent." Mr Hatamani topped up his and Berdo's coffee cups. "I can see you are extremely well informed."

Berdo developed the Shiite theme.

"After the death of Nizar, the last Imam, his followers waited for the Lord of the Resurrection. Qa'im al-Qiyam. He is to return and announce the rebirth of the world."

"And what can you say about the role of Jesus in this context?" asked Mr Hatamani, nodding tactfully.

"Well, eschatology is not my favourite topic. But, to be brief, it can be summed up in a few basic points. Firstly, at the time of the fall, the Mahdi will appear, guided by Allah himself. He will establish the Golden Age. Then the fall of the world, customs, religions and mankind will be even more profound than before the Golden Age. Dajjal will appear. The Christians would have no trouble recognising him: for them he will be the Antichrist. Then the prophet Isa will return to Earth. The Christian Jesus. The Jewish Joshua ben Joseph. He will kill Dajjal. He will marry and announce to the world the reign of the Islamic faith. Forty years later he will die in Medina. And then the Last Judgement will follow."

After Berdo's lengthy speech silence fell in the Azure Hall. The church bells had already gone quiet. Muffled by the closed windows, the sounds of the city were only audible as a low, steady hum.

"Incredible," said Mr Hatamani. "You remembered all the essential, even the rather folkloric elements! There is a difference between lacking knowledge and having ignorance, as I am always explaining to my pupils. But you are on quite another plane! The angel Ridvan would throw the gates of paradise open to you. Whereas the angel Malik would not let you through the gates of hell. But seriously, your *tariqah*, your path of faith starts from knowledge. And how would you define faith?"

"Nothing that requires a lot of explanation is perfect," replied Berdo decisively. "So perhaps the best definition of faith is a medicine? As the prophet says: 'God did not create suffering without also creating some remedy against it.' Such a remedy is faith. Or at least that is how I understand it."

I suggest leaving Antoni Julian Berdo with this confession. You will fully realise that by saying this, he was contradicting his own plainest beliefs. He should really have told Mr Hatamani, the Mufti of the northern part of our country, that according to his intuition faith is something that exists for ever, but has no beginning, while also being something that always has a beginning and never exists. In short, like God according to Berdo's theory. However, I don't want to take this theme any further or describe Mr Hatamani's compliments or closing remarks on the topic of the oldest religious revelations known to mankind, received by Zarathustra from Ahura Mazda, nor to mention the Mufti's assurances that he had never met anyone as exceptional as Berdo before on his journey through life.

As Hatamani slowly escorted him arm in arm to the door of the Azure Hall, Berdo, would you believe it, was no longer thinking about anything to do with religion. Instead he was remembering an article he had recently read in the *Scientific*

American about a certain species of tunicate. These little creatures, *Ciona intestinalis*, had found an atypical solution to the problem of evolution. In their larval form they had a brain essential for moving about and hunting, but once they found a permanent niche where they could be sure of securing food and safety they instantly got rid of it. According to the biologists, this astonishing phenomenon is dictated by the evolutionary mechanism of survival: in stable conditions the brain is an over-sized, energy-consuming burden for the microscopic *Ciona intestinalis*.

Only as he was passing through the final door of the Free University did Berdo awake from his inner lethargy, and suddenly in a flash of consciousness he remembered that years ago he had already met the man now playing an important role at the university as Mr Hatamani's right hand, who bore the undoubtedly assumed name of Ibrahim ibn Talib. He was the same man who had intruded upon him at Mihajlo's cottage with a Kalashnikov slung over his shoulder.

Something snapped in Berdo's soul, but he did not let it show. Right by the door, which that man had opened for him, he asked: "Do you like motorbikes?"

"No less than you do," came the answer, "maybe even more."

As he headed for the Maska café, once again Berdo could smell the scent of that mountain river, of cheap tobacco and a well-oiled gun.

CHAPTER VI

The Twelfth Man

NOW LISTEN TO A rather different story.

The house on the hill had many secrets, like corridors no one knew about that led to some surprising places of a kind even the spiritually initiated could never have imagined might exist. Sometimes, as he set off on various nocturnal wanderings, he went such a long way that he'd start to feel panic, fearing he'd never be able to get back again. Inez – Mistress of the Dawn – put up with a lot, but if any of her courtiers wasn't in his place in the morning, she flew into a rage. He had experienced it at first hand: he'd spent several days being painfully stabbed with needles. Immobilised in bed, he had suffered terrible cramps and constipation caused by the poisoned food. The biggest secret hadn't yet been revealed then: events lay helplessly like beads scattered at the bottom of a drawer, waiting for a thread of light to come and join them together. There had in fact been some unclear signs or omens earlier on that he could remember, but for fear of such a great burden he preferred not to think about them.

It had happened for the first time in a remote era, when he didn't yet know anything about the city on the bay or the house on the hill. All he knew was where the room with the stove was, the loft, the granary, the barn, the cowshed and the knoll behind the house where the large oak tree grew. Though no one had ever told him about it – neither at home nor in church – he could tell it was a tree that had been growing here since the beginning of the world. By climbing up its boughs he could reach heaven, where the angels were on watch all the time. He used to greet them, and they greeted him too. By sliding down the roots he could reach the centre of the Earth: terrifying caverns where worms and maggots as big as calves lay dozing. But he hadn't often gone on that sort of journey, only when he was sure no one was going to call him home to chop firewood, fetch water or drive the runaway pig into the sty. More often he simply whiled away the hours sitting under the oak tree, gazing at the world laid out at the foot of the knoll: vast meadows with a small stream winding its way between them, the surface of a lake full of clouds, and on the other side of the great water there was always the dark line of the forest. Below the knoll the herd he tended went their own way among the dry junipers. That was where he first heard the voice. He took an axe from the woodshed, unstaked the young billy goat, led it under the tree and struck it a few blows on the neck. He had been found like that, with the animal's head in his hands, all spattered in blood, leaning against the tree trunk and staring into the sky. As his father and brothers flogged him, tied to a beam in the barn, he had not uttered a single word of complaint. The voice that had told him to sacrifice the kid had said it was his destiny to suffer.

He had ended up in the city on the bay when the voice insisted he do it a second time with a heifer. He wasn't beaten again. In a long white shirt, wrapped like a fly in a spider's cocoon, he had crossed a vast wilderness in a strange horseless vehicle. When he got out in the courtyard at the house on the hill, two servants had escorted him to a beautiful, shiny room. He had been washed, his hair had been cut and he had been given an outfit of a kind he had never worn before. The voice had told him that from now on he was lord and master of this castle, and would live in it until the time when he'd receive a sign from a box with a windowpane. Stupid, completely ignorant people called it a television, not knowing what it was really for. He loved it at once, and could spend hours on end staring at the moving images that passed before his eyes.

His subjects named him the Prophet Jan when he prophesied that a lake would soon appear at the foot of the house on the hill, in the vale full of allotment gardens. He had stood by the high wire fence in a yellow dressing gown, watching the people busily weeding their plots and picking strawberries, as he shouted: "Great water, then even greater! Great water, then even greater!"

The servants had gently led him away from the garden to the rooms, but a few days later, when it poured for several hours, and the little stream that ran through the allotment valley swelled at an incredible rate, carrying the wooden cabins, huts, sheds, tools and whole trees off to the city, crushing some cars parked in the vicinity along the way, they quietly started to speak of him as a prophet. And a year later, when the bulldozers and diggers appeared on the site of the disaster they said it out loud. From the open windows (the ones with bars as well as the ones without), all the residents of the house had watched the transformation with bated breath: the valley was surrounded by a bank of earth covered in turf, and the old allotments were replaced by an artificial lake, on which lovers, drunks, truants and anglers soon appeared. At the time even Inez – Mistress of the Dawn – who was not one to show affection, had stroked his cheek and said loud enough for everyone in the television room to hear: "You see, you predicted the whole thing to us!"

He never revealed that the same voice as before had told him about the flood and the lake. But not from the box – it still hadn't given him the sign to leave the house on the hill. Until one morning when, after Inez's visit, he had left his own room on the sly and pressed the button in the common room. He was amazed when he was summoned to help: explosions at all-night shops, the injured being taken to hospital, people with masked faces throwing bottles at the fence round a building site, policemen shooting rubber bullets at them – everything that was shown and talked about to the camera on the streets and in the studio was like an obvious message for him. He must leave the house on the hill and head for the city to restore peace. In a flash of revelation he suddenly knew the truth. After the Father and the Son, he was the Third One, coming to fulfil the prophecies.

He was not naïve. Twice, when they had been taken on an outing – once on a boat, once to the Old City – they had had to get changed so no one would envy them the comfortable outfits they wore in the house on the hill. Money was necessary too, as in their little shop that sold sweets, newspapers and tobacco. He switched off the box and went back to his room. His subjects were already playing cards as usual. Shortly after, they all went off for breakfast in the dining hall. Calmly and quietly he ate his porridge, until one of the maids, after leaving a food trolley in the hall, went back into the kitchen without slamming the door. As he walked past the coat rack, he took down a white tunic that had been hanging there since the day before and put it on over his nylon pyjamas. He passed the kitchen, from where the usual bustling noises were coming, and took the service lift down to the ground floor without anybody noticing. Once outside the building, he spotted a pair of old clogs someone had thrown away in a basket full of apple cores and cardboard. The servants often went about in shoes like these. He instantly got rid of his slippers and put them on. His appearance did not cause any surprise: on his way to the third pavilion he passed two nurses, a servant and a doctor, each of whom responded to his nod with a similar greeting and went on their way.

He had no trouble twisting off a symbolic padlock to get into the storeroom. A row of bags full of clothes greeted him in its kingdom of lost souls. He spent a long time looking for something in his size. Finally he was wearing a smart black suit with pinstripes and some equally stylish loafers; only the lack of a suitable shirt was preventing him from leaving. Finally he found one that fitted perfectly, though it had a mandarin collar instead of a normal one.

Once dressed, he turned towards the door, and there stood one of the Envoys of the Prince of Darkness. He must have been lurking in the shadows for a while, watching him searching for the clothes, because he didn't seem at all surprised. On the contrary, he was standing there smiling, with his arms folded and his legs astride. On his dark uniform top, with a phone case clipped to one side of the belt and a holster to the other, shone seven silver buttons.

"They're waiting for me," he said slowly. "You can't stop me."

"Of course," said the envoy. "So we're going together. Just raise your arms a bit. I'd like to see your hands."

He didn't oppose this request. He just said: "You see, no holes in them yet!"

As the Envoy of the Prince of Darkness let him through the doorway first, he suddenly turned around and head-butted him right between the eyes, on the bridge of the nose. The Envoy fell to the floorboards groaning, but he was conscious, and reached for his holster, or maybe for his phone. He couldn't leave him like that – they'd soon have the entire house on the hill captured. So he jumped on his neck a few times, and once the Envoy had stopped moving, he unbuttoned his top and removed his wallet from an inside pocket. He took a few banknotes out of it, and a photograph of a Harlot. Then he undid the holster and hid in his jacket pocket the cold, heavy object that as he knew from the films gives power over ordinary people. As he left the house on the hill, where he had spent just about all his adult life, he felt neither joy nor regret, because he knew for certain he was heading towards the destiny ordained by the voice of the Lord.

For now, the Lord guided him through the gates of the large park surrounding the house on the hill without making any specific demands. From this he concluded that he could indulge in a little pleasure. He had always wanted to take a walk by the lake on the other side of the fence, like the courting couples or the single people, and to go right round the reservoir along the top of the bank, then stop at the sluice and take a look at the roaring cascade or the tower of the gutted church reflected in the water. He walked slowly, thrilled by the blue of the sky and the clouds that went sailing across the greenish surface like the thoughts crossing his mind, because that was how he always imagined them. At more or less halfway, where the bank came close to the fence around the park, he stopped to look into the windows of the house he had left. There was one thing he regretted – his nocturnal expeditions down the corridors leading to unfamiliar places. It was one of the secrets neither the servants nor the subjects, nor the doctors had access to. Only a rare few, touched by the hand of the Lord, finally came upon the passage in the underworld of the old laundry.

Where once upon a time dozens of serving maids had lit a great oven to heat cauldrons of water, where sheets, duvet covers, towels, pants and vests were boiled, where those women used to poke about in the cauldrons with long wooden spoons like witches, now there was a junk room full of things no one needed, or of unclear purpose. The first time he ended up there at night he didn't know what the old, long abandoned honey churn was for, the wooden ice-cream maker or the wicker-framed orthopaedic prosthesis. But somewhere among the millions of dust particles, mould and mites the old smell of cleanliness was still there: the smell of starch, huge bars of "Jeleń" soap and hotplates that he remembered from his first months, or maybe years, at the house on the hill. He had found the passage in the wall behind the oven: some bricks had been removed, making a small hole, through which you entered a corridor that immediately forked into a labyrinth.

As he lay down with a blade of grass between his teeth instead of a cigarette, he thought back to his first expedition: he had come to a chamber lined in tiles, where a Harlot was bathing in a large tub. She knew magic spells and tricks. She told him to strip naked, pulled him into the water and soaped his body. Then she played with him like a doll, until he felt a shock: it was sweet, stronger than an electric one. The Envoy of Darkness he had had to restrain in the storeroom today had her picture. Now he tore it into tiny pieces and threw them into the wind, watching as some of them landed in the water.

He was drawn down the corridors by surprise: you could take the same route as before a second time and find nothing, or end up in a completely different room: that was what had happened to him one night when he felt a desire to submit to the charms of the Harlot again. In the middle of the chamber there was a small cage. Inside, a little man sat huddled on all fours, the size of a child, but horribly mutilated. His severed nose and ears, gouged-out eyes, grazed elbows, sides and knees made him look like an animal. Beside the cage an old man was sitting on a footstool, dressed in a long white patterned robe. He was passing the poor wretch a piece of sausage skewered on the end of a stick, but in such a way that the cripple couldn't grab it in his mouth, but banged his hideous snout against the bars of the cage every time he tried.

"All right, Telesphoros, you'll learn," sniggered the Lord of the Footstool. "Patience is the last human feature left to you!"

"Why are you doing that?" he had asked timidly, gulping. "Why did you do that?"

"Some say I was once Lysimachus. A tyrant – that's what Seneca called me. But it's not true. I am the dream of all philosophers. And madmen. As far as you understand what all these names mean, you country bumpkin!"

As he spoke, the Lord of the Footstool began to laugh, the slice of sausage fell onto the floor of the cage and the monster called Telesphoros sucked it up. Only now could he see that his tongue had been cut off too.

It was that very night, as he ran down the corridors in

terror to get as far as he could from the Lord of the Footstool, that he had lost his way and not been in time for Inez' morning round. But even the injections and electric shocks administered to him weren't as dreadful as what he had seen.

Sometimes he came across a character out of a film. Lieutenant Kojak, with his big bald head and a lollypop in his mouth, was interrogating a Harlot.

"You'll rot in here, you whore," he shrieked, "for a miserable line of stolen coke!"

The Harlot was crying with her face buried in her hands. He walked on, and came to a room where two chess players wearing pyjamas were having a game.

"What do you want?" the first one had asked, on seeing the intruder.

"Leave him alone," said the second, "he'll never know our secret anyway!"

"So what's your secret about?" he had boldly asked.

"About the fact that there is no secret," the first one snapped.

"We've already found all the possible versions," explained the second one politely. "It's not true there's an infinite number of them. However unimaginably large, it's finite."

"It's our game that's finite, because we'll never get it started," sighed the first.

He opened his eyes and spat out the almost entirely chewed-up blade of grass. The sun was making his forehead and cheeks very hot. Why should he worry? Once the mission was completed he could come back to the house on the hill any time, and set out any night for the old laundry with all the corridors branching off it. He stood up, brushed off his suit and walked along the bank to the sluice gate. A flock of ducks was swimming there, a mother and seven ducklings. A man fishing was wearing a shirt with the same pattern he had seen on the Lord of the Footstool's long robe. Perhaps it was him? By day he caught fish, and by night he tormented Telesphoros. Just in case, he slowed down and spent a long time staring at the back of the fisherman's head and neck, squeezing the gun in his jacket pocket. He had seen how to do it in films. And he wouldn't have hesitated for a moment, if the lad hadn't turned around and asked him: "Have you got a light?" He shrugged and walked off – it wasn't the Lord of the Footstool.

As he was approaching the bus stop, he saw an ambulance and a police car turning off the main road at the traffic lights towards the house on the hill.

The bus took an unbearably long time to crawl to the city centre. Tired and sweaty, he immediately bought some dark glasses and a light baseball cap outside the bus station. Then he went to McDonald's, where he spent a long time eating and drinking. He left this sanctum feeling very pleased, holding a blue balloon and a paper bag with a supply of sandwiches and cola. The balloon cheered him up: it fluttered gaily above the heads of the passers-by and was like his flag. The sandwiches and cola ensured he wouldn't be hungry before his mission was completed. He also had quite a sum of money left. He was waiting for a sign, but it hadn't come.

He spent ages roaming the narrow streets of the Old City.

He stood before the scorched fence of the mosque, which was surrounded by police. As he passed the huge brick cathedral he noticed a rather funny man: he was walking around the church at a fast, nervous pace, glancing at his watch now and then and audibly muttering to himself, until finally he vanished down a side street.

He found a place to rest by the river. He sat on a bench and watched the tour boats full of happy people going by. He liked the old granary very much, which had a huge picture hung on it, showing snow-capped mountains around a green meadow with a herd of large cows. He had seen the same ones on the chocolate bars he got from Inez before every big holiday, except those ones didn't have the letters F&F on them, which were flying from under the cows' tails. He had a little to eat and drink, then feeling drowsy because of the sun, he dozed off. The instant he was awoken by a ship's siren he heard the voice, saying: "First the Antichrist will enter the glass house, then come running out of it. Leave him to me. Wait until the brothers summon you. You mustn't forgive the harlots any more, nor must you seek them."

He understood that first he must find the glass house. But where and how was he to look for it? He wandered the labyrinth of streets in the Old City with no result. Twice he even plucked up the courage to ask a passer-by: "Excuse me, where is the glass house?" In reply they just smirked and shrugged their shoulders. By now he had eaten and drunk all his provisions, so he threw the paper bag into a waste bin, and had just the balloon left. He walked down an airless arcade, and as soon as he reached open ground he sat down in a café garden for a drink of water. He tied the string to his chair, and then, as he was waiting for service, he saw a building that was obviously the right one. In fact it was ugly and angular, made of dull sandstone, but at the front, and maybe all the way around, the entire high ground floor was made of big slabs of glass. He ordered some water and asked: "What is that building?"

"A theatre," said the waiter. "Can't you read?" He was a bit surprised, but then he looked at the customer's dark glasses and added more politely: "There's no performance today, Sir."

He sat there in a state of extreme tension. The world was reflected in the big glass walls: the nearest buildings, the square full of cars, the passers-by, the clouds, and even himself, slowly sipping water from a tall glass. He identified three entrances. The one on the left belonged to a bookshop. The one on the right was for a café, which, like the one where he was sitting, had small tables outside too. So the most important entrance must be the middle one, the main one. But there was nothing going on in its vicinity. He signalled to the waiter to ask for another glass of water and to say he'd be right back. He walked across the corner of the square and pushed the glass door. It gave way. With a trembling heart he entered a spacious foyer. It was empty. Suddenly, from a small adjacent window that he hadn't noticed, came a woman's voice.

"Who do you want? Oh, you must be here for the photo

shoot. For the Last Supper." She smiled. "You have to go in the back way, through the stage door. Round there." She pointed. "But you might be early – everyone's late today. A proper Armageddon," she said, nodding sympathetically.

He went back to the café table shaking. The woman must have been initiated and was letting him know that. No one would have used words like "the Last Supper" or "Armageddon" just like that. So he was in the right place at the right time, as she had added "everyone's late today". He didn't finish the second glass of water, paid and set off down the narrow side street, at the very start of which he came across a public lavatory, which he made use of, losing only a moment at the urinal.

He had no trouble finding the entrance to the stage door. There was always someone going in or coming out of that door. To be able to watch it, he crossed to the other side of the street and sat on a low wall bordering a patch of grass gone yellow with dog piss.

Now he felt calm. Time wasn't dragging at all, and the blue balloon he was holding on its string in his right hand was gently swaying on the weak breeze. His only doubt concerned the glass house. It was glass on that side, facing the square, but here the sandstone rose from the ground floor, divided only by a line of narrow little windows. But as the woman had revealed the secret to him, it must be part of the overall plan. He could feel the great moment approaching, it was just around the corner, and seconds from now it would engulf him like a tidal wave and carry him wherever it wanted.

You're guessing of course that soon he'll catch sight of the guests invited by Mateusz entering the theatre through the stage door, and will recognise Berdo as the funny man he saw a few hours ago, buzzing around Saint Mary's cathedral like a bumblebee. Also the ones he doesn't know, but you do, of course – Wybrański, Lewada, Siemaszko, and the others, of whom this chronicle will only say a few words in passing. And of course you are rightly bound to suppose that the one called the Twelfth Man in this chapter will have his five minutes too. But never fear – he won't use the gun he has in the right pocket of his smart jacket at the long table, on the theatre stage.

"If not there, then where?" you're already asking. Very smart. But I'll tell you later. Even so, by accompanying the Twelfth Man I have already forestalled events a little. But a chronicle is a chronicle, so we have to go back a few hours: Berdo is just leaving the Free University, Lewada is only now driving into the first of our three contiguous cities on the bay, Wybrański is still stuck in a traffic jam, and Siemaszko, as he enters the Maska café, is bumping into the Engineer, who was due to meet Wybrański there and has been waiting for him in vain for the past half hour. Angry and malevolent – as usual. But as for the Twelfth Man's balloon, it's not my sentimental invention, but a fact. Everyone who appears in the photograph asked afterwards, why did he come with a balloon? Even if he was a nutcase, and he really was, he must have known what he was coming here for, so why didn't he want to leave it at the stage door? Now listen onwards.

CHAPTER VII

*will be about lots of important things, such as
the Engineer's creative career and his argument with
Siemaszko about art; also about Zacharias' scroll at
Father Monsignore's church; but we shall start with
Lewada who*

could not take his eyes off the hitchhiker's pretty face. There was something girlish about her, though she must have reached thirty not so long ago. Whenever she asked him a question, her eyes began to sparkle.

"Would you prefer to be John or Peter? Your friend, the artist, should have told you in advance. It might be easier to pose, even for a photograph, knowing who you're going to be. And why on earth paint the Last Supper these days? Who could that possibly interest?"

In reply to this last question Lewada shrugged. But he did have an answer to the one before.

"These days no one could name all twelve, even after a lot of thought. Even eight would be difficult without cheating. You try."

She laughed, spreading the fingers of her right hand.

"Just a moment, just a moment, all right: Simon, Peter, John, Andrew, James. There you are, I've got five already."

"Four." He came down a gear. "Simon and Peter are the same person. If you mean that Simon."

"Really?" She wasn't faking her surprise at all. "There was another one too?"

"Simon the Zealot, or Zelotes."

"You're a priest, not a doctor. And you've been lying to me for the past forty kilometres. Then what?"

He was already regretting the two minutes of frankness during which he had told her why he was going to the city. "Any moment now," he thought, "she's going to ask me if I believe in God."

"Don't you believe in God, Father?" he heard her say. "But please don't feel accused. Most of the priests I know do not believe. Maybe not as totally, atheistically, as the communists once did. But they don't believe in God. Or else they believe in something, some sort of force. A principle. Maybe in good? No, their belief in good must be weak, because they don't do much of it, or at any rate no more than ordinary mortals. And if anyone should do more good than others, it's the priests, isn't it? And not, let's say, the sleepwalkers. Do you agree with me, Father? The sleepwalkers…"

"I'm not a priest," he almost roared, but managed to get a grip on himself. "I once read a book about it."

Silence fell in the car. Near the flyover the police sent them down a diversion. Instead of driving down the main artery that linked all three cities on the bay they were forced, like the container lorries heading for the port, to crawl slowly along the streets. After a while Doctor Lewada saw a trolleybus ahead of him. There wouldn't have been anything strange about it if not for the fact that the electrical operating system for those vehicles had been dismantled a good twenty years ago. Where on earth had it sprung from? It was moving normally, occasionally spitting sparks from its pole. Then his gaze was automatically drawn to the Ocean Lines administration building, where no shipping firm had resided for years, just banks and funds. The old neon sign with its distinctive lettering and the proud outline of an ocean liner was on display again. Near the Admiralty building – because the diversion for passenger cars led all the way down there – instead of a shabby pizzeria, he noticed the entrance to the Kapitański bar, just like twenty years ago. Several young people, as well as a merchant navy officer, were just coming out of it. Their long hair, bell-bottom trousers, ribbons and beads reminded him of very ancient history. They happily headed towards the tourist anti-torpedo ship and the sailing yachts along the quay. Just past the roundabout, as he was turning back towards the high street, the doctor caught sight of the Roxana café terrace, which hadn't existed since the late communist era. As in those days, when he used to admire the ladies of the night from afar as they waited for their foreign sailors, now too he noticed a colourful crowd of them. Even the large awning inscribed "Co-op" that was flapping above the flock of prostitutes had something surreally nostalgic

about it. Surely Fellini wasn't making a film that day in one of
our three cities on the bay? The images kept appearing and
disappearing before the doctor's eyes like snippets of time
pulled by surprise from a dark well, just to baffle him like a
mirage for a few split seconds, God knows why. But was it just
an illusion? After all, the trolleybus was real, and so was the
gang of prostitutes on the café terrace.

When he caught sight of a large shop sign on the high
street saying PEWEX – as the long-gone communist-era duty-
free shops were called – and a dense queue of several hundred
people outside another shop marked RTV – the former television retail firm – he realised that for some mysterious reason
he had driven into a lost side-shoot of time – in short,
something had happened to him that he had only ever read
about in Schulz or Lem.

He was not sure if his passenger could see the same thing,
but as they crawled at a snail's pace past a grocery shop with
another communist-era sign and a swarm of people teeming
outside it, and as sleet suddenly began to fall on them from a
dark cloud, he heard her say: "At this time of year? And do you
see how they're dressed?"

The car was moving forwards very slowly, driving in single
file through the muddy slush. The pedestrians' anoraks,
overcoats, sheepskin jackets, berets, hats and shoes would
have looked like something from a film costume hire shop, if
not for their owners' faces, tired and grey, with an expression
of hopelessness and a touch of determined cunning. Those
were just the sort of hostile looks they were casting at the

doctor's car.

"Where on earth have we ended up?" she asked, clearly anxious. "Was there no other route we could have taken?"

"This is the way we were sent," said the doctor bluntly. And as he switched on the windscreen wipers, he added: "It really is a very strange diversion."

The sleet was getting thicker. From opposite, splashing through the large puddles, two army transport trucks drove past, followed by an ambulance with its siren going.

The doctor's passenger was on the edge of hysteria.

"But it's just not possible." She was almost in tears. "There has to be some order. At least in the seasons of the year! It doesn't make sense!"

They were stuck in a queue of similarly lost cars and completely disoriented passengers. Finally the doctor said: "You asked if I believe in God. I could truly answer that yes, I do, although I am not a priest. But I once had a certain... encounter. Do you see? Not a revelation. Not a discovery. But just that: an encounter."

"With God?" she asked instantly, and immediately supplied the answer: "But it's not possible."

Yet as she listened to the calm, measured phrases of Doctor Lewada, who would probably never have had the nerve to make this declaration if not for this particular situation, her attention increased by the minute.

"I never said that," the doctor began, "and I'm not saying it now. No miracles. Anyway, I can't bear miracles. They just increase the numbness. It was in Paris. I'd gone there to work.

On a building site. Just after getting divorced. I didn't care, I just wanted to earn some money for a flat here. No one could see the changes coming in those days. The generals were still kissing the hands of the widows of the pre-war generals. To cut a long story short, one day I really did want to die. Do you understand? Not to commit suicide, but to die. Can we achieve the latter without the former? We can, if we go down to hell. But what is hell? Being all alone. Not leading a lonely life, because millions of people live like that. Hell is cold, studied loneliness, that once adopted, cuts us off from everyone and everything. That's when a man enters the state I desired: pure and absolute nothingness."

"Did you achieve it?" she asked timidly.

For her it was astounding to follow his footsteps from the rue Boudon, where he lived in a rented cubbyhole on the sixth floor, all the way to the Jardin du Luxembourg, the Bois de Boulogne or a boulevard by the river where he spent hours on end lying on the grass or sitting still on a bench.

To begin with, the void that filled him brought him relief, even something resembling happiness. But after a while, once he had abandoned his flat and become a vagrant, he felt ever more afraid that this sort of existence would continue into infinity. Finally he was lying in the underground at a closed-down metro station alone. A whole day went by, maybe two. He had stopped getting up for water, or even reaching into his bag for a roll. He had reached a state of total abandonment; if someone had wanted to do anything at all for him, give him a drink, feed him, or take him up to the surface he would have cursed them for interfering.

And yet the person whose steps he heard in the darkness did not make him feel irritated, not even when he briefly lit a match to avoid treading on him, and another one immediately after, in order to sit down beside him. For a very long time he said nothing, Lewada could hear his calm, regular breathing. Finally the man said: "I am helpless too." Not getting an answer, he added: "And completely abandoned." And when Lewada still said nothing, he went on: "I have died, just like you."

"So what have you come for?" asked the doctor quietly.

"To be with you," the man replied.

It was a shock. "If he had consoled me, encouraged or appealed to me, not to mention given me advice," Lewada continued, "I would have cursed him with all that was left of my strength and told him to go to hell. But that was all he said: 'To be with you'."

She heard out the rest of the story, which did not in fact develop into a long tale full of unusual twists and turns. It continued in silence and darkness, just as it had begun. The man did not say anything else. Doctor Lewada had merely heard him lay something on the ground (a scarf perhaps?) next to his head and lie down to rest beside him, without a single sign, gesture, word or touch.

Then he had fallen into a deep, dreamless sleep, and when he awoke, the man had gone. Lewada had stood up and followed the labyrinth of stairs out into the street, blinking at the brightness of the lights. A week later he was back in Poland, thanks to the help of a quiet, modest community of brethren.

The heavy sleet cloud was being chased away by a wind from the sea. Bathed in sunshine again, the high street looked as if time had returned to its normal dimension. There was no more trace of any puddles or heavily dressed people suffering away in shop queues. The acacias were providing the pedestrians with shade.

"So what was that?" asked the reassured passenger. "No one will believe me. A blast of winter at the start of summer!"

They were just passing the memorial cross marking the spot at the intersection where some demonstrators once fell to the bullets of the People's National Army.

"You have to assume," said Lewada, driving into the middle lane, which was slightly less congested at last, "that the so-called laws of nature are only conditional. And there's no theory we're as quick to accept as one we find beautiful. I have forgotten where you're heading," he added after a pause. "That is, I meant to ask where should I drop you off."

"I'd come to the photo shoot with you, but I guess your friend hasn't planned for any women in his painting. Naturally," she huffed, "according to tradition!" Then she added: "One more city to go. Please stop at the tram loop."

"Why did I tell her all that?" fretted Lewada. "What on earth for? But then who would you want to tell about a guy who spent a couple of days lying in the underground?" he reasoned. "She didn't say what she thought about it, not a word. She reckons I made it up. Fine."

But Doctor Lewada was very much mistaken. Already imagining the meeting with his old friends, all the "So what's up with you, pal? You're looking great", combined with slaps on the back and a generally exhilarated atmosphere that was sure to get even more excited once the camera clicking was over and the bottles of red wine were uncorked (Mateusz must have mentioned it in his letter), he failed to notice they had already gone past the second city quite quickly and were getting near the tram loop at the edge of the third.

"It's here, please pull in at the bay, where the buses are," she said, opening her handbag. "Just in case I'll give you my card." She handed it to him. Once on the pavement, as she was closing the door, she added: "I think you're most suitable for Saint John. The one who's nearest. Even in the darkness."

As he rejoined the traffic, Lewada furtively watched her go. She had lovely, thick, golden-red hair. Mateusz would have said it was the colour Titian. Two kilometres further on, as he sat in the next traffic jam, the doctor could not stop marvelling at the way she had alluded to his story. Her name was Anna Kłodowska and she ran a photography firm. It had not escaped his notice, that as she spoke about Saint John, she had used the present tense. Was that just a coincidence?

It was certainly no coincidence that that name Titian, which the doctor had thought of as he gazed at the hair of the disappearing Anna Kłodowska, had cropped up a little earlier at the Maska café, where over a glass of gin the Engineer was expounding his views to Siemaszko.

"That Mateusz of yours is an idiot! You know what he said on the wadio? 'One must paint like Titian!' What a dope! A wight cwetin! Anyone can paint like Titian these days. *Nihil novi sub sole!* There'd be no pwogwess, you fool, if the bwats at the Academy took that sort of wubbish to heart! But some of them fwom his studio do. But art's like widing a bike! When you lose momentum you lose your balance and you have to stop. If you haven't fallen off the bastard already! So either you fall off, or you come to a standstill. There's no third option, damn it. What's the matter with you? Not dwinking? Afwaid of the Awabs? Shawia law isn't in force – not yet! Even if you fuck over all the night shops! You used to smoke ganja at least. You wetired now?"

Indeed, Siemaszko didn't have his pipe. But he smiled knowingly, sipped his tea, and extracted from his velvet jacket a small tin box of Okassa Zarotto cigarillos, a brand that was extremely popular in all the tobacco shops in our city over a century ago. Out of it he took something that looked like a bar of chocolate. But it didn't have a smooth surface, and the grooves between the little squares were much deeper than in a standard bar, no doubt to make it easier to split them. He broke off a piece against his saucer, put the rest back in the tin and carefully placed the dark brown cube on his tongue. Then he slowly chewed the medicinal substance, looking extremely contented.

"First communion?" wondered the Engineer.

To which Siemaszko began to hum:

Andrew, Andrew,
Here's some hemp for you!
God let me discover
Who's going to be my lover.

"Off your wocker? Got a scwew loose?" The Engineer was actually intrigued. "Well, come on, say something!"

"That's what the girls in my village used to sing. On Saint Andrew's night. Sowing hemp. Then they'd run around like crazy. From barn to house, from house to barn – some in nothing but their shirts. Or naked. For the fortune-telling."

"They sowed cannabis?" wondered the Engineer.

"Uh-huh." Siemaszko had just let the cube crumble and was swallowing the crushed-up, bittersweet mush. "In the Bible it's called aromatic cane. *Kanas* in Breton. *Canaib* in Celtic. *Hampaj* in Swedish. *Kanapes* in Lithuanian. And all from the Greek, *kannabis*. In the Gospel of Basilides, where Jesus isn't crucified, but Simon of Cyrene dies instead of Him, the disciples give him an infusion of it, so he'll suffer less. And so he won't tell the truth."

"What twuth?"

"That they've handed him over to the Romans and the Sanhedrin instead of Jesus."

"So what?"

"Nothing. It's completely differently from the texts recognised by the Church."

"But what does it say?"

"That Jesus went on teaching in Galilee for seventy-seven years until all His disciples had died. Then, on Mount Hermon, He changed into a ball of light and disappeared."

"A ball of light, you say."

"What's so extraordinary about that? Mass and energy transformed into light. Anyway, if you'd been there, on the slopes of Mount Hermon, you'd have understood it."

"Understood what?"

"The waterfalls," said Siemaszko dreamily. "Meadows like a grass harp, the springs of Jordan! The cedars! And higher up, the snow! You can see it at the hottest time of year! And below, at the foot of the mountain, there are pastures all around, then just desert. Can you imagine it? I've been on a pilgrimage. I know what I'm saying."

"With Berdo?" smiled the Engineer.

"What's that got to do with it?" Siemaszko reached for his tin, broke off another square of the chocolaty substance and stuffed it in his mouth. "With Berdo or not with Berdo. The main thing is I saw it all. And I'll tell you, you cynic, Jesus had been all over the place. You can feel it. Except they mistook Him for someone else entirely."

"Bloody hell, what a sensation!" The Engineer ordered another gin and tonic. "So who, in your humble opinion, was the carpenter fwom Nazaweth?"

"What do you mean, who? He was one of the Archons! Certainly not a human being! Intelligent beings from the higher world are too pure to mix with matter. The body is visible. Tangible. It has weight corresponding to its mass. But did Jesus?"

"Yes, did he?"

"He walked on water, which terrified his disciples so badly that He had to calm them down. In Luke they recognise Him after His apparent death, but then He vanishes from their sight like an apparition. They're terrified then too. But that's peanuts. The most vital thing was on Mount Tabor. I went there on the pilgrimage too."

"Bloody hell, somehow I don't wemember that. He vanished from their sight? So tell me, is that sort of twick so very difficult? It's just cwap! Pure circus."

But Siemaszko knew his stuff. And he could quote by heart something that kept the Engineer riveted, at least while the issue was being aired.

"A glowing wobe," repeated the Engineer incredulously. "You say his clothing 'shone whiter than any fuller on earth could possibly have bleached it'?"

"Right, it was so brilliant the disciples simply keeled over. They were stunned." Siemaszko nodded. "Anyone who looks at a light like that for too long is sure to go blind. Has it ever occurred to you that no human being could suddenly light up, just like that, like a hundred halogen bulbs? He must have been an Archon. One of the seven lords of the planets. The Son of Supreme Light, the Mother of All."

The Engineer heard out this last piece of information with his typical, ironical grimace. Somewhere at the very bottom of his so-called educational memory the word "archon" evoked the image of some old men sitting on an Athenian council. But it was just a faint glimmer, like his recollection of a postage stamp depicting the ruins of the Acropolis, which for some unknown reason he had swapped for one portraying Adolf Hitler in third class at elementary school. Just in case, he did not probe the subject any further, but started asking about something that really did intrigue him.

"Hemp, you say. In your village? But how? They sowed it, picked it and smoked it? Or chewed it? It's not exactly on the Afghan trail! Or maybe you're weally from Medellín, not the bloody Ukwaine!"

As he said this he sniggered, very pleased at his own joke. It wasn't the least bit politically incorrect, because on the Engineer's lips the word "bloody" was a compliment, admittedly of a lower degree, but it was a compliment. If he had said "fucking", of course, that would have been on a far higher level of courtesy. Siemaszko sighed and got on with his lecture.

"Our civilisation lost its way long ago. Ever since we chose water, that's to say alcohol, we've been bankrupt. Hemp was known the world over. And do you know why? It's self-seeding and self-pollinating. It gets help from a shield bug called *Pyrrhocoris apterus* that spreads its seeds around. But that's not what I wanted to tell you. Here in the north, up until the nineteenth century we still cultivated so-called early, northern hemp. It's weak, up to fifty centimetres high. Tiny fruits, not much branching and a very short growing season, up to ninety days. If it's a rainy summer that comes late, sometimes it's no use at all. You see? But nothing compares with the Caucasian or Indian kinds. Those are powerful. So ever since the reign of the alcohol makers began, cannabis has been excommunicated. You had to work in order to drink, and drink in order to work. Why were the Indians in Peru forbidden to chew and cultivate coca? For the same reasons why the once universally popular hemp was excommunicated.

Alcohol, just like money, became the real ruler of Europe. In millions of pubs or bars, just like this one, you can dope yourself up on liquid filth, because that's what the economy of whole nations depends on. Concerns and cartels run everything! Prohibition? That was invented to rebuild the American economy! Perhaps you don't agree? Beer," said Siemaszko, pouting in disgust, "is the foundation of German national unity! I'm right, aren't I? Our most ancient rituals, prayers and customs were all connected with cannabis, not alcohol!"

"What about wine?" said the Engineer, just catching a glimpse of Antoni Julian Berdo coming into the café. "What do you say to that? Dionysos wasn't invented by the capitalists, was he?"

"Well, of course not." Siemaszko was ready for this sort of question. "But hemp was still a permanent folk element. Only when industrialisation came and people migrated to the cities for bread did our kind of civilisation finally change. How would you put it? Fuck 'em up with vodka and bugger off! Right? Next please! But hemp was always connected with a ritual. With songs by shamans, folk healers, with the waxing and waning of the moon, with femininity. The triumph of alcohol marked the final ousting of the Great Mother. The victory of the bearded satrap, whom many fools took for a god, because they found it more convenient."

"You're a harsh fucker, aren't you?" Despite Siemaszko's remarks the Engineer took a swig of gin and tonic. "I like this. But that stuff you're munching, that's not hemp, is it?"

"Oh no, it's majoon!" Siemaszko smiled. "A very ancient discovery. A sweetmeat, hash for chewing. They had it in Isfahan a thousand years ago! Probably even earlier. They say Alexander the Great used to add it to his wine."

"And that's why he came to such a sticky end," said the Engineer, who was plainly tired of Siemaszko's theories by now. "It's all just the same as speed or ecstasy or any other shit. Just chemistwy, that's all. Do you weally believe in all this nonsense? Let's shoot up. And once you're stuffed with it, you talk cwap. The Gweat Mother? Femininity? The moon? What else?"

Siemaszko wasn't offended. He just felt, like the Apostle Paul at Ephesus, that he was talking to someone incapable of understanding him.

"I'm off for a piss," announced the Engineer. "You take a look at our head pouf. He's invited too!"

Only now did Siemaszko notice Berdo, who had sat down alone on the other side of the room. And suddenly he understood the meaning of the Engineer's last remark: he was sore because Mateusz hadn't invited him to the photo shoot. As he stood up and walked over to Berdo, Siemaszko felt a mild, but unimportant sense of satisfaction about it: at least he wouldn't have to keep hearing the words "fuck" and "bloody" on stage at the photo shoot! He was just about to tell Berdo, but he smiled, shook Siemaszko's hand warmly, and immediately launched a bombardment of questions.

"What's new at the Academy? Had any exhibitions? How are the children? And your wife?"

Siemaszko gave a short, businesslike report, probably so he could finish by talking at length about his favourite youngest daughter, who the day before her own wedding had dropped out and become a novice.

"Teresa's gone to the convent..." Berdo could not hide his amazement. "The most beautiful of your girls has had her head shaved and is singing hymns. What's got into her? These days?"

Siemaszko shrugged.

"These days especially. Maybe she's the only one who understands what the gift of freedom really is."

"In a nunnery." Berdo laughed. "How can it be?"

"As many things and experiences in the shortest time for as little money as possible." Siemaszko stressed each word, tapping his Okassa Zarotto tin against the tabletop. "That's how you understand freedom! Special offers, cut prices and bargains are the Father, Son and Holy Ghost. Meanwhile no one takes any notice of the human being as he's pushed, hurried, lured, driven and finally forced through the pack of salesmen, running in circles, faster and faster, like a mule on a treadmill, until he drops dead – that is, until the moment he stops being a consumer. She can paint there, play the violin and do gardening! Who'd allow her such luxury these days? A husband? A lover? Children? The department head in an office? A pension fund? A mortgage loan? You must be joking." Siemaszko raised his finger like a prophet. "She has other obligations there, of course, but she's free of the rat race generally known as freedom. The Hildegard of Bingen Society of Free Sisters was established with this very aim: for women who have no desire for any of the forms of life offered them by modern society to be able to develop like their patroness. That's it." Siemaszko said it with satisfaction, as if it applied to him personally. "Their aim is to perfect the talents given them by God. Their artistic and nature skills."

"I see," said Berdo, nodding. "But can't you do that normally, outside the convent?"

Siemaszko just waved and took out another cube of majoon. For what in this context did the word "normally" mean? He might even have taken the trouble to explain, but just then the Engineer appeared, coming back from the toilet.

He waved his right hand at Berdo, while in his left he pressed a mobile phone to his ear; he was plainly shouting the end of a conversation into it that he'd started in the lavatory.

"But yes, Father Monsignowe! I assure you the artist will be delighted! For sure! After all, you understand the awkwardness of his situation: he didn't dare contact you at the last moment, Wevewend Father, as if you were just a substitute. All the more since he hadn't thought of this simple idea earlier. He's embawassed. But I can act on his behalf – after all, I work at the Art Institute, don't I? Of course, Father Monsignowe, it's a gweat and enormous pwoject: for the gweater glowy of God! As for the facts, I can't imagine he won't suggest a significant wole for you, Wevewend Father. Excellent! Then thank you very much, in the name of art and on behalf of the city!"

As he said this, the Engineer sank into a chair facing

Berdo, shut down his phone at last, nodded to the barman to order another gin, and roared with laughter.

"Now I've got him! The gweat artist won't be able to wefuse him! Who'd dare? The Wevewend Father Monsignowe himself has agweed to come to the photo shoot!"

"Well, well," muttered Berdo, "sure to be there, medals and all."

"Wight on." The Engineer was almost dancing on the spot. "Full wegalia!" He glanced at his watch. "He'll be starting to get dwessed up wight now!"

"You know what, Engineer?" said Siemaszko, then broke off to order a double espresso and some mineral water. "I've known you for years," he resumed, "I've seen all your dirty tricks, overt and hidden, but I've never seen anything like this before. Why are you doing this to him? What for? If you can't stand Mateusz, beat him with your art, not by scheming. And what a stupid trick too. Are you really that badly hurt because he hasn't invited you to take part? Why should he anyway? You win over the journalists, you slag off every one of his exhibitions using their poison pens for your filthy language, and when he got the prize in New York for *The Dead Class* you yourself wrote – the one and only time you did it in your own name – that of course the class was dead because painting is dead! Couldn't you have waited until the picture's ready? What's got you so bothered? Anger?"

"Fucking hell." The Engineer raised his voice. "Didn't he phone wound to evewyone today to say Fwanek's in hospital and he's missing a Twelfth Man?"

"Yes," confirmed Berdo, "he called me too."

"So what?" said Siemaszko, refusing to give in. "He's sure to have found someone himself. And even if he hasn't, why dump something like that on him? Yes, you're a swine, and your art – perhaps it's time I said it loud and clear – is complete shit. You hear me, Engineer? It's shit. And you can't bear that. It pains you. Three strokes of Mateusz's brush demand more skill and imagination than all your media-hyped flatulence."

"Which bit do you mean?" asked the Engineer dryly.

"All of it," replied Siemaszko, "from start to finish. Thirty canvases painted red and cut into strips with a razor. Isn't that idiotic? Of course it is. But who'd dare to say it's nonsense? Who'd be brave enough not to jump on the express train labelled 'youth' and 'modernism'? Everyone wants to travel fast and in comfort! Your 'Sanitary Towels of the World' series was disgusting! And what's more it was fake. The media worked up the idea that you collected them from rubbish bins in the hotels, brothels and public lavatories of European capitals! But what really happened? You ordered them wholesale." Siemaszko addressed Berdo. "He spray-painted them, crumpled them up and glued them onto canvas and boards! What a cunning fellow! 'Women's menstwual blood has as many shades as the splendour of the Euwopean metwopolises. And as many hints of darkness. That's why I wondered whether to call my sewies 'Blood of Euwope', but ultimately I wefused to do that, to avoid making a political statement. My art is a pwotest against the enslavement of women by nature, not politics.' Isn't that what you said?" Siemaszko poked a finger at the Engineer's chest and gave him a gentle push. "And isn't that how you got the sanitary towels?"

"You can attack me all you like, because I don't give a shit." The Engineer was self-controlled. "Mind you," he said, addressing Berdo, "the guy who's talking spent twenty-five years sticking old bits of carpet onto canvas stwetchers!"

"First I've heard of it," said Berdo in surprise.

"What do you mean, haven't you ever seen those stwips of his?"

"Yes, once perhaps."

"Do you know what they called him down at the market? The wag man! Because he used to buy all the old wugs and carpets. Then he cut them into nawow stwips and stuck them on canvas: howizontally or vertically. Never at an angle. A stwip of border here, a load of bullshit there! The Malevich of Kozia Wólka! How much of that cwap did I take off you for the museum, you fool?" he turned back to Siemaszko. "They're sitting in the cellar waiting for a flood, because they're not even worth the paper for a damage weport. The moths have eaten them long ago. And each one cost a couple of thousand, fuck it! Not the moths, the collages!" He sniggered.

"If it weren't for me," said Siemaszko, smiling into his empty cup, "you could have ended up as the janitor at the archaeological museum, not the great head of the modern art gallery. Anyway," he looked at Berdo, as if seeking his approval, "what could be stupider than a name like that? What's a modern museum?"

"Now you're talking wot. What have you ever done for me in life? A packet of condoms in the commie ewa! You couldn't even pull stwings at the Pewex shop, let alone later! You're scum, Siemaszko, just a common junkie, not an artist. All the west are just bumpkins too. Nothing but village idiots! Just get out." The Engineer waved a hand to show Siemaszko the door, though he could just as well have meant the next table.

"That evening," said Siemaszko, addressing Berdo alone now, "he came to see me, shaking all over, pissed as a newt, all puffed up from a three-day bender. 'Bwother, give me something for my head, I'm cwacking up!' What's the matter, I ask. 'It's the bloody competition. I don't know what to do!' It was a novel idea – the future head of the museum had to be an artist, and apart from a programme of exhibitions he had to present a project of his own devising for a new series, something to bring the capital city and all Europe to its knees. Can you imagine?" Siemaszko leaned closer to Berdo. "His own series of installations. But we'd already had the lot here. 'Pwison underpants have been done, fuck it, piss in transpawent potties, dolls with cactuses up their fannies or arses, peeling potatoes has been done too, just like abortions filmed with a hidden camewa, embwyos in formaldehyde, and a necwophiliac with some old biddies at the morgue have been caught on camewa, the wanking general's been done too, even the pwiest who instead of pwaying to the Virgin Mawy pways to a portwait of Evita Pewon's been done' – in short, plenty of old rope but not much cash to show for it! So I told him how to write the project," continued Siemaszko, "make it simple, very expensive, ecological, international, multi-city, and above all with room for development, for sequels, like a Brazilian soap. And I said: 'City Air' is your future. He didn't get it – can you imagine? He didn't twig. Not at all. So I dictated the whole thing to him, first just a couple of pages of preamble: art should be open to the city, and the city must enter into art. Best imagine it in the form of a gigantic hall, entirely made of glass, with sliding walls. When you slide them back, the city really does enter inside: the din, the noise and exhaust fumes are in there at once. When you shut them, the interior becomes the exterior. You wouldn't need anything else inside if not for the wretched bourgeois conservatives, that's what I dictated to him, who will never stop insisting that anything at all should be put in there at the taxpayers' expense.

"But what the fuck should be put in there, he moaned and whined. So then I gave him the greatest project in the history of our city – hang it, our country. 'City Air'. Huge rectangular boxes made of glass, three metres by ten. Sealed shut tight before witnesses – the first box, for example, would be 'Jerozolimskie Avenue, Warsaw, at ten a.m. on the tenth of June such and such a year. Air sealed by witnesses X, Y and Z...' and a modest plaque with their names. Random passers-by, of course. The next box could be from, let's say, 'the Marketplace in Krakow, by the statue of Mickiewicz, on the eleventh of November, at three p.m.' And so on and so forth. Can you imagine the possibilities? The contacts to be made? The exchange exhibitions? The efforts of all the mayors and city councillors who'd want to be in on the act too, who'd issue an invitation and want to add their brick to the only collection of City Air in the world?

"And he won. And what went on display in great long rows in that new gallery the size of an airport? Block after block, two hundred identical boxes. Tokyo, Łódź, Toronto, Brussels and so on! Three or four years later the museum building had to be made wider and longer. How does Socrates put it? Hellas is great, my friend, and there are some brave men in it, but there are also plenty of barbarians."

"I know, I know. I even liked it to begin with." Berdo smiled. "Because how can you tell Tokyo air apart from Moscow air? But later on it got…"

"What did it get later on?" snapped the Engineer.

"Boring," Berdo calmly replied. "More and more boring. The idea's quite amusing, but you soon realise how childish it is."

"Did I ever say it was clever?" said Siemaszko, rubbing his hands together. "I can safely claim that, first of all, only projects like that one passed muster in those days, and still do nowadays too, and secondly, our great Mr Museum Head didn't even think of it himself!"

"You lout," screamed the Engineer, "you'll take that back in court!"

He took a swing at Siemaszko, but failed to slap him on the cheek; the table tilted, the cups and saucers fell to the floor and there was a crash of breaking glass as the Engineer almost lost his balance on the chair.

"Gentlemen! Geeeentlemen! It'll all pass," said Berdo,

separating them just in case, "but not so very quickly," he added, as the barman began to clean up the broken china. "After all, it's obvious that our times are marked, in art at least, by an infinite regress. The whole spectrum of our various human cultures is ultimately bound to fall into the void produced by our madness! We're only going to witness the very first rockbursts. And you're trying to argue about the results already."

The Engineer leaned on the table top and stood up; thinking this was the next stage in the action, Berdo stood up too, and that was how they both greeted Jan Wybrański and Doctor Lewada, who entered the café just then. During the general exchange of greetings the Engineer immediately took Wybrański aside and began to spout at him, and then just about coerced him into sitting down with him at a faraway table, to which, though reluctantly, he agreed.

"So what have you been talking about?" asked Lewada. "I can only go on about the bloody traffic jams! Who's going to be Judas? Shall we draw lots?"

"That's the best thing I've heard for the past half hour. They've done nothing but quarrel about art, but stupidly, with no imagination." Berdo sighed.

"Actually we were talking about money, just as those two are doing now." Siemaszko nodded towards Wybrański, who was offering the Engineer a cigar.

"How do you know they're talking about money?" Lewada wondered.

"Because I know the Engineer. As soon as there's wind of

any project in town that's not to do with his organisation, or rather his person, he immediately declares an interest and goes running after the sponsors, just in case. Even if he doesn't get anything, at least he can blacken the competition right at the start. Do you know what he's telling Wybrański now? That the whole Last Supper idea is a big mistake, as out of fashion as granny's bloomers. And that it'll end up being kitsch, so if Festus & Felix are planning to get involved, they'll be making an error: the reviews will be negative."

"Good heavens! Are you always like this here?" Lewada ordered a coffee. "We never used to talk about money at the Actors' Club."

"Or about terrorist attacks," added Berdo.

"Can you really tell what the reviews will be like in three or four years' time, when the painting is finished, if it hasn't even been started yet? And they said such a lot about the attacks on the radio that I had to switch it off. Has there been another one?" concluded Lewada, then added: "So what were you saying about art?"

"That it's mediocre," Siemaszko responded, "because there's something missing in it. I only realised that today, a quarter of an hour ago. You know what? In a Bach fugue we follow the main theme in rapture. It keeps vanishing, like the thread in a cross-stitch pattern. And whenever it disappears, it's still there in our heads, and we wait in suspense for it to reappear. Whenever it comes back – because that's the principle of a fugue – we're thrilled by the masterful way it has been transformed. And most of all by its reappearance."

"Beautifully put," judged Berdo. "You hit the nail on the head."

"That's not me, it's Miciński," admitted Siemaszko with sorrow in his eyes.

"Well, really, take a look at their table," said Berdo, changing the subject. "The Engineer is handing him something!"

"I bet it's some new project of his," whispered Siemaszko. " 'I only need half a million, so you can sponsor me!' But you know what? It's really strange: he usually gets the money, even though he never uses the word 'please'."

"It's psychology." Berdo was closely inspecting the Okassa Zarotto cigarillo tin, until finally he opened it tentatively and whispered: "Oh, it's majoon! May I have a tiny bit?"

"Have a whole piece." Siemaszko nodded. "So you reckon he's got a sort of psychological trick worked out?"

"Definitely." Berdo broke off a square of majoon against his saucer and put it in his mouth like a pill to be ashamed of. "But quite apart from any tricks, there is such a thing as a domineering personality. The tone of voice, the way of talking, the look, a certain insolence. Only very few people can see through it and are able to say no to dominators."

"And avant-gardists," added Siemaszko.

All three of them burst out laughing.

"When I think," continued Berdo, happily chewing the plug of majoon, "how much Wybrański has earned on all his enterprises, sometimes it makes me go weak. With envy too."

"You wanted to say: on all his scams," Siemaszko threw in

at once.

Lewada couldn't restrain himself.

"Does anyone who has money in this country immediately have to be a criminal? A racketeer? It's an ugly trait in those of us who don't have much. The *Homo sovieticus* syndrome."

"It's more in the sphere of facts," replied Berdo, "not all of which are known to us. I mean to say that some of my former boss's enterprises do prompt reservations. But is that why we're sitting here today?"

"Some of them?" snorted Siemaszko. "What peculiar arithmetic! Remember the Happy Fleet? Out of every hundred old people on each cruise several of them always kicked the bucket! And Festus & Felix got a bonus per item deceased. When the number of deaths began to rise from one cruise to the next, they launched an inquiry. At that point Wybrański switched to other, more lucrative things."

"I don't believe it." Lewada was sceptical. "How many old people would have to die to make a fortune? It's like an idea out of a horror film. But a weak one."

"He made a real fortune," said Berdo, developing the theme, "as we all know, on 'pajomacho', the Andean herbs imported here via London. I don't know if they really raised potency, but do you remember the frenzy? And his first *Pajomacho* colour magazine? If it weren't for Viagra it'd still be going strong. But he's nobody's fool. He immediately found and introduced a new herb, for cancer and prostate trouble. Now a new magazine called *Ticcacora* comes out each week to report on miraculous recoveries in hopeless cases. And all those interviews with the happy parents! The secret wisdom of monks and Andean Indians plus advertising equals over a hundred million a year."

"Net or gross?" asked Lewada.

"It's a very simple equation," continued Berdo. "A small bag of ticcacora costs forty zlotys and lasts for about a month. The average punter buys it for three months, until he dies or finds to his disappointment that his state of health hasn't really improved. So he spends a hundred and twenty zlotys on herbs plus at least thirty-six on three successive issues of the magazine. Altogether that's a hundred and fifty-six zlotys. Fine. Now multiply that sum by about one-and-a-half million people who are suffering from or afraid of the illness. That makes a total of over two hundred and thirty million zlotys of gross income in a year. Take away forty per cent in taxes and you're left with about one hundred and forty million zlotys. Even if all the costs – advertising, transport, cultivation, sales – added up to half that sum, and we know they don't exceed it, you've got a net figure of over seventy million zlotys left on the collection plate. At an average rate of three point eight that's about eighteen million euros a year. For at least twelve years. The only thing I find surprising is that he goes around without a bodyguard."

The magic of the numbers cast a momentary silence at their table.

"I know what the plantations look like," said Siemaszko and sighed. "I worked for him briefly too."

But he had no time to tell them about ticcacora farming, because after saying goodbye to the Engineer, who left the café moments later, Wybrański came up to their table and without ceremony sat down to join them.

"We were just debating whether the Engineer would wangle some money out of you or not. And for what project," Berdo addressed him.

"I never answer that sort of question," he answered coldly, but with a smile. "After all, you know, because you used to work for me. I've ordered us a bottle of champagne, because we've got to go in a moment, haven't we? And by the way, who'd have expected those explosions? And fires outside the mosque at once? It's too well orchestrated."

Immediately a debate erupted about the jihad and McDonald's, which I shall not recount, because slowly, but inevitably, we are coming to the end of this chronicle. All I'll tell you is that there was a moment when even Siemaszko wetted his lips on a glass of champagne. And so they argued.

Now let us follow David Roberts for a while, who two hours before dusk is turning off a narrow little street called Suq Khan, where since the 1940s the Zelatimo sweetshop has been located, up some steps that run between blind walls. They lead to a passage closed off by a small wooden gate, with a knocker coated in grey patina. The beams in the doorframe date from Roman times, while the many nails holding the iron bars in place have evidently been replaced over the past few centuries. I do not know if David Roberts was aware of it, but having made an appointment by letter (via a translator) with the prior of the Ethiopian monastery, he was the first subject of the British Crown to enter its gate. Led into a tiny courtyard by a gatekeeper monk, as he waited for the prior, he was astounded by what he saw. He associated the word "monastery" or "abbey" with a number of buildings distributed around a place of worship, as in old England, Scotland or Spain. Here, in a cramped space between closed walls, he saw something like clay cottages – hermits' cells, with tall, dark, mysterious people in long robes peering out of them. The cupola rising above it all still admitted enough light for him to perceive the beauty of the monks' slender figures and heads. He could easily have drawn them in the retinue of the Queen of Sheba on its way here, to this city, during the reign of Solomon. Just as the prior and the pre-paid interpreter approached him, Roberts was doing his best to remember the dates of the great monarch's reign, but in vain. His memory failed him, and all that remained was like something out of a fairytale – "a long, long time ago".

That was how he felt as the prior uttered his words of welcome. He knew it was Amharic, which in Ethiopia had replaced the ancient Ge'ez language. He could not understand a word of it. Not a single one was like anything he had ever heard before. He had only had a similar impression once, on his travels across Spain, when he had encountered some drunken Basques who were furious with an innkeeper. However, this did not in the least imply that the Basques had anything in common with the Ethiopians.

First he listened to the information that here, underneath

them, right where they were standing, was the crypt of Saint Helena, mother of the Emperor Constantine.

David Roberts expressed his surprise: he had already been in the Church of the Holy Sepulchre and also in the imperial crypt, to which one descends by following the cloister to the right of the anointment stone. As he came in here from Suq Khan street, he had never imagined he was so near to the Church of the Holy Sepulchre.

The prior explained that the present monastery was once part of the great Basilica of Constantine. Burned down by the Persians in 614 AD it had been rebuilt, then razed to the ground in 1009 by the Caliph Hakim. Shortly after he added that the door, to which he was pointing, led to the present basilica, and the Ethiopian monks could go in there at fixed times of the day and week, because apart from them the Copts, Greeks and Armenians regularly held prayers.

David Roberts expressed no surprise at the fact that the Ethiopians are not members of the Coptic church, as he had thought, because he did not wish to show his own ignorance. Instead he asked if this meant they were standing above the very spot where the Empress Helena had found the wood of the True Cross.

This was duly confirmed. Then they walked over to one of the clay cottages. It was the prior's cell; inside the entire furnishings consisted of a bed, a table, one stool, a bowl on a wooden trestle and a small, narrow cupboard. Out of this cupboard the prior took a large book. It was once a scroll of papyrus that had been cut into quartos and carefully glued onto small boards. David Roberts listened attentively to the interpreter's explanations, but to tell the truth, it was a mixture of extracts from the Coptic Gospels, the Gospel of Basilides, the Gospel of Thomas, the Gospel of John and the Gospel of the Twelve. The texts had a mixture of alphabets too, among which Greek featured least of all. After this presentation the prior kissed the book and then put it away, but he took another thing out of the cupboard too: it was a single sheet of papyrus glued like the previous ones to a small board. Around an extraordinary beetle with a human face, as if scrawled by a five-year-old, ran some Coptic letters. The beetle was oval; in its left limb it held a sort of shepherd's crook. Above it three lines ran crosswise, and beneath it there was a circle with holes in four places.

"This is an amulet," the interpreter explained the prior's words. "It represents King David holding a harp. The inscription in the language of the Copts is a spell against eye disease and ghosts. It dates from the second century. It may have been preserved here because it was consecrated, and also because among the Coptic words there are three words written in Ge'ez, the ancient language of the Ethiopians, but in the Coptic alphabet."

David Roberts asked what those words were.

"Eye, wind, desert," came the answer.

"Why did the Copts, who were probably already Christians by then, represent King David and his harp on the amulet, rather than one of the apostles, for example?" asked Roberts.

After a lengthy silence the prior replied that ancient magic
often referred to Moses, David and Solomon. Their images
appeared on many amulets. The one kept at their monastery
was among the oldest. More amulets made of bronze, copper
or stone had survived than ones on papyrus. No one knew if
the creator of the amulet was a Christian or not.

The tour was coming to an end. Back in the small
courtyard David Roberts asked the interpreter if he might
pose one more question. The prior nodded.

"What is the basis for the belief that the Ark of the
Covenant is preserved in one of the Christian churches in
Ethiopia?"

"During the time of the Crusaders there was a monastery
here," replied the prior, "bigger than our present one. One
day a scroll was found in the scriptorium, written in the Ge'ez
language. It described the journey of the Ark from Jerusalem
to Sudan, and from there up the Blue Nile, all the way to Lake
Tana, which is its source. The Crusaders wanted to go there in
a small company, but Jerusalem had fallen, Caliph Hakim had
given orders for the books and scrolls from the scriptorium to
be burned, and so it remained a legend."

As he gave the prior his hand, for a moment David
Roberts felt as if he were in a strange, other world. This world
was not the invention of a poet or a novelist: it expressed itself
in the naïve image of King David, the exotic letters of the
gospels he had never heard of before, and finally in the words
"eye, wind, desert", written down in Coptic style. As he
walked along Suq Khan street towards the Christian district,

where he had lodgings in the house of an English merchant, David Roberts thought it would be worth going to Ethiopia one day. To draw Lake Tana at dusk. Or the church of Debre Birham Selassie in Gondar, the capital of that state. I know he will never make the journey. Too much publishing and painting work will keep him busy in Scotland on his return. As I leave him in the purple dusk of Jerusalem, I am just as grateful to him as to the chance that one day led me to buy a poster with a reproduction of his work, right by the Jaffa Gate. The same gate that in his book René de Chateaubriand called the Pilgrim's Gate.

But Berdo, Lewada, Siemaszko and Wybrański are walking down Theatre Alley now, past the mediaeval pharmacy, to the stage-door entrance. The cobbles in the alleyway are just as dangerous as the uneven stones in Suq Khan. If you don't look where you're going, you can trip and end up with a bruise or even a bump. Luckily they're walking slowly, chatting and waving their hands about, Siemaszko next to Lewada, with Wybrański and Berdo behind them. As they go past the theatre's loading ramp and come around a slight bend, the Twelfth Man will notice them. He will recognise Berdo – he has seen him already today, pacing around Saint Mary's cathedral, muttering under his breath. But the Twelfth Man knows his moment has not yet come, because none of the four is the Antichrist. He tries to make contact with them, but as they ascend the steps to the stage door none of them takes any notice of the man with the balloon making faces and gesturing at them, mainly because he's sitting a good twenty-five metres away on the low wall of the parking area. Siemaszko was humming his apparently meaningless entrance song – *Jaldabaoth Zozezaz – Zaozoz Jaladabaoth*.

A few minutes later, a dark blue Maybach with tinted windows drove up to the stage door. First the driver got out, who looked like an adolescent, and then another of Father Monsignore's assistants, who was just as young. He opened the rear door and helped the Reverend Father out of the car. Dressed in a modest white cassock and crocodile skin shoes of exactly the same colour, Monsignore surveyed the scene and noticed the Twelfth Man, who had just got up from the wall and was moving towards the car.

"Give him a few pennies," he told the assistants, "and get the wine out of the boot." Then without looking back, he set off up the steps, a little surprised there was no one to meet him at the door.

Why am I always finding questions about Father Monsignore in your e-mails? There are some three hundred priests in our city who perform their difficult everyday job more or less correctly. Among them we could mention several outstanding pastors, theologians, community workers and scholars. The Holy Scripture really does speak the truth, so believe it – "by their fruits ye shall know them". But how typical for a journalist – all you ever ask about is Monsignore! You know why that is, don't you? The other three hundred aren't as attractive for the TV screen or the newspaper column. The ones who solemnly do their duty are positively boring. Not so Father Monsignore! He only has to insult the

Jews, take someone to court, slander someone from the former opposition or himself be accused by the mother of an altar-boy, and the wheels start to turn!

The furious bee that stung the youngest of the Oczko brothers really did fly out of the bottle of Monsignore wine run over by their car tyre. When I sent you a picture of the wine label, there was no end to your amazement: how is it possible for the sale of alcohol to be promoted by the Catholic church? "Do you know this country?" was my instant reply, and you were mildly offended, so now let me ask you: in New York where you live now, does any of the Catholic priests sell whisky with a picture of himself on it? Not even an Irishman? Nor do I think any of them would be photographed in a uniform with an admiral's insignia that no one has ever awarded him – the local bishop would be sure to send him for therapy, if not straight to the asylum. But enough of that: as you pestered me about Monsignore, here he comes in full regalia. As you know from what Berdo and Siemaszko heard of the conversation with the Engineer, he immediately agreed. Why? You may well ask, since the invitation wasn't very gracious or polite. At the last moment? And evidently from the reserve bench? I don't wish to speculate, so instead I'll state the facts.

About a year before the meeting at the theatre, Father Monsignore had got into a new scrape. This time it wasn't a case of "ephebophilia" (a term coined by the country's leading sexologist, while commenting on the harmlessness of priests kissing altar-boys), Mercedes Benzes, Maybachs, banquets, medals, titles, company shares, monuments to himself, rebuking the Jews or the Russians, or humiliating various political parties. In my humble view, this time the hand of God was at work, and that was why Father Monsignore was somewhat on the defensive.

Imagine the following scene: at his church, during the transubstantiation of the wine into the Blood of Christ and the bread into His Body, instead of looking at the chalice or simply downwards in the traditional way, the eyes of the congregation are aimed upwards, straight at the ceiling, where the vaults were finished off in Hanseatic Gothic style a few hundred years ago. There's a loud rustling noise coming from up there, something like the flutter of a large bird's wings. The altar-boys are ringing their bells, the formula has been uttered, but everyone seems to have forgotten about that – they're all looking up, many with their mouths hanging open in astonishment.

What they can see is quite unfamiliar to them. They can neither name it nor relate it to anything they have ever seen before. The scroll of sizeable dimensions that is fluttering under the vaulted ceiling looks at first like a sealed tube or a pipe, then like a poster, until finally it takes on the shape of an unrolled page of the Torah. As they go to take communion, it gets even worse: they can see the scroll coming to rest right under the tabernacle, at the foot of the altar. Obviously, the mass is coming to its end, the blessings have already been said and the church is gradually emptying, but the thing that was seen fluttering under the vault is already the topic of conversation all over the city.

Once the congregation has left, Father Monsignore tells two altar-boys to pick the thing up from the floor and bring it to him in the presbytery; he senses some insolent provocation. Nothing but Hebrew letters!

"The Jew boys are taking revenge!" he whispers to Jaś and Krzyś. "Burn this for me at once!"

The instruction is carried out to the letter.

Probably if Father Monsignore had applied himself better in Bible classes at the seminary, he would have remembered the Book of Zacharias, chapter five. But he didn't. Maybe that was why, a couple of months later, when the situation repeated itself to the last detail, he hardly glanced at the scroll. This time the text was in Latin, but he had no desire to read it and, as before, it was consumed by flames.

Chief Inspector Zawiślny was invited to supper and promised to catch the culprits, but he might just as well have offered the moon. He soberly demanded that next time the *corpus delicti* be preserved.

Fantastic rumours about the contents of the scroll were already going around town, which I shall not venture to summarise. In the Jesuits' community periodical, as if quite by chance, an essay appeared by the biblical scholar Professor Świder on the prophecies of Zacharias. It was partly reprinted by the newspapers, selectively of course and tendentiously. From the long, extremely erudite text two points were usually extracted: firstly, that the flying scroll was unique. In the Bible birds and angels fly, but never, apart from this one occasion, scrolls of scripture. Secondly, the commentary was important. The angel who showed Zacharias the scroll that "rises in the air", and says "every thief" and "everyone who swears falsely will be banished", and that a curse "will remain in his house and destroy it", was thinking of those who appropriated the money entrusted to them for the rebuilding of the Temple in Jerusalem. Or those who pledged impressive sums and then gave nothing. The incident took place in the holy city, after the return of the Jews from exile in Babylon. When one of the journalists used the word "brick", it all came to a head. In fact, Father Monsignore had had nothing to do with the campaign run by the Reverend Father who headed the religious radio station; years ago, in an effort to save our local shipyard, he had distributed several million symbolic bricks to be sold for charitable donations all over the country (forgive me, but I can't remember how many zloty they cost) and had apparently never accounted for this campaign. All these facts were combined in the editorials. A joker writing in the local tabloid summed it up in this headline: *A Letter from Heaven to the Shipyard Workers*. The poison pens, which are never in short supply, also brought up the money Father Monsignore was said to owe to jewellers making amber baubles for him as part of an ambitious plan to eclipse the king of Prussia: the German monarch had had an Amber Chamber, so Father Monsignore wanted to put up an altar in his church made of the same precious mineral.

Two or three weeks before the photo shoot the scroll had appeared again, not during the elevation, but after the candles had been put out. According to the eyewitnesses (who included Zofia Wybrańska), there was nothing there but the above-mentioned quote from Zacharias, this time in a translation by Father Wujek. Nevertheless, when one of the altar-boys unfurled the large roll of paper and a second one slowly and rather clumsily began to read out the declaration of the Lord of Hosts, the handful of communicants still standing by the altar were thoroughly dismayed. Someone advised calling the police at once. Someone else suggested the television instead. But none of them thought of calling the Archbishop. Father Monsignore came back from the vestry, saying: "Don't read that here, no!"

But it had already been read. As Monsignore tried to take the scroll from the altar-boy's hands, the Scripture rolled up of its own accord, flew skywards and hovered briefly, high beneath the Gothic vault; then, as if guided by the invisible hand of God, it calmly sailed through an open skylight in the stained-glass window. Early that afternoon the unusual scroll was spotted at several sites about town, but among those who saw it there was no consensus over where exactly it had unfurled like a papyrus and hung for a few seconds above the heads of the astonished passers-by like an advertising banner, nor could they agree on its dimensions. In Zacharias it was twenty cubits long and ten wide; according to the biblical scholars, a cubit was equal to forty-five of our centimetres, so it is easy to calculate that it was nine metres long and four-and-a-half wide. It must have been as vast as the hoardings for Wybrański's firm, but this was not unanimously confirmed by the witnesses to the paranormal event. Very large – that definition was repeated in several accounts, of course, but how large, no one could agree.

"Like a sheet," said some. "No, a little smaller," replied others.

But what sort of sheet? A double one? Or a single?

Apart from that, it wasn't necessarily a scroll exactly like the one in Zacharias: some people saw a list of names there, others saw nothing but columns of figures, others yet saw the face of Father Monsignore wearing a huge crown, not of thorns, but an imperial one.

According to the information gathered, the flying scroll first appeared at the shipyard gate, just above the monument to the fallen workers, then later it was seen near the Main City Town Hall, fluttering above the fountain of Neptune, armed with his trident, but it spent the longest time circling the Municipal Council building, which was closed for business because it was a Sunday.

Now you can understand that Father Monsignore, as the object of gossip and controversy, was for the first time not happy about it. If it had been about another medal being awarded to him by some strange people, an aristocratic title, ephebophilia, a new Mercedes or the wine trade, he would certainly have brushed it aside and gone on doing his thing. But matters took a different turn: Zacharias' scroll weighed on the heart of the Reverend Father in a dreadful way, so badly that he was even refusing to give any more interviews and had sent the journalists packing. Maybe because it was the first time he had ever come up against something truly unpredictable? And that could happen again at any time? This was why – in my humble opinion – when he received the call from the Engineer (whom he cannot possibly have remembered) with the offer to pose for the Last Supper, he agreed at once.

How surprised the Twelfth Man was when one of the priest's servants handed him a few small coins, and then, helped by the other one, took four boxes of wine from the boot of the limousine.

How many bottles were there? Twenty-four in all. They gently clinked together like the bells of the trams that once had a terminus here, which no one in our city is likely to remember any more. But they weren't opened on the stage. Just wait a little and you'll find out why.

CHAPTER VIII

Flash

I HAD HEARD THAT SONG BEFORE. Jaunty and wistful all at once, as if it were by Goran Bregović. Now, as I gradually approach the end of this chronicle, it keeps coming back to me and refuses to leave me in peace, falling like light upon the people and events I'm describing. Why this particular folk song about two feuding clans, of whom no one or just about no one in our city knew any of the facts? Why should we care about some esoteric characters called Obrenović and Karadjordjević from a kingdom that no longer exists? But maybe it was because of Milan's voice that my memory, as it offers up an endless series of images from that evening, has retained the words and tune of the folk song as something it will keep for ever?

It was like this: first a fellow called Nowik had made

himself at home at the bar in the Actors' Club. Who was he?
An avant-garde theatre activist. What was he doing there?
Passing the time, as usual. What did he have to say? Not much
really, or almost nothing: just that all theatre to date is crap.
This original thesis, sending all the directors and actors that
ever were to the hell of non-existence, did not get any particular acknowledgement, so to speak. Of course, someone over
there nodded, someone else raged at the so-called theatrical
establishment, but on the whole no one was interested in
pandering to Nowik. Maybe that was why he had the performance ready? Just accept that it was meant to be provocative,
like everything produced by Nowik, who was a fundamental
modernist in those days. So as soon as the concert was over,
several boys jumped up on the bar top. Their garters, singlets
and boots left us in no doubt at all – we were up against the
militant gay faction, who were greeted by eager applause. So
these boys got up and – I don't know quite how to put it –
joined together in a strictly carnal attitude, in a breach-loading
position, on all fours on the bar. For a moment everyone was
dismayed, but then, to the rhythm of techno music, their
swaying bodies began to move like a locomotive piston:
effectively, rhythmically, time and again. And Nowik was
conducting them like von Karajan with an orchestra of emanci-
pated Germans, the tails of his velveteen jacket flapping like
wings in the wind. Someone shouted: "Disgusting!
Scandalous! Filth!", but they were in the complete minority
and failed to prompt further protest, because even those who
did not find this performance all that revelatory were still keen

to watch the action, curious to see what would come next. In fact nothing in particular happened: the tough, burly Nowik went round the crowded room and in time with the music and that theatrical activity, so to speak, kept waving his arms about and shouting: "We want twelve! We need twelve!"

With a sweeping gesture he kept pointing at the spectators, then at the stage, inviting them to join in, because this performance was meant to be a democratic, audience-participation show. Can you imagine it? Volunteers were found very quickly, and another five joined the seven performers on the bar. When after a few moments of pretend or genuine group spasm Nowik jumped onto the bar, his twelve happy followers relaxed and gathered around him. Like the Master among his disciples he spread his hands wide in a gesture of benediction. Some of them, plainly to play up the clownish premise of the performance, kissed the Maestro on the calves and thighs. Now I don't think it was clowning, but a serious debate about modern art. Eventually Nowik, who a few years later became director of the National Centre for the Dramatic Arts, transferred the experience he had gained at the Actors' Club to the country's main stages – with immense success. No one, or practically no one, was outraged by it. Do you remember *Hamlet*? How all the gravediggers spoke in reedy little voices, slapping each other on the bum, smacking their lips like babies and feeling each other up in a coarse manner while the Danish prince was delivering his monologue? The critics liked that idea – there's no question, it was a huge success. But for now we're at the bar in a Sopot pub. Nowik gives the signal and his entire Laocoon group disperses: the disciples go and wander about the pub, bearing the news of the new era of new art.

Just then Mateusz came up to me and asked: "Have you been to the seven cities?"

I wasn't sure how to answer, but as he went on it gradually dawned on me that he meant Ephesus, Smyrna, Pergamum, Thyatira, Sardis, Philadelphia and Laodicea.

"These things saith he that holdeth the seven stars in his right hand, who walketh in the midst of the seven golden candlesticks," he thundered in a mighty voice, "remember therefore from whence thou art fallen, and repent, and do the first works!"

"My God, what bullshit he's talking," said the enthusiast sitting on Doctor Lewada's right knee. "Is he cracked or what?"

Her ample bust, on which the doctor's hand was resting, rippled, giving a rhythm to the words as she spoke them.

"What's got into you, Jolka?" wondered the girl on the doctor's left knee. "Maybe you're the one that's cracked? The guy's shit-hot! Let him go on. Who's got such a great story?"

She was the tomboy type: hair cut short, with a checked flannel shirt loose over jeans with a solid pair of bovver boots peeping out from under them.

"I know where thou dwellest," thundered Mateusz, not in the least put out, "even where Satan's seat is: and thou holdest fast my name" – here he gazed triumphantly around the assembled company – "and hast not denied my faith!"

"What a load of tosh," remarked Berdo, emptying his glass. "It's just words!"

"Now now, doctor," replied Jan Wybrański. "Who, if not you? When, if not now?"

"Just don't bore me with the Talmud," snarled Berdo. "At least not in this place!"

"What's wrong?" said Siemaszko indignantly. "Isn't our life like Jacob's ladder? Nothing but dreams and common beliefs? And do you know who Vishnu is? The god dreaming the world, who dreams that he himself is being dreamed…"

"Jesus, what a bunch of losers," sighed Jolka. "Can't you behave normally?"

"Ah," Mateusz enthused, "sure we can!"

But I don't wish to quote you the next bit of the Scriptures that Mateusz immediately recited, out loud and no doubt faithfully. By then I was already tipsy, to tell the truth, and tired of everything that was going on in the pub: the way everything was completely confused with everything else, as if nothing could mean what it actually did mean.

"Oh Lord, how we revere our pipes and our rakia!"

Who was singing those words?

Who kept repeating that jaunty refrain?

It was Milan, leaning his right arm on the bar, and holding a microphone in his left.

I'll add that there was someone accompanying him, on a concertina, a saxophone, a guitar and a fiddle.

The Balkans had invaded the sad northern town where we were busy spinning around our own axis. Are you familiar with that sort of singing? A slightly faltering voice, as if acquired sometime somewhere from a muezzin. Or a Jewish kantor. I don't know to what extent consciously. And all those quavers, semiquavers and demisemiquavers – bashed out over and over by the accompanying instruments. There's a natural, unabashed dramatic tension in this way of singing, infinite lyricism, and an epic sweep, because each song – just like a Scottish or English ballad – tells a complete story.

So as Mateusz was unfurling the wings of his erudition, as Berdo was eyeing up the two boys kissing on the sofa, as Jolka and Mariola were snuggling with Doctor Lewada, as Jan Wybrański was explaining to Siemaszko that our civilisation doesn't have to perish at all – although it is dreadfully permissive – Milan was just finishing the warm-up with this refrain, "Oh Lord, how we revere our pipes and our rakia!" (unless I'm mistaken, I heard that song many years later in war-destroyed Mostar) and at once he went straight into the song about Djordje Karadjordjević, who swooped down like a falcon from the mountains and routed the invaders, and then about how that uprising went on for several long years, until the blasted Turks had drowned it in a sea of blood. As I listened to the sad end of the first verse, in which Karadjordjević goes off into exile in Vienna, I gazed at the faces of the future apostles. Sweaty and excited, there was a touch of sorrow about them: their youth was just coming to an end, never to return.

By the time the crowd gathered in Saint John's church for the unveiling, a couple of years had passed since Berdo's death. He died in Alexandria, where he was lecturing at the university. Wybrański did not come back from Switzerland because, as he wrote in a letter to Mateusz, he was stuck there on urgent business. He was lying. Since his divorce from Zofia, which resulted in him losing more than half his property, he had been living in peace and quiet with a former chambermaid from the Hotel Adler in Zurich, and no longer spread his wings as he used to. Siemaszko had vanished somewhere in Tibet or Burma, where he had gone on his own Pilgrimage of Truth, organised by himself alone. Apparently he became a monk at one of the monasteries there, but those rumours, which had no confirmation, were probably made up. Doctor Lewada frankly admitted that he didn't want to use any of his leave, which he planned to take with his family and not necessarily in our country. For some time now he had been working at a hospital in Dublin: he and his lovely Anna had twin girls. He sent Mateusz their photographs by e-mail.

Maybe that was why I was looking forward to the unveiling so impatiently? Ultimately, as in a way their fate was already sealed, and as they weren't going to be there, I was hoping for some sort of déjà vu. To remember voices and conversations from the Actors' Club or the photo shoot wouldn't have been all that strange, but nor would it have been entirely normal, considering they'd be staring at me from an enormous canvas, embroiled in another story for once and for ever. In fact, as it was to turn out, not for ever.

The lights had just been switched on, and Mateusz's Last Supper had only just appeared before the eyes of the assembled company, when from the back of the gathering we heard a strange noise. Twelve young men lined up like the vanguard pushed their way to the front, rather sharply and firmly, not without shoving. As the enquiry later revealed, they had driven up to the church in a hired minibus from the river and got inside through an unused entrance from the chancel. If they hadn't done that, they might have been stopped: they were wearing capes, they had flippers on their feet, and their bare, shaven heads were painted pink. The crowd giving way to them as they moved forward must have thought it was a comic performance: after all, in our city people were used to seeing stronger stuff than that. Halfway to the painting they started chanting loudly: "We are artists too! We are apostles too!" Then events progressed at lightning speed. They flung back the capes, and with a single, practised movement pulled gas masks over their faces. I had once seen figures like that at the theatre, perhaps in Szajna's *Replika*. From under the capes, cylinders appeared fixed to their backs, with pumps attached. Twelve streams of chemicals spurted onto Mateusz's canvas. At that point there was an attempt to restrain them, but in vain. Two sluggish security guards were immediately pushed aside, but then a few more pugnacious people from the audience launched a scrimmage. Soon after the police arrived and had no trouble taking control of the situation: as soon as they could see their task had been accomplished as intended, the avant-gardists gave themselves up without further resistance. Several people had holes burned in their clothes by the chemical substance. Luckily no one had been splashed on the face or head. Filmed by two hidden cameras, the whole thing brought the avant-gardists incredible success: their version of the Last Supper was a big hit at the Venice Biennale, where they won the silver medal; later they got first prize at the Berlin Festival of Committed Art, and finally a distinction for Open Art of the World at an exhibition called "Crossing Borders". Mateusz was taken to hospital by ambulance suffering from a heart attack. And once it was all over, as I was leaving the church I could hear Milan's voice from all those years ago, singing the second verse of his ballad: about how Miloš Obrenović led the next uprising, a successful one, and how because of Turkey's concessions he was named Prince of Serbia, at which Djordje Karadjordjević, leader of the earlier uprising, flared up in mortal rage and secretly came back to the fatherland to overthrow Obrenović, but was captured by his people and murdered, so Karadjordjević's faithful followers and relatives swore vengeance on the Obrenović clan, to the very limits, to the end of the world.

Next day the Engineer, who was the godfather of the action, said in a newspaper interview: "Those young people are going to be fined, but we should be showing them our sympathy, ladies and gentlemen, because here we have the struggle of real modern art against kitsch."

The reader was unable to discover what had been used to distort the faces of Berdo, Siemaszko, Wybrański, Lewada and the other eight. The debate was deftly steered along the lines of an academic argument – what is and what is not art. Father Nienałtowski from Saint John's church did manage to salvage a few small pieces of the canvas: to this day he still has the face of Christ with one eye burned out and a hole in the cheek. A *bon mot* issued by the critic Janina Szydlakowa saying that thanks to the avant-gardists' action our city had not had to see a modern image of Judas rapidly did the rounds of all the editors' desks, to the journalists' delight. On the wall of the Academy, right under Mateusz's studio window, somebody stuck a reproduction of Leonardo's *Last Supper*, with Coca-Cola cans added in the hands of the apostles. A psychologist called Doctor Wańka was invited into the television studio to express his outrage at the repressive treatment of the avant-gardists, who had each been fined from five hundred to one thousand zlotys. Zuzanna Wiatrak, former solo mime artiste, stated on camera that there was no great loss because we were dealing with kitsch. And so it went on in this refined manner for several days, until our city sank back into its usual cultural state: the Engineer accepted four new rectangular boxes full of air for the Museum of Modern Art, sealed in Buenos Aires, Glasgow, Włoszczowa and Anon, which prompted the experts to debate the anonymity of life in the modern metropolis. Meanwhile an artist called Halmann exhibited a restaurant car from the communist era in a railway siding: the humble, disgusting dishes of those days, including sauerkraut stew, frankfurters and lemon squash were served.

So you think if we had had just an inkling of this course of events we would have talked Mateusz out of his plans there and then, at the Actors' Club? Or that later on none of us would have turned up for the photo shoot? Your question is bizarre: if we knew what the results of our actions would be, we'd be bound to abandon most of them, in trivial as well as serious situations. Naturally, it's about more than that – yes, it's about art, but I don't have to explain it to you, because you are an artist and you live in the city where Damien Hirst exhibited some ashtrays full of dog-ends, some empty coffee mugs, old newspapers and a smeared palette as a work worth a couple of hundred thousand dollars, but next day a cleaner called Emmanuel Asare threw the whole lot out because he had no idea he was destroying a work of art. The Turner Prize – yes, Turner – was won by a guy who switched a light on and off in an empty room. Why don't you do just the same? For the same reasons as Mateusz. Meanwhile the avant-gardists have long since passed sentence on us – we are démodé, passé, just like painting. The world has gone in another direction, and you're behaving as if you live on Mars. Aren't I right? Whatever you paint, the Engineer, Ms Szydlakowa or Ms Wiatrak will instantly cry kitsch. Why are they so aggressive, you rightly ask. But although it may be very important, that question is not crucial; whatever answer we give, it cannot change the main fact of the matter: these days the power to cast judgement belongs to those who can impose and maintain it. So now I'm going back to the Actors' Club for just a little longer, to finish the story.

Milan sang several more verses, telling how the next Obrenović – Mihailo, son of Miloš – was removed from the throne and replaced by Alexander Karadjordjević, son of Djordje who had been murdered years before. Then Mihailo

Obrenović was restored and reigned again, to the fury of the deposed Karadjordjević clan. Mihailo in turn was murdered as the result of a conspiracy, but this time the throne was occupied not by a Karadjordjević, but by Mihailo's son, Milan Obrenović, against whom however, the Karadjordjević clan continued to plot.

"It's enough to drive you mad," laughed Lewada. "I'm completely flummoxed. Who came after whom and who did what to whom?"

"That's the Balkans," said Berdo. "It all keeps changing faster than the notes in their music."

Once Milan had been rewarded with a rowdy ovation, he sat down at our table, then Wybrański fetched a bottle of vodka and said: "Now we must establish who's for Karadjordjević, and who's for Obrenović."

"I'm for Ogniwo Sopot," said Lewada naming the local team, "though I can't stand rugby!"

Out of the corner of my eye I saw Mateusz and Maryna quietly slipping away. Milan – I can't remember if he was pro-Obrenović or Karadjordjević – was telling us about his production of *Acting Hamlet in the Village of Mrduša Donja* at the theatre in Novi Sad. Also about why he had stayed in our city and was never going back to his own country for good.

"Boy, I wouldn't like to go back to that mess either," muttered Siemaszko.

"If you think it's going to be any better here, you're wrong," Wybrański scolded him.

However, he wasn't entirely right, I thought to myself

years later, looking at his face as in almost exactly the same company he stepped onto the small stage, where apart from the chairs and the long table covered in white cloths there was nothing. Would you believe that as soon as I saw them, hesitantly walking across the large, empty space, I immediately started humming the tune of that ballad to myself?

> *On the bed are stains of blood,*
> *Murdered in a royal feud*
> *Djordje, Karadjordjević*
> *Slaughtered by Obrenović*
> *He flew like a falcon.*
> *God, O Lord, our good Lord God.*

A restless stage manager was bustling about, an electrician was setting up lights, and the photographer was fiddling with his equipment on its stand.

"There you are," the actor Jerzy Zając greeted them loudly. "That's almost the complete set. We're only missing Mateusz and one apostle. Do you know who it's going to be?"

No one knew. There was a conversation about Franek, who had been seriously injured in the first of the morning bomb blasts. He had regained consciousness, but his condition was critical. Zbigniew Awistowski the poet had talked to a doctor he knew at the hospital.

"He's probably going to lose his right foot," he said. "It's dreadful."

Father Nienałtowski's mobile phone rang. After a brief "yes, incredible, yeees, what a cheek, well no, all right, all right, yes, of course we'll wait!", he hung up and announced: "You know what's happened? Mateusz has been arrested! At his own studio! About three hours ago... They've only just released him. He's rushing here in a taxi, or at least as fast as you can rush through those awful jams."

We all stared at him inquiringly.

But I could tell what must have happened. The police had been on red alert all day, and Mateusz's neighbours, Mr and Mrs Zielonko, must have taken advantage of it, reporting that some very suspicious things were going on above them in flat number three. They must have sounded credible, because an anti-terrorist squad had burst into the studio and without listening to any reason at all had taken Mateusz to the police station in handcuffs. Only after preliminary questioning and some phone calls to and from the president of the Academy was he let go, without a word of apology, of course.

"It's incredible," concluded Father Nienałtowski. "They asked him several times where he keeps the explosive materials. Can you imagine?"

"Just like during martial law," said Maciej Kurzawa, the sculptor, gloomily. "Except that in those days they beat you up first."

"It's always the same," added Professor Janusz Cytryński with a sad smile. "The terrorists calmly fly away, and they arrest completely random people."

"Where do they fly away to, where?" fretted Marian Małkowicz, who in those days lectured on psychopathology. "Shouldn't they be stopped?"

"How should I know? Wherever," replied Cytryński, shrugging. "Frankfurt, for example, and from there to Dubai…"

Just then Father Monsignore came into the rehearsal room. The electrician had just switched on a strong, deathly pale light, and as the worshipful servant of God began to walk across the stage, his snow-white cassock became whiter than Christ's robes on the mount of the Transfiguration. Naturally, it was an unintended effect and only lasted a moment, but even so it dazzled the assembled company. Moreover, no one was expecting this particular guest at this gathering. I saw Siemaszko lean across to whisper something to Berdo, who then nodded in agreement: they must have been reminding each other of the Engineer's tirade on the telephone. Lewada clenched his jaw and walked over to Awistowski, who, standing to one side of the room where there was a pail full of water and dog ends, rather ostentatiously lit a cigarette.

"Too much light," said Monsignore, standing centre stage. "Don't blind us!"

And when the electrician shifted the lever to almost zero and we were all left in virtual darkness, with only some small wall lamps for lighting, Father Monsignore's two assistants came in clinking twenty-four bottles of wine together in four cardboard boxes.

"On the table," their boss instructed them. "How long might this take?"

The light returned to its middling state.

The question was aimed at everyone and no one.

Finally Professor Cytryński broke the awkward silence by saying politely: "No one knows. We're just waiting for Mateusz."

"That's the... artist." Father Monsignore went up to the professor. "So what has he painted before now?"

I could see Father Nienałtowski was feverishly writing a text and I could guess to whom and about what.

"Just naked dolly birds on the whole," snapped Kurzawa the sculptor under his breath, as if only to himself. "Saints just once in a blue moon."

It wasn't pleasant for either side: the conversation clearly wasn't taking off, and waiting for Mateusz could go on for a while longer.

The photographer decided to get down to work: he arranged the chairs on one side of the table and asked us to sit down, as we wished.

"But who is meant to be who?" asked Father Monsignore. "Hasn't it been established?"

"No," replied Jerzy Zając, "each of us should remain himself."

"No one knows who he'll be in this incarnation," said Siemaszko, clearly livening up. "Don't you believe in the transmigration of souls, Father? Reincarnation? I think in a former life I was a high priest of the god Ra, in Memphis."

"Listen, hey, listen." Only now did I notice that Małkowicz, the psychopathology lecturer, had a small receiver in his ear and had been picking up the news on the radio all this time. "They've found the perpetrator of the bomb attacks, he gave himself up! Incredible, do you hear? A member of Alcoholics Anonymous, Andrzej K., gave himself up to the police. He hasn't drunk for twenty years and says in his statement that the sight of the unhappy faces at the all-night shops, and the very smell of those places too, highly specific, that stink of human downfall – as he perceived it – oppressed him so much for all his years of abstinence that at last he decided to take action. It's on all the channels! The interrogation's continuing."

"It's the Arabs," said Father Monsignore. "It's rubbish to say it's an alcoholic. One of ours would never do that."

"Even if he's an abstinent alcoholic," said Berdo, glancing at the white cassock, "he must have had some accomplices. Aren't they saying anything about that?" he addressed Małkowicz.

"No," came the curt reply, "but they are saying another one has handed himself in now, nothing to do with the first one, but also an AA member apparently."

"It's an epidemic," sighed Wybrański. "It's sure to get worse by tonight."

The photographer snapped a few test pictures without adjusting the lights.

"And I heard people in town saying it was your handiwork," said Doctor Lewada, sounding truly theatrical, "because not all the shops were willing to sell Monsignore wine!"

"What rot." Monsignore waved dismissively and drummed his fingers on the table. "Let them chatter! When I start advertising dynamite I'll send you a pack for free, Doctor."

This reply amused at least some of the assembled company. And just at that moment, as the not quite crazed, but pretty loud sniggering over the tabletop fell silent, onto the stage walked, or rather ran, Mateusz.

Do you remember his favourite saying, which I've already quoted in this chronicle? Well, exactly – it was no different now. He stood in the middle of the stage, holding his head in both hands and repeating: "What a nightmare! Ghastly!" However, this time it wasn't about finding a glazier on a Saturday afternoon. Arrest, interrogation, a taxi journey through a massive traffic jam, listening to the news about the bomb attacks, being late for the photo shoot, being unsure everyone would get there – all this at once was enough to upset Mateusz, but not as much as the fear, or rather certainty that he wouldn't be able to cope with the expulsion of Father Monsignore. Like an agitated bumblebee he turned a few circles about the stage, and suddenly, as if he had gone off course, came up to the table.

"Father, may I have a word with you alone?" he asked, leaning over the white cassock.

It looked like a confession: the two men stood facing each other in a corner of the room whispering, with Mateusz's voice getting louder and clearer from sentence to sentence. Father Monsignore can't have been insisting on being an apostle, but he did want to hear some logical explanation for his discomforting situation, and here they could not find common ground. A couple of times the Engineer's name came up, and we heard just as clearly that this was a meeting of a private nature for close friends, then finally Mateusz raised his voice and announced: "You're not even fit to be Judas!", which decided the matter of course. As the whole trio were leaving, Monsignore muttered: "I'll get my own back for this." Bordering on frenzy by now, Mateusz ran up to the young assistants, turned them back from the door, pointed at the boxes of wine standing in the middle of the table and cried: "Get that out of here!"

Then he stood on the stage for a while, perhaps unsure what to do next.

"Set up the lighting," he said to the photographer and rushed out of the rehearsal room.

"Surely he's not going to apologise." No one found Kurzawa's doubt amusing. "Why's he running after him when he's just bawled him out?"

Once again the photographer asked everyone to take their places, but this time he kept telling us to change seats – this one here, that one further down, no, maybe here after all. The electrician lit each successive arrangement, now with strong, now diffuse light: I was sitting – from the camera's point of view – third from the left, next to Jan Wybrański and Jerzy Zając.

As the sharp blade of the floodlight made me squint, yet again I saw a light as bright as in Jerusalem in the month of Tamuz when the heatwaves begin: I had seen it on leaving the lecture hall while Professor Aristoteles Demetrios was finishing his talk on one single papyrus, the famous Relegatio in Oasin, which is a letter from presbyter Psenosiris to presbyter Apollon, whom he calls "beloved brother in the Lord" and to whom he relates some sad events, namely that some gravediggers had brought to Toeto a woman by the name of Politike, the one whom "the governor's office had sent to the Oasis".

"When her son Neilos arrives," writes presbyter Psenosiris to presbyter Apollon, "he will give you evidence of what they did to her". Probably as a result of torture suffered during interrogation, Politike died on the journey into exile from Alexandria to Oasin: they had had to embalm her and deliver her like that to the destination, following the orders of the highest authority. What exactly they did to her we shall never know: Politike's son Neilos, who was probably a Christian too, disappeared into the desert sands, just like the other characters in this hazy drama from the early fourth century at latest; as I learned at the lecture, the papyrus was found in the early twentieth century, so for one thousand six hundred to one thousand seven hundred years it had lain preserved by the desert. Professor Demetrios also cited an article by our scholar Adam Łukaszewicz, whose findings on the woman named Politike had cast new light on the research: she may have been a martyr for her faith who was sentenced to forced prostitution, which was often meted out as a punishment; in which case her death would have assumed a different character.

I had seven hours before leaving for the airport, and wanted to walk through the old city once more, gaze from the

Tower of David at the cupola of the Church of the Holy Sepulchre, walk to the Last Supper chamber, take another look at the Mount of Olives and the Cedron valley, and make a brief stop at the Armenian cathedral, because I sensed I would never see it all again a second time: so I sacrificed the denouement of the lecture on one of the world's most famous papyri to bid farewell to the holy city, and so I cast my eye across it all in the sharp, almost blinding light of noon. I have already told you it was the month of Tamuz – the second half of our June: it felt as if the heat of the Negev desert were sending a fiery breeze to fill the little streets of every district, Jewish, Arab and Christian, so all I shall add is that it was then, walking back to the Jaffa Gate, from where I took a taxi to the hotel, that I bought a long, narrow poster from a souvenir stall, a colour reproduction of a view of Jerusalem by David Roberts – what a superb draughtsman he was, I thought, as I opened my eyes on the small stage in the rehearsal room at our theatre. Now you know where I was in my dream when your phone call woke me.

Mateusz brought in the Twelfth Man. He looked a bit like someone from another world: the blue balloon in particular added something to his aura that clashed with his smart suit and dark glasses, and could have prompted concern. He hardly said a word, just bowed to everyone, grunted: "Praise the Lord," and took the place determined by Mateusz.

"Aren't you going to tell him to take off those shades?" the photographer asked.

"No, it's fine like that."

Just then the Twelfth Man did take off his glasses. On the photograph I sent you, you can study his smile. You pointed out that the corners of his lips are curling upwards, but his eyes are motionless, in other words, I'm trying to say, is it that his eyes aren't laughing? Only now did Mateusz give us some instructions: we had to keep changing places, and the lighting never stopped changing too. Again and again the shutter clicked. Had the Twelfth Man already made his plan by then? I doubt it. It looks as if he acted spontaneously, on the spur of the moment. Anyway, who would he have shot at in that room, sitting at the table with the white cloth? Maybe once the last picture had been taken and the stage manager had brought in the wine, when we were standing about in small groups chatting, maybe if one of us had stopped him, the tragedy might not have occurred. He left without anyone noticing. At the station he got into a bus that took him to the stop near the house on the hill. As we were on our way down to the Maska, he was probably standing by the pond. There behind a clump of tansy he saw a woman with a cigarette in her mouth and a bottle in her hand. No one knows if he spoke to her. He must have recognised her as the Whore of Babylon: he fired two shots at close range, and then, elated by a euphoric sense of completing his mission, he realised that now he could go back to the house on the hill over the surface of the lake, across the water. Next day at about noon, the firemen fished his body out by the sluice gate. The current had swept it along until it stopped at the grate. But all that happened later. As he sat at the long table with us on the stage, he must have felt he was experiencing what the voice had told him about.

"Now, to end with, just one more picture," said Mateusz, standing by the tripod. "First we'll turn out all the lights, then please don't move until the flash fades."

I was sitting as at the start between Wybrański and Zając. As the lights dimmed gradually, gently, in the left wing I saw the face of Nowik, and I wasn't sure if he had just come in, for this final scene, or maybe had been watching us for some time already. It didn't really matter, though: pitch darkness reigned, slashed apart by the sudden glare of the flash.

"But where is Jesus?" someone asked rather quietly.

For a long while the electrician left the stage unlit. There we sat, without moving in the deepest darkness, and no one said a word.